IXTAPA

ALSO BY E. HOWARD HUNT

UNDERCOVER: MEMOIRS OF AN AMERICAN SECRET AGENT

THE BERLIN ENDING

THE HARGRAVE DECEPTION

THE KREMLIN CONSPIRACY

THE GAZA INTERCEPT

MURDER IN STATE

BODY COUNT

CHINESE RED

Jack Novak books:

COZUMEL

GUADALAJARA

MAZATLÁN

IXTAPA

E. HOWARD HUNT

DONALD I. FINE, INC.

NEW YORK

Library of Congress Catalogue Card Number: 94-071101
ISBN 1-55611-404-4

Manufactured in the United States of America

10 9 8 7 6 5 4 3 2 1

Designed by Irving Perkins Associates

Crime like virtue has its degrees.

—RACINE
Phèdre, Act IV, Sc. 2

ONE

FLIGHT 491—NEWARK-MIAMI

Eddie Wax had himself a deal.

A deal whose very size made him think of a double deal as he sat in the unaccustomed luxury of the 757 and gazed down at the blue-green Atlantic. The flight attendant served Eddie a second Cuba Libre, and as he sipped it, Eddie reflected that Life, at last, was treating him well.

The third illegitimate child of a Cuban sugarcane cutter, Eddie Wax had had to scrape hard and use his wits all of his thirty-four years. In Bayamo, Eddie's black market dealings had been denounced by the block captain, and in Havana he'd been sentenced to six years in Combinado del Este. He'd survived three when Fidel opened prison gates, and along with other prisoners he'd been trucked to Mariel harbor for the long, sickening boat trip to Miami.

As a *Marielito*, Eddie hadn't been able to get work in Miami—too many refugees flooding South Florida—so he'd taken an INS bus ticket to New Jersey, and found work as a dishwasher in Union City, where there were almost as many Cubanos as in Miami.

Eddie Wax wasn't his real name, of course. He'd been born Eduardo Cera, and his Anglo boss had begun calling him by the name's English equivalent, as a sort of joke. Nevertheless, the name stuck, and in Union City's underworld of petty thieves and drug pushers, Eddie Wax could be counted on for night work as a getaway wheelman, and narcotics courier. Chato, the fellow *Marielito* who usually hired Eddie, would hand him the key to a locker at Penn

1

Station or Manhattan's Port Authority, and Eddie would go where bidden, open the locker, and deliver the contents to Chato.

For those services Eddie received two or three bills from the thick roll in Chato's plump hand. Not bad for a few hours' easy work, Eddie always told himself, but today was different. Today's score was going to be worth ten times more than Chato had ever paid him.

Three thousand dollars—for what? Eddie sipped the sweet rum and Coke mix, and stretched his thin legs. For taking a locked briefcase to Mexico.

Already Eddie was deciding how to use the money; with it he could buy into a street distributorship, maybe with Juanito Almeida, who was always looking for extra financing. Or Pablo Santiago's widow, Ramona, who must be having a hard time supplying Pablo's customers ever since her husband had been wasted by three .38 slugs when he'd tried to run from a pair of undercover waterfront cops. Yeah, Eddie could move in there, maybe share Ramona's king-size bed, in time.

All in all, the prospects were immensely pleasing to Eddie Wax, and his fingers strayed to the briefcase at his side.

He speculated that it contained eight or nine keys of *polvo blanco*, refined, cut and ready for snorting, but there were other possibilities. A pair of MAC-10s would fit nicely into the locked case, and their combined weight was about right, he thought, as he surreptitiously hefted the handle. No, couldn't be weapons, for the briefcase had been X-rayed at the Newark airport, so *cocaina* it probably was.

Or money.

The thought of that weight in green bills made Eddie lick his lips. If the bills were tens, their sum would be several hundred thousand; if in hundreds, he was holding on to a couple of million American dollars. Just out of curiosity he wanted to know how much. But Chato hadn't slipped him the key, and even if he had, Eddie couldn't be sure the contents weren't booby trapped. No, he wasn't going to open the case or even try. His three thousand dollar payoff would overcome his thief's curiosity.

Through a break in the clouds Eddie could see green water far below again. The Atlantic. Must be at least halfway to Miami, he mused, and upended his glass, savoring the last swallows.

There'd be more rum and Coke in Cancún when he got there later today. Chato hadn't gone into detail, he just gave Eddie the Mexicana ticket and told him he'd be met after he left the plane. At the airport or his hotel room, by a contact called "Pedrito."

Or, Eddie speculated, it could be Chato himself, doing things roundabout to trick DEA. Eddie wasn't crazy about going to Mexico—it would be the first time he'd left the U.S. since coming from Mariel, and the *narcotraficantes* in Mexico played at least as rough as in Union City or Miami, where the weekly body count was higher than you could believe.

All Eddie wanted was to make delivery and get paid. In and out, for a fast three thousand cash. He wasn't even sure he wanted to overnight at the hotel, but he decided he'd at least check out the pool and beach for good-looking, available *chicas*.

A large unattractive-looking blonde woman was coming down the aisle, probably from the lavatory. Near his row she stumbled, caught herself and eased into the empty seat beside Eddie. "My heel," she said quietly. "Have to get it fixed in the airport."

Eddie glanced at her and said nothing. He'd have fixed the heel himself if she'd been a young, good-looking chick, but this broad had coarse, thick features, a big nose, and too much makeup. Besides, she was five sizes larger than girls he usually took to bed. Hell with her.

He resumed looking down at the Atlantic.

"Live in Florida?" she asked.

"Naw, just visitin'," he said, without looking around.

"Me, too—boyfriend."

Oh, yeah? Eddie Wax thought. Have to be some kind of *loco* to climb *her* frame. Or try.

The seat-belt sign went on, and Eddie hoped the big broad would go back to her own seat. Instead, she half rose, leaned across him and peered down through the window.

"Must be the Bahamas," she said gutturally, "whadda you think?"

Eddie glanced out and saw the surf-outlined tip of a distant island. "Yeah," he said, "that's them," and felt a sharp prick in his left arm. He yelped, thinking it was her hatpin, or some piece of sharp jewelry. "Look out, willya?" he snarled, and started to push her away.

Then he felt the flooding rush, burning his arm and chest. "What the fu—" he began, unable to say more because his throat was paralyzed. His arms went limp, he couldn't fight off her crushing weight. His head lolled to one side, and the cottony clouds seemed to surround him, cutting off vision.

Eddie Wax saw nothing more.

The woman pinched his nostrils shut. No reaction. She groped under his seat for the briefcase, lifted it free, and got out of the seat.

Across the aisle a young man said, "Hey, lady, that's his case, leave it there."

"You gonna make me?"

"Maybe." He got up lithely, ducked as she swung the heavy case at his head, and when that missed, she lunged at him. The man stepped back and spun, catching her on the side of her neck with the heel of his hand. She dropped in the aisle like a sack of cement, sprawling outstretched. Passengers screamed, a female flight attendant hurried toward them. The man stared blankly at the fallen woman, then knelt and felt for her carotid artery.

"Nothing," he said huskily, and let the flight attendant push him aside. He looked around blankly. "Self-defense," he blurted. "You all saw how she came at me."

Over the intercom the captain ordered passengers into their seats to prepare for landing at Miami International Airport.

The man picked up the fallen briefcase and laid it on the empty seat beside Eddie Wax. When Eddie's open eyes didn't register, the man shook him. "Hang on to it," he said hoarsely, then gasped as Eddie's chin dropped against his collarbone. "Oh, God, oh, Jesus," the man gasped. "She musta killed him."

Then he looked down at the fallen woman, seeing that it wasn't a woman at all, because the wig had come off, showing short hair in a male cut.

The copilot arrived, balancing himself in the aisle as the landing gear ground down. "Mister," he said, "you don't leave this aircraft until the cops get here. Understand?"

Dumbly the man nodded. "I—I don't know what happened, exactly." He looked over at Eddie Wax. "She musta killed him for the case, then came at me," he said, sat back and closed his eyes. The copilot strapped himself into the seat beside the body of Eddie Wax. "Christ," he muttered, "I seen heart failure before but nothing like this. Two dead passengers. God Almighty!"

The landing gear locked into place. The 757 banked and settled into final approach while the flight engineer radioed MIA tower for a police ambulance. Lots of crazy things happened on the way to Miami, he told himself, but aside from one half-assed attempted hijacking, he'd never been in anything as serious as this. And in practical terms, it was going to be a good many hours before the cops screened everyone and got their stories, and he'd miss the turnaround to Newark, making his wife madder than she usually was.

Shit!

Wheels hit the runway, rubber shrieked, and reverse thrust slowed the huge plane.

COZUMEL, QUINTANA ROO, MEXICO

The sailfish came out of the water like a Poseidon missile, mid-morning sunlight silvering its long graceful body. Its blue sail fanned out against the wind, and for a moment I thought the *pez vela* might soar away. Then gravity supervened and the sailfish sliced down into the blue-green Caribbean, and disappeared.

From his fighting chair my client let out a whoop of pure joy. Then the line zinged taut and the stubby rod bowed. "Drag off!" I yelled, too late. The rod straightened, wind caught the slack line and whipped it across the whitecaps.

My client blurted, "He's still on, I can feel him."

"No, you can't," I told him. "Just reel in."

"You *sure?*"

"I'm sure," I said, "and he was a beauty. Not many like that *macho* around."

He was reeling in, but I gestured at my boat captain, and Ramón took over. My client, a portly broker from Austin, sighed remorsefully and unstrapped himself from the fighting chair. He wore Aca Joe khaki shorts, anaconda belt hidden by the overhang of his paunch. His torso was unhealthily red despite my warnings to keep covered. He got up and came toward me, balancing against the roll of the boat. His midriff blubber rolled with the sea. "That's the biggest damn fish I ever hooked, Novak."

"*Mister* Novak to you," I said pleasantly. "Jack to my friends. Yes, a big, beautiful fighter. Run maybe one seven zero on the hoist."

"That all?" He seemed disappointed.

I handed him a chilled bottle of Tecate. "We'll never know, will we? But with sixty-five the local average, not bad at all."

"But the line broke," he complained, sucking at the brown bottle.

"The line broke because you kept on the drag too long."

"He coulda snapped through it."

"Unlikely." I opened a bottle for Ramón and one for myself. "That's forty-pound test line, *amigo.*"

"Maybe we should use stronger, like sixty."

I smiled at him. "I've seen big sail landed on twenty test—but the fishermen knew what they were doing."

"Meaning I don't?" His red face grew uglier than it normally was.

"Meaning you can't learn it all in two days, Mr. Fettick. No, forty pound's the max we use out here. This is sport fishing, not market hauling." I drank deeply and regarded him. Mrs. Fettick was in her air-conditioned hotel room recovering from yesterday's *mal de mer* and sunburn. Like her husband, she'd worn a lot of zinc oxide on her nose, but neglected chest, arms and back.

Fettick finished his beer and tossed the bottle overboard. I handed him the dip net. "Fish it out," I told him.

"The hell you say."

"We don't spoil the waters around here, *amigo.* You can fish out the bottle or pay Ramón ten bucks."

"Suppose I tell you to go fuck yourself."

"I wouldn't like it," I said, "and I'd invoke the Novak experiment."

"What the hell's that?" he snapped.

"Whether a surly client can swim to the beach from here."

Fettick squinted at me for several seconds. "Ah, what the hell," he said, fished a twenty from his pocket and handed it to Ramón.

My captain pulled out his .45 hawg from its leg holster, sighted briefly, and fired. The Tecate bottle disintegrated.

Fettick licked his lips. "Holy Gawd! Forty yards if it's an inch."

Ramón blew smoke from the revolver muzzle and stuck it in his carved leather holster. He tucked the twenty in his hip pocket.

"Some shootin'," Fettick murmured. "How'd he get so good?"

"Sinking other people's litter. And in these waters it's a survival skill. Not every craft you come across has innocent intentions."

He hitched up his sagging shorts. "Meaning what?"

"Smugglers, dopers, *contrabandistas* . . . pirates." That was enough for him to know. In self-defense I'd had to waste a pair of wretches last year, but that was my secret—and the Lord's. I turned to Ramón. *"Carnitas,"* I told him. Bait up.

7

He'd just secured the line to an outrigger clothespin when I heard the ship-to-shore radio signal. "Buckle in," I told Fettick, and picked up the radiophone. "Zebra Tango four niner," I said, giving my call sign.

"This the *Corsair*?" a voice crackled.

"Aye."

"Jack Novak?"

"Who wants him?"

"Manny."

Manny Montijo was an old pal from DEA days, and after. I'd saved his ass a few times, and he'd once saved my life, so I didn't hang up as I would have on any other DEA or government asshole. "You're not Manny," I said. "Where is he?"

"About four thousand miles away, which is why I'm calling for him."

"There's such a thing as satellite communications," I said. "Tell Manny to haul his butt to a phone if he wants to talk. I'll be out here for maybe another two hours." I glanced at the ballyhoo skipping over the water seventy yards off the port quarter, then at Fettick's Day-Glo back. "Make that another hour, max," I said, and signed off. Manny had become a DEA regional supervisor on merit, not because his name ended in a vowel, and there was a time when we'd coast-watched together. Now and then I still did a job for Manny if the pay was right and I needed funds, but at the moment I didn't, so I wasn't particularly interested in hearing what Manny's spokesman had to say.

Nevertheless, when the radiophone buzzed again, I answered.

"Mr. Novak?"

"Zebra Tango four niner. Speak."

"Manny's in a big meeting with the presidential task force, but because this is an emergency he asks that you *please* listen. It's very important."

"To whom?"

"Well, to all of us. It's a question of a very few hours if we're to bring it off."

8

"Bring *what* off?"

"Well, I can't give it to you by radio—the bad guys monitor, you know—so . . . is that old plane of yours still flying?"

"Like a gull."

"Then, please get over to Cancún airport. You'll be met at General Aviation by a man who'll lay out the whole thing."

"Including money, I trust?"

"That, too."

I considered. Melody was competing at a Caracas diving tournament, but before leaving she'd suggested I add a tiled patio to my bungalow, with a screened enclosure. Yesterday's estimate was twenty thousand U.S., and I didn't have that much available cash. Unless I broke into some Mex CDs that were earning 96 percent interest, and I was reluctant to do that, even to please Melody. Besides, it had been five months since Manny had hired me for anything. Old wounds and bruises had healed, and I was bored with charter fishing—clients like Sam Fettick served as a reminder.

I said, "My plane's a Fairchild amphib pusher, only a dozen still flying and none in Mexico. I can be there in under two hours. Say noon."

"That'll be fine."

"Is onward travel involved?"

"No, it's all to go down in Cancún."

"I'll be there," I said, and signed off.

Just then Fettick got a strike. The sail erupted like Godzilla, tail-walked the surface, shaking its beak ferociously, and I grabbed the rod, yanking back so the sail slammed sideways onto the water. That would take some of the fight out of him.

To Fettick I said, "Drag off, for God's sake. He'll run now, and sound, so give him all the line he wants."

Ramón had thrown the clutch, and my boat was moving with the current, bow into the wind. Fettick said, "Think he's well hooked?"

"He swallowed the ballyhoo," I told him, "so he's deep hooked. When he rises, pull him off balance the way I did."

9

I looked at my watch. "You've got half an hour to bring him alongside."

"Half a—hey, I'm paying for the whole *day*."

"You'll get a rebate. I've got business ashore."

"Lousy way to do business," he muttered.

"Listen," I said, "watch the damn line. When it's slack, reel in."

The sail soared skyward again, its whole body shaking like spring steel, droplets glistening like silver beads. Fettick pulled back the rod and the big fish fell horizontally. The impact was like the crash of a tree.

Fettick reeled hard, shoulder straps cutting into his sunburned flesh. He was gasping and I got worried about heart failure—but that was between him and his medics. I opened two Tecates, sipped one and watched. Ramón drank and kept *Corsair* turned into the wind, engine idling.

For the next twenty minutes the sail's leaps were shorter and closer to the boat. Finally, he began swimming close to the surface, back and forth, Fettick reeling him closer to the stern transom. I said, "If we land him, do you want him mounted, or will a photo do?"

"How much is mounting?"

"A lot. And it's all make-believe. Just a foam replica, hand painted. Plus air cargo to Austin. Lotta money. Tell you what, we'll get a sling around him, winch him up and get some photos."

"And let him go?"

"He's too big and tough to eat. Real sportsmen release game fish so they can reproduce and provide excitement for other sportsmen. That's my recommendation."

Fettick was more tired than the sailfish. "Okay," he said. "My Nikon's in that red bag. I just gotta have something to show the fellows back home."

"And you will." I told Ramón to get the net sling ready, and after the sail slammed the hull with his beak a few times and tried to dash away, we drew him into the sling, and winched him free of the sea.

Fettick was almost too exhausted to stand beside his

catch, but I gave him the rod for steadying, told him to smile, and clicked off six frames. Ramón cut the line at the fish's mouth, and lowered him into the water, then pulled him by the sail alongside the hull until his gills took oxygen, and the big fish moved off on his own.

Fettick lay down on the transom cushions and closed his eyes. To Ramón I said, "Head for my pier, then take Mr. Fettick back to the town dock. He owes five hundred for yesterday, three for today. Keep his camera until he pays. Traveler's checks or green."

Ramón nodded, hit the throttle and headed for home.

At the bungalow I fed my two Dobermans, César and Sheba, packed an overnight bag, and opened a hidden wall cache that held an assortment of weapons. From them I selected a nine millimeter Walther PPK, and fitted it into a thin, nylon shoulder holster, DEA issue five years ago. Ramón's wife Margarita was ironing my freshly laundered slacks and *guayabera* shirts, and I told her to lock up when she left.

Then I walked across my back lawn—where the new patio would be—and went down my pier to where the Fairchild was snubbed and waiting.

I turned over the 260 hp Lycoming and taxied seaward. A fifteen-knot wind shortened takeoff, and the amphib slapped up on its hull step and got airborne in no time. As I flew northward toward Cancún I climbed to two thousand feet, passing Cozumel's main town, San Miguel, off to starboard. Cozumel to Cancún was a mere forty miles and, with tailwind, I touched down at the resort's airport just nineteen minutes after takeoff. My aircraft wasn't fast, just very reliable. I parked near a gas pump, got out my overnight bag, and headed for the General Aviation office. Before I reached it a white two-door Ford intercepted me. The driver said, "Mr. Novak? Get in, and we'll talk."

I put my hands on the door ledge and looked at him. He was about thirty-five, tanned face and hands, dark hair, and I saw a neck scar that could have been from a bullet. He

11

said, "I'm Al Wolcott, out of Mérida." I got in beside him, and he steered out of the airport, turned right at the crossroads, and pulled off the road beside the big lagoon called Inglés. He kept the windows closed and the air-conditioning on. Wolcott said, "All I'm telling you I got by scrambler phone from Miami regional."

"Not from Phil Corliss, I hope."

He looked surprised. "You know Phil?"

"He's one of the main reasons I left DEA."

Wolcott grinned. "They've got him in Toronto—finally. Incompetence finds its own level of responsibility. All right, Mr. Novak, here's how it lays: This morning, on a Newark-Miami flight one passenger killed another by heroin OD. The killer was taking a briefcase from the victim when another passenger, a karate student blackbelt, unintentionally killed the killer."

"Must have caused quite a sensation on the flight."

"I guess. Anyway, Miami police met the plane and took off two corpses. The killer was dressed as a woman, but she weren't no lady. Turned out to be a New York contract killer named Sid Fertig. His victim was a *Marielito*, Eddie Wax, small-time crook around Union City—theft, drugs, and so on."

"The Karate Kid should get a medal."

"You're right. Our guys persuaded the cops not to hold him for anything, of course. Under the circumstances—"

"Wait a minute—how come DEA got involved?"

"Ah, this is the beauty part. When the cops opened the briefcase they found—"

"Coke?"

"Uh-uh. Four million dollars, cash. Obviously for a big buy."

"In Miami?"

He shook his head. "Wax's ticket was to Cancún, with a prepaid hotel reservation at the Hotel Maravillas." He gestured. "Up the beach near the Convention Center. Miami speculates Eddie was going to be met either at the airport, or in his room. Probably his hotel room. He was to turn over the four million to a contact, and return tomorrow, according to his round-trip ticket."

I shrugged. "Standard procedure. Why does Manny want me?"

"Because you're here."

"And I'm supposed to do—what?"

"Pose as Eddie Wax."

TWO

I opened the door, got out of the car and stood outside. The sun burned my forehead. The air was about ninety-eight degrees and no breeze. The lagoon looked like molten gold. I took a deep breath and got back beside Al Wolcott. "It's goofy," I said. "The contact may know Eddie Wax, or have a photo of him, which is a lot more than I have. If I'm figured as a plant, I'll get a fast burst from an Uzi, end of story."

Wolcott nodded. "No one said it was safe or easy—which is probably why Mr. Montijo selected you. After all, Mr. Novak, you've got a big reputation."

". . . that won't help me when I'm dead. *Caramba.* I take Wax's room and—wait. That it?"

"Well, depending on what happens."

I smiled. "Go on."

He swallowed. "The idea seems to be that if you're accepted as Wax the money courier, you'd be in position to find out who's selling the coke and how it's to be smuggled into the States."

"That's a possibility—but this is Mex jurisdiction. Why not just bring in the Mexican federal narco guys?" I was starting to have a little fun with this case.

He didn't smile. "I wouldn't feel comfortable relying on them, and I don't think you would."

"True enough. The big drug *jefes* buy officials the way they buy cigarettes. So it's to be done without Mexican 'cooperation.' "

"Until they try and convict the men who actually killed

14

Camarena, and tortured Vic Ortiz. I don't mean the two big *narcos* they jailed. Also, the Mexicans haven't been helpful in identifying whoever shot one of our men near Nogales a couple of months ago. Broad daylight, too." He shook his head. "You'd think every bystander was blind."

"All right, that was just a test question. I'll do what I can so long as it's unilateral, no Mexican involvement."

"There's none, I promise you. Anyway, this project just came up this morning, wouldn't have been time." He glanced at his digital wristwatch. "What else?"

"That matter of my fee."

"What did you have in mind?"

"I play percentages so I work for percentages. Four million dollars is the stake. I'll take one percent for following through. Forty thousand. If this turns to be either a no-show or a one-night stand, pay me a thousand for my time."

"Fair enough." He sighed in relief. "Plane ought to be coming in about now. Carrying the briefcase and Eddie Wax's billfold. Pete Valeriano's bringing them from Miami, plus whatever collateral information that's been developed." He started the Ford engine. "In Union City Eddie Wax ran narcotics errands for an underboss named 'Chato,' true name Isador Campestre. Welterweight boxer on some old Cuban team. Got his nose flattened, thus 'Chato.' We assume he gave Eddie the briefcase and instructions."

"Then I'm adding a stipulation. Have Chato picked up and salted away while I'm on this case. I don't want him available for checkbacks on me." I remembered something. "Are the cops keeping the plane killings quiet, especially the names of the deceased?"

"Valeriano should know. Seems elementary, doesn't it?"

"Exactly. And thus easily overlooked."

He bent down a few inches and squinted through the windshield. "That may be the plane now. Yeah, Gulfstream."

I shaded my eyes against the sun's glare. It was a sleek white Gulfstream jet, unmarked. DEA probably had confiscated it from a major dealer, the same way the low-budget agency acquired expensive cars, real estate and high-powered boats. Wolcott backed around and braked. "You better wait here, and I'll bring Pete."

Reluctantly I got out. "Just make it fast. Otherwise, all you'll find is a grease spot." I slammed the door and headed for the shade of a palm.

Insects buzzed, I slapped a few away and gave up. From where I sat I could hear surf washing the nearby beach, and thought how cool and pleasant it would be scuba diving about three fathoms down, watching coral fans wave invitingly in the current. I'd trained for the SEALS at St. Thomas, but the underwater viewing off Cozumel and Cancún was a lot more interesting. Especially the drug-factory ship I'd sunk off Cancún some five years ago. Melody had helped me that night, shooting down the ship's attack helicopter so I could get back aboard *Corsair*. Memories, I thought, and wondered where my nubile lass was at the moment. Displaying her mastery of the ten-meter boards to an enthusiastic crowd, I hoped, not wrapped in the hot embrace of some handsome Swedish stud in his hotel room. But at twenty a girl has a mind of her own, and I'd foresworn matrimony until she had her degree from Suntan U.

Ah, well . . . The noise of tires approaching over the crushed coral broke off my reveries and I stood up to see the oncoming Ford.

I got in the back seat next to Valeriano and shook hands with him. He was a well-built, dark-skinned man from the Miami office, appropriately wearing a white *guayabera* and a touristy straw hat. At his feet lay a brown Naugahyde attaché case about six inches thick. He wiped his forehead, and said, "Glad you're with us for this one, Mr. Novak."

"Jack," I said, and toed the attaché case. "This the swag?"

He nodded. "Also, Wax had a small travel bag in the rack over his seat. I've got it in the trunk with mine." He took a billfold from his hip pocket and handed it to me. "Eddie's."

I opened the billfold and took out a scrap of paper on which had been written: *Cancún—Pedrito.* Pete said, "We assume Pedrito is the local contact's name, but that's only an assumption."

I said, "My cover's so thin it's transparent. From this driving license Wax was five-eight, and I'm six-one. I'm fifty pounds heavier than he was in life, and my Cuban accent is laughable."

Valeriano said, "Do what we do around Miami—use *-ico* as the diminutive, instead of *-ito*, and use it frequently. Also, you'll notice that Eduardo Cera was his true name."

I said, "The contact had better be Mex, not Cuban, or I'll be blown away fast."

"Al here asked me about the cops. They've got the bodies John Doed with the ME, and he's way behind autopsy schedule. Figure six weeks minimum. The karate champ's been warned to keep his mouth shut, otherwise he'll find himself charged with manslaughter."

"The airline?"

"Hell, they don't want that kind of publicity. Murder in mid-air, you kidding?" He gazed at me with innocent brown eyes.

I couldn't help smiling at his goofy straw hat. "You staying for a while, Pete?"

"Long as you want me. I'm booked into the same hotel—you know the Agency's love for close-in control." He grinned widely. "I can just see myself controlling you. Besides, I don't want to end up in Toronto working for Fumbling Phil."

I smiled back. I was going to like working with this guy. So far, he was okay.

"Need spending money?" he asked.

I liked that, too. "A flash roll never hurts," I conceded, "but let's see what happens today, tonight and tomorrow. For all we know, Sid Fertig had a backup on the plane, and he got word back to Chato—and Cancún. In that case they'll either ignore me, or waste me."

"Guess so," he agreed, "and I hadn't thought of a back-up man, so that's one for you." He set the attaché case on his lap and opened it, showing neat piles of hundred-dollar bills, and quite a few five hundred denomination. "I'll be frank with you," he said. "Miami Secret Service hauled in

17

about twelve million in well-made queer two days ago. My supervisor switched three million of it for what Wax carried. A cautious guy. So you've got a million genuine, and three million odd, but I was told only Treasury can tell the difference."

"Let's hope," I said, "but I don't like it."

"Still, if it's a sting, the Agency's only lost a million instead of four."

"So be it," I told him. "The currency's the least of my worries. Now you can tell me this: suppose that Mexicana flight is met and I'm not on it. How do I explain it—say I sprouted wings?"

"It was either fly you to Miami to board the flight or send me here, and the decision was you couldn't get there in time to catch the flight. I guess we have to hope Wax wasn't going to be contacted at the airport." He looked at his watch. "The Mexicana flight is due to arrive about an hour from now." He turned to Wolcott. "Cancún Customs and Immigration slow or fast?"

"If this were Monday it'd be slow—tequila hangovers. But it's Wednesday, and an arriving passenger should be through and out in around twenty minutes. Another twenty to the hotel, and Eddie would be checking in about an hour after touchdown."

"Giving you," Valeriano said, "two hours to kill before you show up at the Maravillas. Which reminds me—" He produced an airline ticket folder and tore off the unused Miami-Cancún coupon. He handed me the folder, indicating the hotel's prepaid reservation for one night. I pocketed the folder and said, "I've got time to make arrangements for my plane, so let's go back to the airport."

━━━━━━━━━━

I paid for the pumped gas, dipsticked the oil, and rented tie-down space for two nights, went into the adjoining pilots' restaurant and ordered Tecate and a plate of steak, eggs and refried beans decorated with nacho chips. From my table I could watch the runway. Through rising heat waves it quivered like a belly dancer. By now, I thought, Pete Valeriano was luxuriating in his refrigerated, seaview room.

Alongside the original, aging airport building, a new one had been erected, attesting to Cancún's growing prominence as a jet-set resort. The building was shaped like an Aztec pyramid, and painted deep brown. Why brown? I wondered. Why not jungle colors? Knowing Mexico, I figured the paint manufacturer had a surplus of brown, and bribed some *jefe* in airport construction to take it off his hands at 300 percent profit. That sort of dealing explained why Mexico, despite its wealth of natural resources, continued to be a financial cripple.

The AeroMexico flight from Mexico City came in, and passengers disembarked. I killed time over a cup of syrupy coffee, paid my bill and carried my overnight bag and Eddie's attaché case into the main airport where I mingled with the waiting crowd. By then the Mexicana flight was in, and I edged nearer to the customs exit. Some of the passengers could hardly stagger under the weight of consumer goods bought in Miami. Porters helped others with large microwave ovens, mammoth TV sets, computers, and small refrigerators. I joined the emerging stream and went out to the taxi rank. Maybe someone was looking for my brown attaché case, maybe not. I let the driver put my bag in the front seat, and I kept the attaché case on my lap. It was weighty with currency, only a quarter of which had been manufactured under official supervision.

I clung to it while registering as Eduardo Cera in the hotel's cool, breezy lobby, and looked around from time to time as I conjectured the late Eddie Wax might do.

I let the *botones* carry up my overnight bag to my sixth-floor room. It was an economy model, but the Caribbean view was unobstructed, the air conditioning worked, and a sign over the bathroom wash basin guaranteed the tap water to be sanitary and drinkable. After stuffing the money case under the double bed, I unpacked my own bag and stepped out on the balcony to look around.

Cancún is a wide sandbar off the Yucatán peninsula

stretching five miles north and south. Hotels face the Caribbean beach side; behind them lie the shallow waters of Nichupte Lagoon, where no one goes except duck hunters during the season. But pleasure-seekers crowd the greater and lesser hotels: Camino Real, Fiesta Americana, Krystal, Sheraton, Hyatt, Miramar, Aristos . . . hell, it reminded me of Miami Beach without the Haitians. The Maravillas had been built early enough in the resort's development to show signs of wear. Worn carpeting, cracked shower tile, blistered wall plaster, and cigarette-burned furniture showed Mayan indifference to routine maintenance. But it wasn't going to upset me—not for one night.

I called room service and ordered a jug of Bacardi Añejo, four bottles of mineral water, and purified ice cubes. With that I could endure even if no one contacted me.

While waiting for delivery I shed my shoulder holster and tucked the Walther under my belt behind my spine. Then I put on a white *guayabera*, sat down in a rustic, leather-covered chair, and set my heels on the cocktail table. As I waited, I noticed that the simulated tile flooring was strewn with native *serapes*, none of whose colors matched the walls, ceiling, bedspread, or each other. Melody, I reflected, would go bananas in my surroundings, given her need for harmonious color. And I remembered how, after the front part of my house had been rebuilt after a grenade blast, she had chosen attractive tints and hues that I had never thought of. But I'd stayed firm about our bedroom: no baby pink for me. So we compromised on curdled cream with a palm-frond mural to break the walls' monotony. Secretly I'd wanted a ceiling mirror, but lacked the *cojones* to order one, so when we lay in bed, side by side, I had only curdled cream to gaze at while lust replenished.

The door buzzer rang, and I got up to admit the waiter.

But when I opened the door no waiter was standing there bearing my order. Instead, my caller was a dark-haired, oval-faced young woman, holding in her right hand a small, deadly looking pistol.

THREE

In cultivated Spanish my unbidden visitor said, "Gently, *very* gently. Just back into the room. Hands up, please."

Hands raised, I took four steps back and halted while she kicked the door shut and locked it behind her back. Her large dark eyes never left mine, never wavered. Nor did the pistol in her hand.

She wore a sheer silk dress, tie-dyed in shades of blue. Her left wrist was circled by what looked like a platinum-diamond bracelet, and a large pear-shaped pearl pendant dipped into the cleavage of her breasts. She glanced quickly at the balcony, showing me a somewhat acquiline nose. Her skin was creamy with the lightest possible dusting of chocolate, teeth white and even.

I'd seen drug molls before—too many of them—but this one outclassed them all. By light years. She looked me up and down and said, "Eddie Wax?"

I nodded.

"Prove it."

"Four million talks for me."

He gaze flickered. "Show me."

"We'll get to that—after I know who you are, who sent you."

"Who were you expecting?"

"Pedrito."

Her smile was brief. "You'll do," she said, "I think."

"Can I lower my arms?"

She shrugged. "Do so, but I'm an excellent shot."

Lowering my arms I said, "Look, I didn't come here for trouble. Chato sent me, that's all."

"The money."

"My instructions," I said, "were to deliver to Pedrito. Whoever you are, you are not Pedrito."

"I serve him as you serve Chato." The gun muzzle lifted until its dark circle pointed at my forehead. "The money," she said icily.

And then the door buzzer sounded.

She glanced at the door and whispered, "Don't move."

"Bullshit. It's room service with drinks." I took a deep breath, turned past her, walked four uncertain steps, and unlocked the door. A dark-skinned waiter grinned at me. I opened the door wider and let him enter. He went directly to the little table and set down his tray, turned and handed me the bill. Fishing pesos from my pocket, I paid and tipped him. As he turned to leave I looked at my visitor. Her right hand was empty, her left clutched a small purse. Before the door closed on the waiter I was standing directly in front of her, my right hand gripping her left. When the door clicked shut I pried the purse from her hand and tossed it on the chair cushion. It hit heavily.

She stared at me sullenly. "That doesn't change anything."

"Of course not." I opened a bottle of mineral water, added ice to a glass, and poured. "Refreshment time," I said, and handed it to her. Then I poured Añejo and iced it for myself. "Sit down," I told her. "Let's do business in a friendly atmosphere."

Slowly she subsided in a chair. I sipped rum and looked at her. "The money isn't here," I said, "but I can get it—after we talk."

She lifted her glass and sipped. "Talk about what?"

"About you. Why you held a gun on me. This was to be a straight turnover meet. A gun makes me nervous, unless I'm holding it, of course."

"I had to make sure of you—who you were."

"Satisfied?" I reached over, took her purse and pulled out

22

her pistol. After drawing out the magazine I ejected the ready shell from the chamber, and put the weapon down. Then I inverted her purse. Change fell out of it, a lipstick, pen, a small address book, and a plastic laminated driving license. It showed her photograph, and gave her name as Paula María Quiroz, unmarried, of Monterrey, N.L. I was beginning to return the items to her purse when she reached for it. "I'll do that," she said quickly.

Too eager, I thought, and kept the purse from her grasp. I began probing it while Paula María Quiroz watched with widening eyes. As I pressed into the soft material my fingers felt something hard and thin. I turned the purse inside out, but whatever it was had been sewn into the lining. Her face was fearful. I tore the lining and pulled out what felt like a plastic card, larger than a credit card. Without looking at it I laid it on my thigh and covered it with my hand. "Tell me about Pedrito."

"What do you want to know?"

"His name, where he is, the size of his operation."

"Why do you want to know so much? You're only a courier."

"I'm curious about him. What kind of man sends a woman into a spot where she needs a gun—" I gestured at her weapon on the bed. When she said nothing, I said, "Not much for talking, are you? Well, I can't risk handing over Chato's money to the wrong person, so you tell Pedrito to collect it himself."

She sighed. "You might as well see what's under your hand."

I picked up the card and saw her photograph and name on one side. The reverse side made it a CREDENCIAL FEDERAL identifying the woman as an agent from the office of the PROCURADORÍA GENERAL DE LA REPÚBLICA MEXICANA—the attorney general. Narcotics Section. I dropped it into a pocket.

She said, "I could have you arrested and jailed."

"Maybe, but any *narcotraficante* of significance carries official credentials. No harder to buy than a magazine. The question is, do you work for the attorney general—or Pedrito?"

"You won't believe me if I tell you."

"Try me."

"Both."

"Double agent? Dangerous agent, *señorita*, wherever your loyalty lies. Is you name really Quiroz?"

"Is yours Cera? Wax?"

"What makes you think it's not?"

"For one thing, your accent isn't true Cuban. For another, you didn't arrive here on the Mexicana flight. I saw every passenger who disembarked, and you weren't one of them. Oh, I saw you blend in with them and take a taxi to this hotel, but you weren't on that flight."

"Interesting," I said. "Whoever you work for, you do good work."

She nodded. "You have dangerous knowledge of me, and I have dangerous information about you. That's called a standoff—a Mexican standoff, I believe."

"I wouldn't know," I said, "coming from Bayamo, as I do. But I think it's time to sort things out. Go into the bathroom."

"The—? Why?"

"Do it or you'll wish you had," I said, and gave her my best mean stare.

Shrugging, she rose and went into the bathroom. I secured the door from the outside, then called Valeriano's room. When he answered I said, "Room six-nineteen. We need to talk. Now."

"On my way."

━━━━━━━━━━━━━━━

We talked on the balcony, out of earshot. Pete fingered the federal ID card, and muttered, "You're so right, this needs sorting out. Any thoughts?"

"Too many," I said. "Call the Mérida office and have Al or whoever's there vet her name with Miami." I paused. "The name on this doc."

He nodded.

"That'll take a couple of hours at minimum," I went on. "Meanwhile, I have this kitten who could become a wildcat at any moment, so time is crucial. If she's an actual federal agent that doesn't mean she hasn't sold out to Pedrito— whoever *he* is. In which case, we turn over the money to her, and put on a tail to see where she takes it."

"Maybe Wolcott could come up with a tail, but I can't. I'm Miami office, remember. You got anyone local?"

I shook my head.

"How about you, Jack?"

"Hell, she's seen me, knows my face. She'll be expecting a tail, and could drag me around for hours. When she tires of running, she could call Pedrito and have me erased." I looked at him. "But she hasn't seen you."

Valeriano said nothing, but I could see he didn't like the idea. "At least," I said, "you could tail her until she decides there's no surveillance, phone me her location, and drop off."

He brightened a little. "Yeah, I could do that much."

"Watch your own rear end," I said, "because for all we know she didn't come alone. If I were Pedrito I'd have an escort nearby, possibly without her knowledge. Four million is a lot of bucks, especially in Mexico." I took her ID card and studied it. "The major unknown is whether she's a true-blue fed working against Pedrito. If she is, her superiors aren't going to like anyone interfering with her, especially in the absence of what we used to call 'mutual trust and confidence.' I've been in Mexican custody and barely survived—wouldn't have but for Manny Montijo."

He nodded. "I heard about that. They traded you for Parra."

"I took him later," I reminisced, "so it wasn't a total wash. Anyway, whatever her role, she can blaze the trail to Pedrito, and that's what this is all about. Right?"

"Right." He grimaced. "A few hours ago this all seemed so simple."

"Well, it's far from that now, so maybe I'll try a recruitment."

"Meaning?"

"Let her think I accept her as a federal agent, and invite her to make this a joint op." Before he could protest, I said, "She knows I'm not Cuban, meaning I couldn't possibly be the courier Pedrito expected. So far she hasn't figured me out, but if she's as smart as she is good-looking that won't take long."

He looked astonished. "You can't let her know you're DEA!"

"I'm not. I'm an independent contractor."

He grunted. "She won't make that fine distinction, Jack. To her you have to be one of Chato's people or a *gringo* agent. So, if you want to work this out with her I can't tell you no. I'm not your supervisor, just a cut-out and commo channel." He looked at me. "The dough?"

I pulled out the case from under the bed and set it on the coffee table. Valeriano opened it and glanced at the stacks of currency. He closed it. I said, "My strong inclination is to jaw with her for a while and let her take the money. By then you'll be watching the elevators for her departure. You won't need to know if I've cut a deal with her, so assume worst case and keep after her until she lights. I'll stay by the phone."

He thought it over. "In the circumstances I don't know what else can be done." We shook hands and he said, "Aside from DEA, we have something in common. I went to the Academy, too. Annapolis."

"What class?"

"After your time, but I didn't graduate—bilged out on eyesight." He sighed.

"Wasn't the end of the world, was it?" I hadn't noticed his contact lenses before. "Hell, they almost bilged me—for concentrating on Crabs." The midshipmen's term for Annapolis girls.

That brought a grin from him. "How sweet it was. Okay, I'll call Mérida and start the namecheck, then cover the lobby."

"Better have wheels handy," I suggested.

He nodded, said, "See you," and went out.

I finished my Añejo, locked the hall door, and opened the bathroom. The lady from Monterrey was on the toilet seat staring at me sullenly. She rose, and said, "Can we finish our business now? This is all quite unpleasant."

"Provoked by you," I told her. "Yes, we're nearing the end of preliminaries. We can resume after you take off your dress."

"What?"

"Don't be coy, Paula. I have to see if you're wired."

"I'm not."

"Show me."

Slowly she turned from me, and began pulling off her dress. Holding it in one hand she turned completely around, displaying an excellent, small-waisted figure. Pink panties, sheer garter-hose, and a pink mesh bra, about 34C. No mike, no miniature transmitter or recorder. "Thank you," I said, "we'll now get back to business."

I built another drink for myself, and when she joined me she said, "I'll have one, too." She eyed the closed attaché case.

"That's it," I said, "just delivered from safekeeping."

She opened the lid and stared at the piles of currency. I handed her a glass of iced rum.

Sitting down across from me, she said, "Who *are* you?"

I got out Eddie Wax's billfold, and extracted his New Jersey driving license. She looked at Eddie's photograph, then at me. As she returned the license, she said, "You're being very open with me—having proved you're not the contact Pedrito expected." She sipped slowly and thoughtfully. "Why?"

"Who I am isn't important. I brought the money, it's here, and you can take it to your boss—assuming Pedrito *is* your boss."

"Is Chato yours?"

"Good question. At least I'm carrying out the assignment he gave Eddie Wax." I got out her federal identification card and looked at it. "If this is genuine and Pedrito saw it he'd have you tortured and killed. Right?"

She nodded, and crossed her knees, displaying a pair of extremely well-shaped legs.

"On the other hand," I went on, "if you denounced me to Pedrito, he'd do the same to me."

"Unhesitatingly."

"Which brings us to a particular point. So long as we hold each other's lives in our hands the intelligent thing to do is cooperate."

She sipped her drink and gave me a long, calculating stare that gave me a little tingle. "What do you have in mind?"

"You can walk out of here with those four million dollars if you'll tell me what I asked about Pedrito."

For a while she was silent, looking down at the ice melting in her glass. Then she seemed to rouse herself, and sat forward. "To explain Pedrito, I need to tell you something about myself."

"I'm a good listener."

She finished her drink and set the empty glass on top of the attaché case. "Quiroz is my cover name," she began, "and for now my true name is not relevant. My family was prominent in Monterrey, and my father was once governor of Nuevo León. He amassed considerable wealth, as our politicians do, and was considered by many a potential candidate for the presidency. He was what they call 'eligible.' So, my brother José Manuel and I were raised in very comfortable circumstances. José Manuel was three years older, and after our father died, a strong bond developed between us. He became an architect with a Mexico City firm that had good governmental connections—meaning they got a great many profitable government construction contracts. I studied business administration and accounting at Rice University in Texas, and so my brother and I saw less of each other during those years.

"While I was learning management of our family's business my brother began constructing a resort hotel at Ixtapa for a very wealthy entrepreneur named Francisco Ibarra. His money, my brother gradually learned, came from narcotics trafficking. Ibarra owned ranches in the north where mari-juana and poppies were grown. There were airstrips for his planes that flew narcotics across the border to the U.S., and Ibarra had so much money that he needed to invest it where he could. The hotel was one such investment.

"Buildings, as you know, are constructed and financed on a basis of scheduled payments. Ibarra provided the pay-ments, but threatened to withhold them unless my brother cooperated with him in laundering money through his architectural firm. That involved trips to Texas and California banks, and at first my brother refused. Ibarra stopped the next construction payment, and my brother faced ruin and professional disgrace—so he agreed. José Manuel made trips for Ibarra despite his conscience, and having become entangled in Ibarra's activities he was sub-ject to blackmail." She paused, and looked beyond me to the sunny balcony. "Inevitably, he was told to begin smuggling cocaine to the U.S. for Ibarra, but that was too much for José Manuel. Laundering the proceeds of past crimes was one thing, but feeding the appetites of addicts, and making new ones revolted my brother. So, he killed himself."

"How did you learn of his involvements?"

"Through professional friends, and his secretary. His death almost killed my mother who still doesn't know the reason. So," she spread her hands, "I became involved. The attorney general is an old family friend, and an honest man. I went to him with my story, and he agreed to let me help try bringing Ibarra to justice. But he warned me that any evidence I turned up had to be absolutely conclusive, Ibarra being a very powerful man whose influence doesn't stop at the courts. In Mexico it is one thing to indict a *narcotraficante*, quite another to convict him. Witnesses are killed or intimidated, prosecutors frightened off, judges bribed . . ." She gazed at me bleakly. "I've been almost a year gaining Ibarra's confidence. Delivering this money to him is a test I need to pass. Then in time I can gain access to his ledgers, the names of his dealers here and in the U.S.—perhaps with that kind of solid evidence I can destroy Francisco Pedro Ibarra."

"Also known as 'Pedrito.' "

She nodded.

"I'm sorry about your brother," I told her, "but it's not a unique story. My sister—well, I lost her to drugs." I looked away. "It's not something one forgets." Pam's ravaged, once-lovely face came into my mind, the bony, clawlike hands, the skeleton her model's body had become . . . I'd substituted sister for wife because of Paula's evident glibness. If she'd been spinning me a legend it was well polished, and my counter was to fabricate one of my own. Touching the attaché case, I said, "Where do you deliver this?"

"In Ixtapa. Tonight." She gazed at the case as if it were inherently evil.

"Is it for cocaine?"

"I suppose so."

"How is it to be gotten to Chato?"

She shrugged. "The usual way. A light plane will leave one of Ibarra's strips in Durango or Sonora, touch down in Texas. Someone will board a bus and deliver a suitcase in Union City a few days from now."

"A major delivery," I remarked. "I'd like to abort it if that's possible without compromising you."

"I don't believe that's a danger," she said, "but I don't know when the *fayuca* will leave Mexico or when it will reach Union City. And Chato is only a name to me."

"Isador Campestre is his public name—in case you hear it mentioned." I was considering how much else to tell her. Finally I said, "You might as well know that Eddie Wax was murdered this morning on his flight to Miami. By a man, dressed as a woman, who stuck a lethal dose of heroin into his arm. The killer, Sid Fertig, was killed as he tried to take that case. I was inserted to make the Cancún connection—but I didn't expect to meet you."

She smiled. "Nor I, you. So, you're DEA."

"No, ex-FBI. I was in the Legal Attaché office, Mexico City. I liked Mexico and decided to go into business for myself. Occasionally I'm asked to help out."

"You live here—Cancún?"

"Not far away."

"Explaining why you tried to make it look as if you'd been on the Mexicana flight."

I built another pair of drinks and looked at her. She was as petite as Melody, but her figure—and I'd seen 95 percent of it—was less athletic. In English I said, "In the U.S. we don't score an impressive conviction rate against major drug dealers, so my policy is to eliminate them before they get to trial. Let me suggest that your attorney general was right—Ibarra is going to be very, very hard to convict. If you can think of a way to put me next to him, with luck and some planning I might be able to put him out of your life. Without appeal."

"José Manuel had none," she said somberly. "Why should Ibarra?"

"Exactly." I picked up her Colt .25 and slid the magazine into the grip, put it in her purse and handed it back to her. "I'm going to keep your federal ID," I told her. "You shouldn't be carrying it while you're around Ibarra or his men. When I have reason to trust you completely you'll get it back."

"That's agreeable. And what do I call you for the present?"

"Juan. I want you to phone me when you've made delivery to Ibarra. By then, you may have thought of a way to bring me into his organization."

"Any suggestions?"

"Tell him you met an interesting *gringo* in Cancún—we had drinks, got along well, and you got the impression he was looking for drugs to buy, in quantity."

"I suppose I could do that. But I should have a name to give him."

"I'll be Henry. From Wilmington, Delaware. If things warm up I'll have a last name and some ID. Meanwhile, I'm just plain Juan. Room six-nineteen, Hotel Las Maravillas. Will you phone me?"

"When it's safe."

"If Ibarra wonders why the case locks are broken, tell him Wax didn't give you a key because he had none. You broke the locks to verify contents."

"He'll like that," she said and stood up. "You'll never know how much I hate Pedrito Ibarra. Perhaps in trusting you I let hatred overcome caution, my personal security, but then you did find my *credencial,* and my cover was blown."

"Not entirely. I'll feel better about things when you call."

She picked up the attaché case that had already cost two men their lives, and walked toward the door. "We'll talk again," she said, and went out.

I locked the door after her and finished my drink. I could have followed her down to the lobby and waved Valeriano off, but tailing her would be good field experience for him, and I wanted to know where she went.

Paula's revelations might or might not be true. And I'd withheld the fact that three-quarters of the money she carried was counterfeit—if Ibarra discovered it, her surprise had to be genuine.

In the meantime, she seemed to be everything she'd described about herself: educated, intelligent, cultured, sincere. And dedicated to the destruction of the man she held responsible for her brother's death. Superficially her story held together. Her call might add or detract from its validity. *If* she called.

I went out on the balcony and looked down. The beach was nearly deserted. Swimmers and sunbathers were in the hotel, dining, or enjoying *siesta.* Three men were raking litter from the beach. A sombreroed Tarascan Indian with a load of *serapes* on his shoulders walked across the sand, looking for customers, but the few still lolling on their beach towels waved him away.

The lonely Indian, I thought; a permanent fixture of the Mexican social scene; unwanted, ignored by a stratified system that hadn't in hundreds of years figured out how to deal with him; a tragic contrast to the corrupt and avaricious officials whose grafted billions built palaces in Spain, California and Miami. Compared to them, Ferdinand and Imelda Marcos were trivial despoilers.

Still, I mused, as I turned away from the sunlit scene, although it was said that people got the government they deserved, I'd long felt that the Mexicans deserved better. A sentiment I nursed quite privately.

I was tired from the morning's fishing, the flight to Cancún, the tension of dealing with Paula. It would be a while before Valeriano called in, so I took a long pull from the bottle, closed the window blinds, and declared *siesta*.

FOUR

Pete Valeriano was saying, ". . . took the flight to Zihua-tanejo."

"Huh?" Partly awake I clenched the telephone and glanced at my watch. Nearly two hours had passed. "Repeat, please."

Patiently, he said, "The target personality is airborne for—"

"I heard the destination." Ixtapa was five miles from Zihua, served by the same airport. "Okay, I'll have a wake-up shower and we'll talk when you get here."

Thirty minutes later he was sipping ice rum while I summarized my dealings with the young woman known as Paula María Quiroz. At the end I said, "Bottom line, she took the money."

"I saw her carry the case aboard the plane."

"And may or may not recontact me."

"Think she will?"

"She's got intestinal fortitude, but after maneuvering around Ibarra for a year she may welcome outside help. Whatever she decides she'll give it sober thought."

"Assuming her tale is true."

"I'm playing carefully."

"I checked for phone messages; so far, nothing."

"I wouldn't expect her operational alias to show up, so thank whoever calls you, and leave it at that."

"I shouldn't tell Wolcott what happened?"

"He has no need to know. And I don't want the Mexicans finding out that she's in contact with a Yanqui." I paused. "*Any* Mexicans."

"Got it. Well, what to do now?"

"Against the possibility that the lady can put me next to Ibarra, I need alias ID on an expedite basis. In the name of Henry *fulano de tal* from Wilmington. Better have it sent to Mérida in case I have to move fast. I'll tell Wolcott where to deliver the package."

"Henry somebody from Wilmington. Anything else?"

"She said *papa* had been governor of Nuevo León some years ago, and a *presidenciable*. Also, if she told true, the family was—is—prominent in Monterrey, the state capital. So, run down a former governor with two children, one an architect, deceased, named José Manuel. And a daughter. Having her true name would help me, and you can run it through the indices. If she's clean, fine. If not . . ."

Valeriano looked up from his notes. "What?"

"Eliminate her," I said, "and go after Ibarra some other way."

He looked thoughtful. "Quite a load for the Miami office, Jack."

"Yeah. Shake out those empty suits. If you sense any foot-dragging, invoke Manny's name."

"Will do." He got up. "I'll get back to my room, stay there until Al calls."

After he left I got into swimming trunks and went down to the hotel pool. It was empty, the only action being in the wading pool where tots were happily splashing, belly-flopping, and zapping each other with a big colored ball while their mothers chatted with one another.

I did a dozen lengths and pulled onto a sun pad. A pool-side waiter brought me a Cuba Libre, and I sipped it—merely to replace lost body moisture, I told myself. Half an hour's snooze, and I went back to my room. The phone-message light was on, so I dialed Valeriano's room.

"No file trace on the lady," he told me, "but I laid the rest of the requirements on Al."

"So I can stay liquid and mobile, you might pass me the introductory thousand before you leave."

"I'm leaving?"

"You'll be more help honchoing Miami."

"You're right. Well, I'll take a morning flight back."

In a little while he brought up my initial fee—ten hundred-dollar bills—and I signed a receipt for the money. We traded words of mutual esteem, shook hands, and said *adiós*.

I thought about Pete Valeriano for a while, evaluating him as a reliable case officer, but not a man for heavy field action. He was too nice. He seemed to lack the killer instinct, but then he hadn't been touched by narcotics as I had. And in that Pete was fortunate.

My own future, I reflected, was uninsurable. What I really wanted from life were some satisfying years with Melody, and beyond that I didn't care. Eventually, sometime, a hit man was going to emerge from an alley and blast me into nothingness before I had time to draw. It was inevitable. Meanwhile, I'd do all I could to reduce their numbers.

For a while I read *Time* and *U.S. News*, dozed on and off, and after nightfall, I left the Maravillas and walked to the Caracol shopping plaza, cooled by the offshore breeze. At Keller's I took an outdoor table, ate char-broiled bacon-wrapped *gambas*, and washed down the big shrimp with cold, purple *sangría*.

Strolling back to the hotel I thought again about Paula. I'd give her a day to contact me, then fly back to Cozumel. With a relatively small amount of effort I'd earned a thousand dollars. It wasn't enough for even a down payment on the screened patio, but it would get me to Caracas for a surprise visit with Melody.

No, I reflected, that wouldn't be fair; we didn't intrude on each other's lives when separated. She didn't come unannounced to my bungalow, so it would be wrong of me to pop in on her at Caracas. Still, I thought, I *could* send a telegram. Not having seen Melody for three weeks I missed her.

If nothing materialized from Paula I'd check Viasa flights and wire Melody I was coming.

Before retiring I turned off the air conditioning, and

opened balcony doors to the sea breeze. I fell asleep almost at once.

It seemed only minutes later that the telephone rang. I pulled off the receiver, said, *"Sí,"* and heard a woman's voice begin to speak.

FIVE

"Henry? I can't talk long. Because—you understand?"

"I understand. Go on."

"The man to whom I gave the briefcase is interested. Can you come to Ixtapa?"

"When?"

"Tomorrow. I'll reserve a room for you at the Tropical. What name?"

"Henry—" I tried to think of something. All I could come up with was "—Furlong."

"All right. There's a morning flight from Cancún at around nine-fifteen."

"I'll be on it."

During breakfast in Valeriano's room I covered late developments and said, "Things are moving faster than expected, so I need an alias ID, like, today. Also, a flash roll to impress Ibarra. And make Henry's last name Furlong."

He leaned over to take a sip from his thick black *café.* "No problem. I'll bring it to you at the Tropical."

We took separate taxis to the airport. Valeriano caught the flight to Miami, and I had time to make arrangements for my Seabee. I paid a week's parking in advance, hid personal ID in the baggage compartment and locked it. As I carried my bag into the airport lobby I reflected that even if I'd wanted to fly to Ixtapa, the thousand-mile flight would have meant three refueling stops, the first at Campeche before the long haul over open water to Veracruz, then on to

Puebla so I could climb over the southern Sierra Madres with a fuel margin for bad weather. Solo, I couldn't reach the Zihuatanejo airport much before nightfall. But Áeromexico would have me at the hotel before noon.

As it turned out, I registered as Henry Furlong at eleven-forty. That was after a five-mile taxi ride from the airport along a road bordered with thick groves of coconut and papaya trees, reminding me that I was truly in the tropics. The driver had mistaken me for a casual tourist and tried charging me ten dollars for the drive, but he settled for half after I expressed displeasure in gutter Spanish.

The suite reserved for me included a comfortable sitting room, a bedroom with two large beds, a large tiled bathroom and an ample balcony overlooking a long white sand beach and the Golden Pacific, as tourist pamphlets called it.

Clustered on the sand were the usual palm-thatched conical sun shelters, *palapas.* The largest shadowed a beach bar that seemed to be doing heavy business among the ocean bathers. This was the promotionally named Costa Grande, and any beach four miles long was entitled to the adjective. Looking up and down the beach I counted ten large hotels including a Holiday Inn. I wondered which one Paula's brother had designed for Francisco Ibarra.

From room service I ordered ice and mineral water, sent out my laundry, drank some Añejo, and waited for Paula to contact me. By now, I hoped, Valeriano was in Miami getting my alias ID together.

I answered the phone, and it was Paula. "I'm at the beach bar," she said, "and I'd like you to join me."

Welcome words. After changing into swimming trunks I went down, and found her sipping a piña colada at the end of the bar. She was wearing about two ounces of brick red bikini that barely met the exposure code. All bar seats were occupied, so we walked over to her *palapa* and stretched out on beach towels. After a waiter brought my planter's punch, she said, "Are your accommodations comfortable?"

"For the present. When do I meet Ibarra?"

"Tonight. He was in a good mood because of my delivery,

so I took advantage of it to mention you as a possible customer. He agreed to meet you at dinner tonight." She paused. "At the Andaluz. His hotel." She sipped her creamy drink. "That's what you want, isn't it? Are you actually going to make a buy?"

"Just making a buy would be futile unless it leads into his organization."

"I see your point." She stretched languidly, and her body seemed more sensuous than when she'd tensely disrobed the day before. "Do you like ocean swimming?" she asked.

"Very much. Scuba is a hobby of mine."

She got up and ran into the water. I followed, and we both plunged headlong into the waves. Paula was a good swimmer, not with Melody's trained skills, but for someone brought up inland she performed well. The water was warm and refreshing. When we were out a way, she dove under and disappeared. Suddenly she jerked my feet out from under me, and I dropped down to the bottom. Through the stirred-up sand I could see her legs. I grasped her ankles and pulled until she slid down beside me, her body touching mine. Together we floated upward, and when our heads were above water, I very lightly kissed her cheek. A wave broke over us and I steadied her lighter body with my hands. She began pushing away, then stopped. Current brought us back together. Eyes wide, she gazed at me. "We could have lunch in your room," she said throatily.

"Let's go." My arms circled the small of her back, and she pressed herself to me. I kissed her lips and they opened on mine. She broke away and swam laughing back to shore. After collecting her bag and towels from the *palapa* we entered the hotel and took an elevator to my room.

To our wet bodies the air was chill, so I turned off the air-conditioning and opened the balcony doors. Warm breeze flowed in. Paula took a seat at the balcony table while I rang for room service. Then I mixed drinks and carried them to the table. As she lifted her glass she said, "Normally I don't drink very much, but the last twenty-four hours have been . . . demanding."

"For me, too. Everyone needs to relax now and then."

After drinking she said, "How long have you been ... involved in what you're doing?"

"Close to six years." That long since Pam died. I hadn't thought I'd survive the first year. Now it seemed long ago. The breeze blew gently on the curtains. Ocean music.

The waiter arrived, we ordered drinks and lunch from a thick, ornamented menu. Paula changed into shorts and halter, and hung her bikini to dry on a sunlit chair. I was starting to feel pretty damn mature for all this small talk, and salty, so I jumped into the shower, shaved and put some clothes on. At least yesterday's mutual hostility had dissolved into a kind of tentative acceptance, a feeling of complicity. Paula and I had become accomplices in a dangerous effort that could lead us—no one knew where. Her obsession was revenge, and I sensed that she discounted her own life against the chance of bringing down Ibarra. She was living, I decided, one day at a time. Not carelessly, I hoped, for my sake as well as hers.

I said, "Does Ibarra have any idea who you are?"

She shook her head. "I was in Texas when José Manuel was working for Pedrito. He may have heard his architect had a sister, but there's no way he could connect me."

"How did you manage to meet him?"

"It was quite simple. Once I'd made up my mind I went to the Andaluz, rented an expensive suite, and began buying cocaine and marijuana from the help. Within a few days Ibarra approached me on the beach." She sipped from her glass. "He said, as owner, he liked to know his guests, and he hoped that I found my suite comfortable. I said I did, and he invited me to his dining room table that evening. During our conversation he said there was no reason I should have to pay for my drugs, or my suite. If I were unattached, as I seemed to be, he had a proposition for me. In addition to being his occasional hostess, I would make trips for him now and then—become a confidential courier. I said I'd consider it. Two days later I told him I would agree, but I wouldn't become his lover.

"That surprised him. He's accustomed to having his way with women of all classes, even though he has a wife and several children."

"Where?"

"The residential zone at the edge of Mexico City—Lomas de Barrilaco. I've never seen his home, but I've heard it's large and very opulent." Her lips tightened. "Why not? He's an extremely wealthy man."

"Narcotraficante."

She nodded. "Occasionally I smoke with him, or do small amounts of cocaine to maintain my cover. Several times he's asked me to go to bed with him, even offered to pay me, but I haven't done it."

"That's a complication to avoid," I said. "Besides, you've done well without the sex factor. Clearly, it's not essential."

"Had there been no other way to gain his confidence, I would have," she said stubbornly. She looked at me steadily. "I've found that deep hatred overcomes a good many inhibitions, but making love to my brother's executioner would have been repugnant."

"It didn't come about, why think of it?"

"I . . . I wanted you to understand I'm not Ibarra's woman."

The waiter arrived with our meal. Cold shrimp salad for Paula, cold lobster with drawn butter for me. A bottle of Domecq Chablis, and coffee. A light lunch, for we were not at the altitudes of Mexico City or Guadalajara where luncheon is the heaviest meal of the day to accommodate slower digestion.

I added Añejo to our coffee, and after a while Paula got up and closed the balcony door and drapes, and turned on the air-conditioning. Behind my chair she placed her hands on my shoulders. "In the water," she said, "you kissed me."

"It seemed natural. Besides, you kissed back."

"Because I wanted to," she said, huskily. "I wouldn't go to bed with Ibarra, but we have some hours to pass before evening . . ."

Mentally I completed the unfinished thought. Rising, I turned and took her hands so that we stood face to face. She hadn't asked about Melody and I wouldn't have lied. Now she whispered words that caught in her throat, and moved against me, and my whisper joined hers, thoughts beyond expression. Mouths met, tongues touched, and in the cool darkness of my bedroom two people joined and moved slowly together who didn't even know each other's name.

━━━━━━━━━━━━━━

My balcony faced east so we were denied the sunset I was accustomed to watching from my bungalow at Cozumel. Lovemaking had bonded us, we were lovers who hadn't decided how fully to trust one another. But it was a start.

After Paula left to dress for dinner I showered, not wanting Ibarra to scent her perfume on me, and got into freshly laundered clothes. Instinctively I wanted to carry iron into the lion's den, but as a presumed novice from Wilmington I would have no reason to go armed to dinner. If Ibarra found a piece on me his reaction would be heavily adverse. And he might begin to suspect Paula.

On the chance that my quarters might be searched I slit the foam mattress in the unused bed, and placed the holstered PPK inside. No bulge. I smoothed the bedclothes, turned off the air-conditioning and went out on the balcony.

The horizon was still a deep purple, a few far away clouds tinted lavender and pink. It was a time of evening I love, before blackness envelops the earth, just before the evening stars come out. Off in the distance bobbed a scatter of fishing boats, carbide lanterns their only running lights. Otherwise, the sea began to look dark and forbidding.

Below, on the beach, Hawaiian torches flared up. One after another was touched off until they illuminated the *palapas*, the beach bar, the tiled dance patio to one side. Playing *mariachi* music, a gaudily costumed troupe filed out to serenade patio diners at candlelit tables. I would have liked being at one, with Paula, but we'd made different arrangements. At my request I was meeting Francisco

43

Ibarra, a man who had just received (he thought) four million dollars from a scumbag in Union City for cocaine Ibarra was ready to supply.

Sounds of patio revelry broke into my thoughts. I went down to the lobby and stood by the outside portal until a light yellow Rolls Corniche pulled up. The driver got out and opened the rear door for me. He was a swarthy, muscular man with a Pancho Villa mustache, wearing a white *guayabera* loose enough to conceal a shoulder-holstered weapon. I got into the Rolls, the driver closed my door and got behind the right-hand wheel.

The thickness of the front seat accommodated a built-in bar. Soft music drifted from stereo speakers, and within arms' reach was set a television screen. Soundlessly, the Rolls pulled away.

The drive to the Hotel Andaluz took less than five minutes, the Rolls gliding smoothly as a snake on silk. At the entrance the driver handed me over to a servant in starched white uniform, who showed me to a private elevator on the left side of the lobby. Music whispered softly as we rose to the penthouse where the doors opened.

Directly in front of the opening stood a decorated wooden frame. Except for painted flowers and plastic vines, it resembled an airport metal detector. I stepped through it, a buzzer sounded, and I stepped back. I emptied my right-hand pocket of metal change, gave it to the unsmiling servant, and tried again. No buzzer this time. He returned my change, and I followed him across polished marble floor to a windowed alcove.

A sectional lounge was set into it, curving around a massive free-form cocktail table. Paula was wearing a white linen dress with a black, gold-tassled belt. Beside her sat a white-haired man with an uncreased, intelligent face. His eyebrows and pencil mustache were so black I wondered if they were dyed. The man got up as I approached. One hand smoothed his one-piece leisure suit. The other hand lifted until his index finger pointed at me. His lips barely moved as he said, "I know who you are."

SIX

Paula's face was expressionless. She leaned forward and reached for her drink. Frozen by his words, I said, "You know me?"

"You are Paula's friend, Henry Furlong. And I am Francisco Ibarra." His hand extended to shake mine. *"Bienvenido,* welcome."

My heart resumed beating. Through dry lips I said, "Thanks for inviting me." Then I looked down. " 'Evening, Paula." Your friend's a regular laugh riot, I wanted to say.

"Good evening, Henry." Eyes vacant, she sipped from her glass.

Ibarra said, "Sit down, please, be comfortable. What's your pleasure?"

To the waiter I said, "Añejo on the rocks," and sat across from them. Through the seamless window I could see a sky speckled with stars. The Rolls, the hotel, the penthouse with its view were things a man would kill for. And Ibarra had.

Sid Fertig, the transvestite hit man, hadn't knocked off Eddie Wax for the thrill of seeing another corpse. Someone had paid Sid to snatch the case from unsuspecting Eddie. The same someone who knew when Eddie was flying, where to, and what he had in the case. Chato knew, because he'd given Eddie the attaché case, airline ticket and contact instructions. But would Chato hijack his own money? The other possibility sat in front of me, sleek, self-confident, expensively attired. It would have been greatly to Ibarra's advantage to secure the four million before Eddie could turn

45

it over to him; then he'd have the money, without obligation to provide any cocaine. From Chato, Ibarra had known Eddie's flight and what the attaché case contained. Yes, I decided, having given little previous thought to Eddie's murder, Ibarra had hired Sid Fertig for the job. And now he had—he thought—four million green, and he didn't have to pay off Sid.

Sometimes, I reflected, circumstances conspire to favor the evildoers of the world.

I was noticing Ibarra inspecting me with an appraiser's eye. He said, "So, you are enjoying your vacation in Mexico?"

"Very much." I took my drink from the waiter's tray. "Prosit." We lifted glasses and drank. I licked my lips appreciatively, and said, "This Ixtapa looks like a nice place. I was going to spend time at Puerto Vallarta, but then I met your friend here." I smiled at Paula.

"Perhaps," said Ibarra, "it will have been a fortunate meeting. Yes, Ixtapa is becoming a second Puerto Vallarta, and, so to speak, a third incarnation of Acapulco. Fortunately for all of us, our waters and beaches are still clean and pure. And our hotel association, of which I am a director, intends to keep it that way."

"Praiseworthy," I remarked. "Marbella, the whole Costa del Sol, in fact, became smelly garbage dumps, untreated sewage emptying right into the Mediterranean."

"Speaking of the Mediterranean," Ibarra said, sitting forward, "there is a Club Med three kilometers to the northwest. I own a hundred hectares of desirable land in that area. Paula tells me you are looking for investments in Mexico, and it occurred to me you might be interested in looking over my property with a view to development."

I smiled deprecatingly. "In our brief conversations Paula gained perhaps too broad an impression of my interests—and means. To be blunt about it, my revered father always told me never to buy in Mexico anything I couldn't swim back with across the Rio Grande."

Ibarra chuckled appreciatively. "Excellent advice, in general, but to us Mexicans, land is still sacred."

Paula said, "The two of you are being awfully dull. Pedrito will develop his land with or without outside investors. Henry, you can doubtless find what you are looking to buy without Pedrito's aid."

Ibarra said, "Nevertheless, I feel sure that Sr. Furlong appreciates the profit motive."

"It's why I'm in business," I said.

"And what exactly is that business?" Ibarra inquired with a perfectly charming smile.

"Like yourself, I buy and sell." I glanced at Paula and began my spin. "In my younger years I worked in the office of an oil company in Maracaibo, first as an accountant, then as business manager. I learned enough about the petroleum game to become an analyst for a brokerage house. When the oil business became depressed I was without a job. But I had made a wide range of friends in the investment business, and many of them enjoyed the use of recreational cocaine. An opportunity arose for me to acquire a kilo of high-grade dust. Selling it among these friends, who would have taken more than I had, I made a profit of 400 percent. Since then, Sr. Ibarra, the sale of cocaine has been my sole interest."

"Why did you come to Mexico?"

"Because supplies from Colombia through Florida have become unreliable. Coast Guard, Customs, the Navy—" I waved a hand "—have reduced the availability of what I want. So I decided to explore the situation in Mexico, never dreaming this charming young chance acquaintance might be the connection I needed, the answer to my prayers."

I spotted a glint of approval in Paula's eyes, professional acknowledgment that I, too, could create a legend. Not too thin, nor too thick. Only what the moment called for. Hers had much more detail, but plausible detail was what suspicious men like Ibarra wanted to hear from a consort.

I sat back and sipped my drink while Ibarra thought things over. Finally he said, "Business is not well done on an empty stomach. I see that our table is ready, so let us put first things first."

Rising, he took Paula's hand and drew her to her feet. Ibarra led us around a corner into a large candlelit dining room, furnished in French antiques. The service plates were silver, the place settings English sterling. Irish china, Swedish crystal. Servants seated us, Paula at the head of the table, Ibarra on her right, while I faced him across the table. Wine was poured, vichyssoise served, and we began.

After the salad course came tempuraed fish, veal medallions in Marsala, blanched asparagus with hollandaise, and for dessert profiteroles. Coffee was served in a sitting room whose windows provided an even broader view of the Pacific. I declined a cigar, Ibarra selected one, a waiter pierced the end, and held a light. Through a screen of gray smoke Ibarra said, "You were quite right in coming to me, Henry. I have the commodity of interest in ample quantity. How much do you feel you could handle?"

"That would depend on quality," I said, "and price."

"Price," he said, "is important to us both," and laid on the table something that resembled a small TV remote control. He flicked it across to me. It was a plastic case measuring about two by three inches, perhaps half an inch thick. "Do you know what it is?" he asked.

"Never seen one before."

"Then I will tell you. These electronic devices are used by major banks that take in American dollars. Over the last few years your Treasury has begun using metallic ink in certain portions of its currency. The open end of the validator scans for those inks, and this bulb lights up if they are present. No light, the bill is counterfeit."

"Amazing," I said, pushing it back to him, "what technology can do."

He glanced at Paula. "Only yesterday," he said, "I was paid for a transaction with what appeared to be genuine American dollars." He touched the validator. "Only a portion of the cash was genuine, the greater part was counterfeit—undetectable to even a trained eye, but—" he tapped the plastic case "—this marvelous instrument saved me from making a costly mistake."

"Lucky for you," I said. "How much was involved?"

"Several million dollars." His face hardened. "Of course I will keep the genuine currency, but the man who sent me the counterfeit will not receive his merchandise."

I smiled foolishly. "I haven't got anything like a million dollars to spend."

"How much, then?"

"Enough for a trial transaction. If the stuff's good, you can depend on major business from me."

"You are, may I ask, working for yourself, or . . . ?"

"Strictly solo," I said. "If I'm caught it's my own fault, not because of some informer's treachery."

"I envy you. A large organization such as mine must be constantly watched. The rewards are greater, but so are the risks of betrayal." He drew lengthily on his cigar. "Are you a user?"

"No. For me cocaine is business, not indulgence. I've seen distributors become addicted, snort away their profits."

Ibarra turned to Paula. "As usual, my dear, your judgment has been excellent."

"Thank you," she said with a slight smile. "I'm glad you're pleased with Henry."

A servant brought Ibarra a cordless telephone, whispered something, and he nodded. Rising, he said, "If you'll excuse me," and took the phone out of the dining room. In a low voice Paula said, "You bastard, you didn't tell me the money was counterfeit."

"I couldn't know he'd detect it. And your surprise had to be real."

"It certainly was! I was so frightened, afraid he'd suspect me."

"The thought probably occurred to him, but he had to ask himself how you could have gotten the counterfeit money to substitute, and then realize you couldn't have."

"He was furious, of course, cursing Chato, swearing he'd make Chato pay for trying to trick him."

I said, "These people rip off each other constantly—but Ibarra shouldn't be too unhappy: he got a million without having to part with any product. Who's he talking to?"

"I couldn't hear, but it may have something to do with that money."

I heard Ibarra's returning footsteps, and whispered, "When will I see you again, Paula? Can you come tonight?"

She shook her head, then Ibarra was at his seat, looking at me. "Liqueur?"

"Thanks, no," I said, "but I'd like to discuss a deal."

"Regretfully, other business demands my attention, but tomorrow I will be in touch with you and we will finalize a sale."

I thanked him for a superb dinner, said goodnight to Paula, and Ibarra strolled me to the private elevator. I rode down unaccompanied, and as I waited by the hotel entrance, I noticed the building's cornerstone. Engraved on the marble block were the construction credits: CONTRACTOR, KAMINSKI HNOS. ARCHITECT, JOSÉ MANUEL MENDEZ PERALTA. That told me Paula's family name was Mendez, Peralta the matronymic. As the Rolls pulled up I wondered about her given name. Perhaps Valeriano had discovered it by now.

By eleven I was back in my suite. I checked, found the Walther undisturbed, and complimented myself on not having taken it to Ibarra's penthouse. Paula should have warned me about the metal detector, but perhaps she was too accustomed to it to give it any thought.

No call-in messages. When would Valeriano deliver my operational needs? To convince Ibarra, I had to have enough money to make a down payment, and I couldn't postpone it very long.

In bed I thought over Ibarra's detecting the counterfeit bills and I didn't like it. The Miami office should have treated Chato's four million as windfall money, unaccountable, and passed its entirety to me. If Ibarra had received it from me I wouldn't have attended a dinner party tonight, I'd have attended my own funeral.

So far, luck was riding my shoulders, but I wondered what tomorrow would bring.

Geckos chirped and rasped in the balcony vines. A string of firecrackers exploded somewhere along the beach. I thought about Melody for a while, then I slept.

━━━━━━━━━

I was finishing a substantial breakfast when Pete Valeriano arrived looking tired and disheveled. I chuckled a bit and set him up with some coffee and a plate of tropical fruit, and asked if he'd brought what I asked for.

He handed me a large, sealed Manila envelope. "See for yourself. It was an all-night job, be grateful."

"Hey, I didn't ask for this gig so let's keep proper perspective."

"Sorry, I haven't slept, and I didn't exactly get whole-hearted cooperation." He added sugar to his coffee and sprinkled some over the fruit slices. "There's a core of ill will toward you in Miami, did you know? Some of the guys would love to see you hung out to dry."

"That's news?" I opened the envelope.

Driving license, credit cards, charge cards, club cards, Mexican tourist card, calling cards, all in the name of Henry D. Furlong, with an address in Wilmington, Delaware. Pete said, "Don't forget to sign where it says to."

A sealed white envelope contained a stack of currency. "How much?" I asked.

"Three hundred thou."

"Treasury issue?"

"Yes."

"Welcome news," I said, and told him about Ibarra's unexpected discovery. Frowning, he said, "I'll make a point of passing that on, Jack. The substitution wasn't necessary. Or wise."

"My feeling." I sipped from my cup, poured more. "Everything else buttoned up, flemished and shipshape?"

"Well, one more thing—in New Jersey they're still looking for Chato, aka Isador Campestre."

"What?"

"Yeah, couldn't find him to arrest him. Maybe today." He didn't sound optimistic.

"That's not good," I said, "but at least I'm not playing Eddie Wax any longer. That was a short off-Broadway run."

Pete reached over and pulled from the envelope a sheet of paper I'd missed, a copy of Chato's rap sheet. The black-and-white photo showed a square head that could have been chopped from stone, gnarled ears, narrow piggish eyes and a flat, misshapen nose with flared nostrils and no bridge. I gave it back to Valeriano. "Looks as though Chato's taken a lot of punishment in his fifty years. That's fortunate for him."

"Fortunate?"

"Because Ibarra's certainly going to punish Chato for trying to defraud him. For openers, Chato gets nothing in return for his money, and he's going to look very hard for it—and for Eddie Wax."

He squeezed lime over a papaya slice, chewed and swallowed. "Yesterday, INS included Ibarra's name in a bunch of Mexican visa applications, and ran them through the Mexican consulate in Miami. Ibarra came out clean."

"Money covers a lot of sin," I said, thinking of Ibarra's smile. "What about Paula?"

"State gave us the answers. Her father was the late Carlos Manuel Mendez Gortari, a Monterrey industrialist in textiles and chemicals, and two-term governor of Nuevo León. Daughter Nina Victoria Mendez Peralta, present age twenty-nine. No derogatory information on Nina. State files reflect yearly visas issued while she studied at Rice."

"And her brother?"

"José Manuel, architect, received occasional visas for travel to professional meetings in Houston, Chicago, and San Francisco. No DI on him, either."

"Because he was never caught." I pushed aside the remnants of my now-cold scrambled eggs, got up and stretched. Valeriano said, "What's your approach from now on?"

"Ibarra's supposed to meet me today to work out our deal. I'll have a better view of things after that."

"If you can lure him across the border we can arrest him."

"Sure, but to what purpose? He'd bond out in minutes and be gone forever. Even if he could be held there'd be only my testimony against him, and I'm not anxious to surface as a witness."

"What about Paula—Nina?"

I grunted. "In Mexico City not long ago an unusually corrupt high official was indicted on the basis of sworn testimony by no less than twenty-one witnesses. By trial time those who hadn't been killed had recanted. There was only one stubborn holdout, and defense lawyers destroyed him on the stand. Result, acquittal. How do you think Nina Mendez would fare? They'd kill or intimidate her, kidnap her mother, do whatever they felt was necessary to prevent her from testifying against Ibarra. Let's forget this arrest and trial foolishness. It's the stuff dreams are made of, as Bogie said not so long ago."

"I suppose you're right." He laid down his fork. "I was on the Gulfstream nearly five hours, Jack, and I'm dead. Can I borrow a bed?"

"Help yourself."

Pete stripped down to his skivvies and fell asleep on the spare bed in less than a minute. Meantime, I got dressed. The telephone rang; it was Nina Mendez saying she'd see me shortly.

When she arrived she was carrying a large Gucci handbag, looking fresh and lovely as the morn. We kissed quietly, and she whispered, "How is my little businessman today?"

"Fine, Nina, never better."

Her face set as she stared at me. "So you've learned my name."

"All for the better, too, because you traced clean. Incidentally, I spotted your brother's name on the Andaluz cornerstone."

"It didn't give you mine."

"I had help with that." I gestured at the closed bedroom door. "A visitor from Dallas."

"I see. Then you're just a hired gun?"

"Call it whatever you like." I stared back at her. "What goodies did you bring me?"

"A sample." She took out a small glassine bag filled with a white crystalline substance. It was stuff I'd seen before, too often. Beside the bag she placed a test kit that resembled a swimming pool acid-alkali tester. "I suppose you know how to do this?"

"I do, and I expect first-rate results. Pedrito wouldn't send me a mediocre sample." I opened the bag, wet a fingertip and dusted it with powder, touched it to the tip of my tongue. It had the characteristic bitter taste and numbed the end of my tongue. "Cocaine hydrochloride," I pronounced, and filled the glass tube to the first mark, added dilute acid, and shook. When the mixture was uniformly pink, I added the second reagent as far as the third mark, and set the tube in its small plastic rack. The pink changed to light blue, darkened and became deep purple. I said, "Around 90 percent purity."

I emptied the tube into a flowerpot and handed Nina the bag of coke. "Enjoy," I said, "and tell Pedrito I'm enchanted with its quality. Did he set a price?"

"Thirty thousand a kilo delivered in the U.S. Twenty if you take delivery here. That's for under a hundred kilos; 20 percent less if you buy more."

"On American Express?" I grinned. "Four keys will do for now, and I'll pay him in person."

Her eyes narrowed. "I hope you won't be foolish enough to give him counterfeit money."

I shook my head. "That little validator is impressive, eliminates the guesswork. And I have to remind Pedrito to deliver only highgrade white, no Mex brown. I guess it's worth a hundred and twenty thou to learn where the stuff is delivered, by whom, and how. To maintain Ibarra's interest you might mention I'm also interested in marijuana, both now and in between coke deals."

"I'd rather you took it up with him."

"I will. Do you know how to turn off the metal detector?"

"A small switch on the wall beside the elevator."

"What's the elevator lock combination?"

"Forty-one, seventeen, sixty-three."

"Good girl." I gave her a smile, just to keep *her* interested. "And his ledgers—where are they kept?"

Nina paused. "In a large safe set into his bedroom wall. It's faced with a wooden panel that looks like a stand of drawers."

"I don't suppose you'd know the combination?"

She shook her head. "I only found out about the safe by chance. He had it open and I was walking past his door."

"Any servants sleep in the penthouse?"

"No, just a bodyguard named Ramos."

"Is he any good?"

"Well, he's big, and he's always armed. You've seen him. Ramos drives the Rolls."

"Ah," I said, "the blifit. Two hundred pounds of meat and an acorn-sized brain."

"That may be, but I believe he's killed for Ibarra."

"Who?"

She spread her hands. "Some competitor in Sinaloa."

I thought of Chato and wondered how he'd react to Ibarra's failure to deliver. But he was out of the play for now, probably in Toronto or Jamaica, where the ganja grows. Still, I wondered why Chato had dropped out of sight so opportunely. An informer in the Union City PD was the likely answer—and a principal reason why federal law enforcers avoid local PDs when they can.

Nina gathered the test kit and placed it in her bag. "I really ought to be getting back," she said, and glanced at the closed bedroom door. "I'd looked forward to—but another time, yes?"

"Definitely yes." What a smile this girl had! "Dinner tonight?"

"Unless Ibarra has other plans for me."

"I'll hold the hope he hasn't." I drew her to me, and kissed her forehead, the tip of her nose. She said, "You know, Jack, when you want to, you can be a very gentle person, if a complicated one."

"To say nothing of you." I kissed the dimple below her throat.

She sighed, breathed deeply. "No more, please. I want my mind clear while I decide how best I can help you."

"Help me do what?"

"Rob Ibarra's safe, *querido*. I hope you don't think I haven't been paying attention."

SEVEN

After Nina left I signed the ID materials Valeriano had brought, and stuffed them into my billfold, along with one hundred and twenty thousand dollars in one- and five hundred-dollar denominations. Valeriano had fractured U.S. law by exporting more than five thousand without reporting it, so he was vulnerable to prosecution by Treasury, Justice and Congress if the operation blew. Laws are broken in line of duty, so it was prudent to maintain control and keep the op from being blown. Especially in my situation, because Ibarra would treat me far worse than any Congressional committee. No Fifth Amendment refusal in Ibarra's circles; just torture, death and dismemberment, not necessarily in that order.

When Ibarra called around eleven Pete was still sleeping, so I left a note on his pillow: OFF TO SEE THE WIZARD, and went out. No Ramos, no Rolls. I taxied the half mile to Ibarra's hotel, entered the Andaluz, and walked directly to the penthouse elevator. A phone was set into the wall beside it, and I pressed the call button. *"Bueno?"* came a male voice. "Furlong," I replied, and the servant said, *"Ahorita."* I replaced the phone and waited.

Presently the elevator door opened, the servant said, *"Pase,"* and I stepped in, jingling change in my pocket, heavy metal for the detector. When I went through, the detector buzzer sounded, and I gave a handful of coins to the servant, turned around in an exaggerated way, and spotted the covered detector switch just to the right of the elevator opening—as Nina had said.

The servant motioned me to wait, so I slumped down in an oversized leather chair beside a support column, and heard angry voices. Two men were shouting at each other. I heard Ibarra yell in Spanish, "Son of a whore, you don't cheat Pedrito and get away with it."

"Sister-violator," shouted a rougher voice, "if you don't give me what I paid for, I'll kill you!"

"You'll get a bullet, asshole," Ibarra said in deadly tones.

There was a silence. Then came the sound of rapid footsteps. From semiconcealment I saw two men striding toward me. The second man was Ramos, and he held a .45 pistol against the other man's back. Ramos shoved the man into the open elevator, snarled, "*Vaya al diablo y no vuelve,*" and closed the doors. I heard the elevator hum, descending. Ramos parted his *guayabera* and holstered his weapon, then buttoned the flowing shirt as he walked back where he'd come from.

The ousted man was about five-ten with powerful sloping shoulders and a neck like a buffalo's. He'd walked bow-legged, and his thick hair was gray and black. The rap sheet hadn't given that much detail, but judging from the attached photo, the visitor's granite-block head, his battered ears and porcine eyes, it was Chato himself.

Aka Isador Campestre of Union City, New Jersey.

I didn't have time to ponder whether his coming to Ixtapa was good news or bad news because the servant appeared and gestured for me to follow him.

This was another room I'd never seen. It was Ibarra's office, and it was unique. The heads and hides of big and lesser game were mounted on the walls, as were a half-dozen macabre witch-doctor masks. His desk was covered with elephant hide and set on four elephant legs. A stumpy hollowed-out elephant foot made a waste basket. Carved African figurines stood on the desk top, and behind the owner of all this, a long Watutsi shield with crossed assegais. The color scheme was black, white, and red. Ibarra's face was damp and he was chewing an unlit cigar.

"Sit down," he said curtly, then with one arm swept away

a dozen figurines. As they clattered against floor and wall he looked startled. He yanked the cigar from his teeth and tossed it at the foot-basket. Then he shook his head as though ridding it of water. "That *puto*," he snapped, took a deep breath, and sat down.

"I had a visitor," he said, more calmly. "He called me liar and cheat. It upset me. I had to have him sent away." He breathed deeply again, getting control of himself. "The man was not expected. As a courtesy I saw him. I expected you, Henry, and I have been rude to you. Accept my apologies."

I shrugged. "Now and then everyone has a bad day." I got out my billfold. "Four keys," I said, "on my side of the border." I laid the sheaf of money on his desk. Ibarra pushed it aside with the heel of his hand. I said, "To avoid the possibility of dispute, I'd like you to validate the currency now."

"As you wish." He got out the scanner and ran it over portions of each banknote almost unconcernedly. When he finished he dropped money and validator into a desk drawer. "No problem," he said, "but I didn't expect false money from you. One reason I showed you the device last night."

"It impressed me. I'm not used to violence, don't like it. So I try to avoid disagreements."

"Ours is a violent world, Henry. My business is a particularly violent one. But—life goes on, eh?" He managed a slight smile.

"When do I get my keys?"

"When do you want them?"

"A week too soon?"

"I can accommodate you." He wrote on a pad, tore off the sheet, and gave it to me. "A week from today phone this number and you will be told where to claim your four keys."

"How do I identify myself?"

"Give your name and say you're Pedrito's customer."

"Simple as that," I said in an awed voice. I checked the telephone area code: 415. Philadelphia? "As long as I'm here," I said as smoothly as I could, "how about some marijuana—sinsemilla, right?"

"Available by the ton if you like."

"Imagine," I said as though to myself, "how chance steered me to just the right place. Well, I'll get back to you before the end of the month."

"I'm here much of the time. If not, ask for Paula Quiroz, and she will get a message to me." He stood up and we shook hands. For Ibarra, a minor transaction was ended; he had more important things to do. *"Buen viaje,"* he said, and I left his office. When I glanced back he was picking up the scattered figurines.

I took my time getting to the elevator, mentally drawing a floor plan of his space. Past the office were sleeping quarters, bathrooms and bedrooms. One concealed his safe. The kitchen was off the dining room, and I was already familiar with the open sections of the place.

A servant opened the elevator, and I rode it down to the lobby. From a house phone I called Nina's room, and said, "Business completed. My watch says it's playtime."

"So does mine. Come up."

Her corner suite was on the floor below Ibarra's penthouse. The décor was attractively feminine without a lot of sconces and bric-a-brac. We kissed, and she led me to a light brown sofa at right angles to the beach. There were fresh flowers everywhere, and on the cocktail table an ice bucket and a selection of liquors. I put ice in two glasses and added Añejo to each. After sipping I said, "I paid Ibarra for four keys—and who do you think was with him when I arrived?"

"His wife? No, I can't imagine. Tell me."

"Chato, the man who sent him four million via Eddie Wax." I sipped again. "They had a shouting match, threatened each other, and Ramos evicted Chato with a pistol at his back."

She said, "I suppose it was bound to happen, each accusing the other of treachery." Her tongued dipped delicately into the mellow rum. "Is it threatening? Significant?"

"Chance has put two scorpions in the same bottle. One has the upper hand—or claw—because it's his bottle. But if you had seen Chato you'd know that he's decided either to get his money, his cocaine, or Ibarra's life."

She clapped her hands. "How marvelous *that* would be!"

I considered, and put my glass down. "Chato's on strange turf, he may need a little help, and I'm a natural-born Samaritan. Have you a sheet of hotel stationery?"

"Over there in the desk drawer."

In Spanish I printed:

Ibarra has cheated me, too. If you want to get your money, go at night. The elevator opens to 41-17-64. Turn off detector switch by elevator door.

Good luck.

Nina read the message and nodded. As I was folding it into a hotel envelope her phone rang. She answered at a corner table and came back. "Pedrito wants to see me, he sounded very upset."

"I can imagine." I pocketed the envelope and stood up. "I shouldn't be away long. Are you going somewhere?"

"To find Chato."

He wasn't in either of the hotel's two bars, so I gave Chato's description to the doorman, who said he'd seen the man head for El Capitán, a beach saloon less than a hundred yards away.

It was dark inside El Capitán, no more than half a dozen customers between bar and tables. Chato was one of them, sitting in a far corner morosely nursing a drink. I beckoned to one of the waiters and we stepped outside. "*Sí, señor! A sus órdenes.*"

I gave him the envelope along with a day's wages, and told him to wait five minutes before handing the envelope to Chato. The waiter pocketed my tip, smiled, and said he'd follow instructions.

When I got back to Nina's suite, she had changed into a

pink cutoff negligee, and was adding ice to our drinks. "I'm afraid Ibarra is suspicious of me," she said.

"Why?"

"Because he's begun to think Chato may have told him the truth." She looked at me. "Did you find Chato?"

"Umm. Maybe it won't make any difference who believes whom. Then I can collect those ledgers at leisure."

She said, "Ibarra told me Chato said Eddie Wax failed to phone him from Miami and thinks Eddie could have been robbed, or substituted the counterfeit money. Ibarra had me describe Eddie, which I was able to do from the license you showed me in Cancún. Ibarra agreed the description fitted Eddie, so he's left with three possibilities: that Chato tried to cheat him, that Eddie Wax robbed them both—or I did."

I thought it over. "He said that?"

She nodded.

"If he really thought you were responsible he wouldn't have laid it out for you."

"No, I suppose not. But I'm going to have to be even more careful than I have been."

I put down my glass and drew her body against mine. Our lips met and she moved softly against me. Gently, I lifted Nina and carried her into her bedroom. She stepped out of her slippers, I removed her negligee and kissed her smooth breasts. She unfastened my belt and drew me to the bed and took me inside her.

She was warm and sweet and lovely.

———————

Two hours later I was back in my own suite, where Pete was lunching on the balcony. He said his sleep had been restorative and he was ready to fly back to Miami. I told him what had transpired in my meeting with Ibarra, and described the row between Ibarra and Chato. I didn't mention my message to Chato, feeling that Pete's sensibilities might be ruffled by the provocation. If it resolved anything I'd tell him at a later time.

"You must have had a drawn-out meeting with Ibarra, Jack."

"Well, not really. I spent some time with Nina."

He smiled. "Blanket drill?"

"Not nice to ask. Ibarra has a hundred and twenty thou, leaving me one-eighty. Of that I'll keep forty—my fee—because things may just wind up tonight." I returned a hundred and forty thousand dollars to him. "So soon?" he said.

"I said 'may,' and I could easily be wrong. Whatever happens I'll contact Al Wolcott in Mérida, and thanks for your help." I gave Pete the phone number I was supposed to call for delivery, and said, "Very quietly you could have this traced to location, but for God's sake don't raid the place."

"How about a wiretap?"

"No objection if professionally done, court order and all related formalities."

"Suddenly you're concerned with legal niceties?"

"I don't like to see hard effort wasted. Besides, what goes on here and in the U.S. is entirely different. Mexican laws are ignored. Americans are aware our laws exist, and generally respect them."

Valeriano put the money in his Manila envelope with Chato's rap sheet. "Hope things go well for you, Jack. You've always got a friend in Miami."

"I'll remember that." I folded my forty-thousand bundle in a sheet of hotel stationery and fitted it into an envelope. I addressed it to my PO box at San Miguel de Cozumel, Q.R., and gave it to Pete. "There's a *paquetería* office at the airport," I said, "and I'd be much obliged if you'd have this taken by messenger."

I walked him to the door and shook his hand firmly.

By now it was mid-afternoon. My next engagement was at seven for cocktails in Nina's suite, dinner at eight. So I decided to honor *siesta* and turned in, wondering what the night would bring.

———————————

I said, "How is it you're not married, Nina?"

She sat across from me at her small, candlelit dining table, wearing an evening dress of iridescent Thai silk with a single-strand pearl necklace. "I've been engaged twice. First to a Texan whose family didn't want him marrying a Catholic, then to a young man from Saltillo who expected me to bear children and manage his household to the exclusion of everything else. My own interests had no place in his scheme of things." She shrugged. "I have the rest of my life to be married—if I choose to be. Besides, I live now only to avenge my brother's death." Her gaze lifted to the ceiling, which was directly under Ibarra's penthouse.

"Other than the private elevator there must be another entrance."

"There is a back stairway from this floor for servants' use. The door is kept locked."

"So his servants have a key. Do you?"

She nodded. "During power failures everyone has to use the stairs."

"Did Ibarra buy those African game trophies, or shoot them himself?"

"Oh, he did the killing with a submachine gun. You see, Ibarra was an intimate of a previous president who, in the grand tradition, looted our treasury before leaving office. The ex-president took his closest friends on a long African safari, along with their automatic weapons. Not quite sporting to shoot everything in sight with machine guns, but then they weren't very nice men."

"I remember the story," I told her. "But not Ibarra's participation. I suppose he contributed heavily to the Party."

"Of course. Buying influence is another national tradition."

While she was making espresso I wandered over to the wide window and looked out over the indigo sea. No wind, no whitecaps, just an occasional distant glint reflecting the yellow half-moon. Beautiful Mexico.

Silver tinkled on china as Nina brought over our demitasses. We sipped in silence until she said, "I know the time will come soon when you'll go away. But perhaps you'll return another time."

"I'd like to." I kissed the side of her face, nibbled the lobe of her ear. Her hand drew mine to her breast and I could feel the beating of her heart. This was an unusual woman, I told myself, one with whom I could spend considerable time and never a trace of boredom.

We kissed lingeringly. "I mustn't rumple this dress," she whispered, and led me into her bedroom.

Sometime after midnight we woke from deep sleep in each other's arms. Two shots shattered the silence, then a third. Nina turned on a light and glanced up. "The penthouse," she said, and left the bed to pull on a long robe. She took her automatic from the nightstand drawer and started walking away. "Wait," I barked, "I'll go," and pulled on my trousers. "You need my key," she said, "so we'll go together."

I stepped into huaraches and got into my *guayabera*, recovered my pistol from under the bed, and followed her to the service door.

She unlocked it and we went up an angled flight of stairs. At the top, another door. It opened to her key, and she reached around and switched off the alarm. The room we entered was dark. Nina turned on a light, a butler's pantry. "This way," she said, and we crossed through the kitchen. In the main dining room I pushed ahead of her and said, "Stay here."

"No!"

"Then keep behind me." I turned down the hall leading to Ibarra's office. Seeing a bar of light under his door I snapped a shell into the pistol chamber and moved ahead. "Cover me," I whispered, and shoved the door open.

There were two lights in the office, two bodies on the floor. One lay face down in front of the massive desk, a plate-sized bloodstain covering the left shoulderblade. The other body was against the wall, below an impala head. The body moved, groaned, and the face turned toward me.

Ramos.

The big .45 was still in his hand and he was trying to point it at me. I stepped over and kicked it from his grasp. He groaned again and his head thunked against the floor.

From the shadows a man moved toward me. He wore a black bathrobe and his right hand held a MAC-10 machine pistol.

Ibarra.

From behind me Nina cried, "Pedrito, I was so worried. Are you all right?"

Ibarra laid the machine pistol on his desk, ran a hand back through the mass of rumpled hair. His expression was rigid, stunned.

I didn't need to turn the dead man's head to recognize Chato, but I did. "Who is he?" I asked.

Ibarra wet his lips. "He came to kill me."

I went over to Ramos, half-turned him, and pried bloody fingers from his belly. "He's gut-shot," I said. "We must get an ambulance."

Ibarra sat heavily in his chair, slumped forward. I picked up his MAC-10 and discreetly sniffed the muzzle. Unfired. The fallen men had shot it out, Ibarra hadn't been touched. To Nina I said, "You know who to call?"

Ibarra said, "I don't want them found here."

Nina said, "Where then?"

Ibarra stared dully at me. "Any place."

I wadded a handkerchief, which Ramos clutched at and pressed against his belly, and I stood up. Nina was gnawing her left fist. I took the pistol from her right and pocketed it, stuck my Walther under my belt. I gripped Chato's wrists and began dragging him away. Nina stood frozen, staring at me. "Call a doctor," I snapped, "unless you both want the man to die."

Nina took three rigid steps to the desk telephone. I dragged Chato out the way I'd come, tumbled his heavy body down the staircase, and pulled it into the hall. Then I went back to the penthouse. Ibarra was still slumped behind his desk. Nina sat in a chair staring at him. I wondered if she was considering killing him, for the circumstances were ideal. She looked at me, and I shook my head. Killing in self-defense was one thing, but I wasn't going to kill an unarmed man in cold blood. What Nina did was her business.

Seeing that neither of them was going to help me with Ramos, I dragged him away as I had Chato, and arranged him on the hall floor ten feet from Chato. Then I returned for their weapons.

On the floor below I wiped my prints from the .45 and Chato's piece, a snub Colt .38, pressed them into each man's hands and went back to Ibarra's office. On his desk stood a bottle of cognac, and he was draining a glass. I raised the bottle and swallowed a long slug. Nina said, "An ambulance is on the way."

"Then maybe the driver can be saved." I drank again. "If anyone cares."

In a hoarse voice Ibarra said, "He saved my life. I was sitting here, the door opened and the man came in. He was drunk, crazy. I don't know how he got this far. The alarms—" he waved a hand. "He was going to shoot me."

"But your man shot first?"

"I don't remember. It's all so . . ." He licked dry lips and poured brandy into his glass. "They were down . . ." He stared at me curiously. "Then you were here. Both of you."

"I heard shooting," I said. From Nina's robe our situation was obvious. Let her explain it if she wanted to, it wasn't my job. To the right of Ibarra's desk a wall section stood partly open, a camouflaged door. I got out my Walther, went around the desk and moved the door on its pivot until I could get through.

Around the room stood long guns in racks. A broad table displayed hand weapons and grenades. Slanted in one corner was a bazooka. The place was an armory and it smelled of cosmoline. Under each weapon was a description of the piece and a dollar price. No one had told me Ibarra was also an arms merchant. I went back to the office. Ibarra looked at me and said nothing. Neither did I.

From the distance came the rise and fall of a siren. I sat down and pocketed my pistol. To Ibarra I said, "You were very lucky tonight."

Nina said, "Henry, there's blood on your shirt."

I looked down and nodded. My trousers were also stained. To Ibarra I said, "I'll borrow from you."

He nodded and I left the office. In the master bedroom I turned on a light and opened a walk-in closet. From racks I took trousers and a starched, embroidered *guayabera*. I put them on. They were small for me, but better than my blood-stained clothing.

I went over to the false drawer-face Nina had described and pulled a long drawer handle. On hinges the panel swung out from the wall, revealing a five-foot Mosler safe with three-way combination dial. I searched the steel face and hinges for wires indicating an alarm system or a booby trap.

Nothing.

Unless the lock system was new and exotic I could probably open it. The safe was my target, or rather what it contained. Now was obviously not the time. At any moment Ibarra could come in and take to his bed. I'd expected the drug baron to take a tougher approach to the incident, but he seemed shocked, almost helpless. I moved the panel back into place and left the bedroom.

Very quietly, I walked through darkness to the private elevator and found the metal detector switch. Someone (Chato?) had turned it off, so I clicked it on. Another mystery for Ibarra to ponder.

Through the elevator shaft I could hear voices on the floor below, the creak of gurney wheels. Medics, police, whoever, removing bodies. Ramos had only been doing his job protecting his employer; if he'd been less watchful and efficient Ibarra would be dead and I could have wound up the project now, tonight.

Instead, it was going to take longer.

I went back to the office.

On the desk between Ibarra's manicured hands lay a stack of U.S. currency, the money I'd paid for four keys. He pushed it toward me. "I'm grateful for what you did. Take the money, you'll get the four kilos as agreed."

I shook my head. "I don't want to feel obligated," I told

him, "because I expect to do more business with you. It was a straight deal, we'll keep it that way."

Below, a siren started up, the meat wagon pulled away. We listened as the sound diminished. Ibarra swept the money back into the drawer.

I said, "Get that blood off the floor before it hardens."

Nina said, "Blood sickens me, but Pedrito will do it, Henry. Nice of you to stop by—we'll finish that nightcap another time."

I admired her cleverness in so casually providing Ibarra with an explanation for my presence. "I'll count on it," I said, and went down the back stairway to where a cleaning woman was mopping the last traces of blood from the floor. She glanced at me incuriously and continued her work. I rode the guest elevator to the lobby and walked back to my hotel.

Whether Ibarra traded armaments for narcotics, raw or refined, or whether it was a separate line of business, his involvement had to be reported to Al Wolcott in Mérida. The office was closed now, but I vowed to call him in the morning.

Next I had to gain access to Ibarra's bedroom safe and the books and ledgers that detailed his distribution contacts, the scope of his operations. They were the reason I was in Ixtapa. Only with them could I justify my forty thousand dollar fee.

As I got into bed I reflected that although my plan for Chato had miscarried—Ibarra wasn't dead—I didn't have to worry about Chato discovering my Eddie Wax impersonation any more.

One down, I thought, turning off the lamp, and one more to go.

EIGHT

From a pay phone just off the lobby I double-talked my message to Al Wolcott who seemed mildly interested in Ibarra's line of "agricultural implements," and said he'd pass along the information to an interested party, meaning the Bureau of Alcohol, Tobacco and Firearms. But he sounded disappointed when I conceded the "book cartons" still hadn't been moved from "storage."

"Patience," I told him. "I've been on this less than a week and I'm still having fun."

"Well, well," he said. "Call us when it gets serious." He broke the connection.

I was leaving the phone when I saw Nina crossing the lobby. She was wearing lavender Bermudas, sling slippers and a lavender halter top. I approached from the port quarter, said *"Boo!"* and simultaneously took her arm. She jumped, looking angrily around. "Oh!" she breathed. "Don't *do* that. My nerves are in terrible shape—hardly any sleep last night."

"I'm a brute, I can't help it. Had breakfast?"

"Only coffee."

I steered her into the coffee shop where a waiter seated us at a beach-view table. Water-skiers were pluming the ocean and two parasails were airborne offshore. Nina ordered *huevos rancheros*, and I asked for scrambled eggs, ham and fries. Automatically the waiter poured coffee and left us a basket of buns.

I took her hand. She fidgeted nervously, then her eyes bored into mine. In a low voice she said, "Last night, why didn't you kill him?"

"Why didn't you?"

"I—I thought you planned to . . ."

"My plans are always subject to change. Besides, you have the blood-grudge against him, not me. Once he laid down his gun he was helpless." I stirred tan sugar into my coffee. "Let's review things. You want to destroy him, which includes depriving him of his life. I want to destroy his operations, which means getting hold of his books. If Pedrito tries stopping me there could be violence with fatal results for one or both of us." I sipped strong coffee from my cup. "But after seeing his limp reaction to last night's violence I'd say he's not used to gunplay, so I'd bet on myself."

"So will I," she said, "because Pedrito has always hired others to do the dangerous and dirty work." She looked away, toward the sunlit beach where volleyball was being played. "Others," she murmured, "like my brother."

The loudspeaker system began blaring a song by Roberta Flack. I listened for a while, then said, "So. He had the blood mopped up—then what?"

"I could see it was eating at him that you and I had been together. He hinted around, but after what you'd done for him he couldn't bring himself to accuse me directly."

"Why should he? You've said you don't sleep with him."

"But he suspects that I sleep with you, and that's a slap at his *macho* pride. He tried to conceal it but he's angry at me and jealous of you." She broke and buttered a bun. "Also, he resents that you didn't take back your money. He's not used to having gifts refused, and that makes you much more than an ordinary man. That, plus the other things you did, puts him under obligation to you—and he hates it."

"I won't lose sleep over that, at least until he gets a replacement for Ramos. How is he, by the way?"

"Dead." She bit into her bread. "The hospital called a little while ago."

I grunted. "I don't imagine the police will bother Pedrito with annoying questions."

"Hardly, they've been too well paid. They're saying a hotel security guard killed a violent burglar, who shot and

71

killed the guard. No names, no publicity. It's over with, finished."

"As it should be," I said, and sat back while the waiter served our breakfast.

As we were finishing, Nina said, "Ibarra was muttering that he ought to retire, get out of business, the risks were too great, he had enough money for the rest of his life, and so on."

"That was immediate postcrisis self-examination. In daylight he'll have other thoughts. No, he likes the excitement of illegality, and for his kind there's never enough money to satisfy."

"Still, he'll probably leave here for a while."

"And go where?"

"Oh, I don't know, he owns so many places—Rio, Acapulco, France, Seville . . ."

"But not Mexico City and his family."

"Not when he's feeling frightened and depressed."

I sat forward. "And when might he be leaving?"

"Soon, probably, but he didn't say."

I thought it over. Welcome news if true. "I checked the Yellow Pages, and there's no medical supply house in Ixtapa or Zihua. Where would the nearest one be?"

"The capital, Mexico City, I suppose. It's less than an hour's flight from here. Planes leave all the time."

"Want to go with me?"

"I'd love to—stay at the Camino Real, go nightclubbing, have some really magnificent meals—but Pedrito will need me today. If you have to go, you can be back by evening. And by then I may know what Pedrito plans to do."

━━━━━━━━━━━━━━━

In addition to the expensive boutiques lining the hotel lobby, there was a travel agency. I bought a round trip Aero-Mexico ticket leaving Ixtapa at noon for Mexico City, returning at 7:45. Giving me, I thought, plenty of time for shopping and a few beers.

The DC-9 flight took only forty-five minutes, barely enough time to scan the Mexico City *News* and munch a complimentary bag of peanuts.

As usual, Tenochtitlán was shrouded in a yellow smog, far worse than Los Angeles in preenvironmentalist years. Before leaving the airport I consulted phone book classifieds and noted four medical supply houses, any one of which should have what I came for.

I had my taxi driver wait on Avenida Velasco while I entered the first place on my list. The showroom was clean and modern but the salesman said they didn't have the item in stock. "Imported from Germany," he explained. He telephoned two other houses for me, and very kindly said that what I wanted was obtainable at the supply house on Bucareli, not far from the National Medical Center.

That was my next stop, and the salesman had the item ready for me: an amplifying stethoscope that could be plugged into an ECG machine, cost $589.78, including two batteries.

I tested it on the salesman's heart, and the sound came through with the ear-busting pounding of a bass drum. Plenty of amplification for my particular need.

The black fabric case was about a foot long, four inches wide, and three deep. The salesman wrapped it and gave it to me in a blue plastic bag.

I paid my driver at Monte de Piedad and strolled through the capital's combination pawnshop and flea market. In the hardware section I found a stall displaying a thin brown leather case containing a set of lock picks. Made in Czechoslovakia, they were of blued spring steel; rakes, bars and spicules loosely joined at one end by a rivet. The locksmith wanted twenty dollars and we agreed on five. The leather case fitted easily into the breast pocket of my shirt. Very handy.

From the national pawnshop I walked over to Sanborn's restaurant for a hamburger plate and a chocolate shake, then I crossed the Zócalo, the heart of Mexico City. The broad square was bordered by the marble Palace of Fine Arts and the ancient cathedral, erected on the foundations of the Aztec *teocalli*, where Cortes and his troops had watched in horror the bloody spectacle of human sacrifice. There, in a far corner, subway construction years ago had unearthed the huge wheel-like stone known around the world as the Aztec Calendar. Nearby, the presidential palace from whose balcony Mexican presidents annually echo the revolutionary cry of Padre Dolores, reminding.*chilangos* that his and their revolution continues. Forever.

The foul air was closing my nostrils, irritating my throat. I went to a taxi *sitio* and took a cab back to the airport.

In a dimly lit air-conditioned cocktail lounge I sipped iced Añejo, fondled my two purchases, and wondered how soon I'd have an opportunity to use them. If Ibarra left Ixtapa to settle his nerves, access to his safe would be easier. If he decided to remain in his penthouse, entry would be more complicated. But either way I was going to crack his safe and take everything it held inside.

The scent of marijuana drifted to my nostrils and I glanced at its source, the nearest table, where two well-dressed young whores were smoking and sipping watered anise. Catching my glance, one got up and came over to me. I didn't invite her to sit down.

She and her sister—she gestured—were Salvadoran refugees. They lacked work permits and earned their daily bread entertaining nice-looking men. Did I have a hotel room? No. Then the three of us could taxi to a nearby motel and spend an exciting hour. Very cheap, very inexpensive. Besides, they liked my looks.

I said I liked theirs, too, but I was a Greek priest in civilian garb. The girl said they had no objection to priests and repeated her invitation. I said I was a pederast, and she offered to get me a boy. Finally, I said my plane was leaving, and picked up my plastic bag. She cursed me for a priest and a pederast. I advised her to attend Mass more frequently, and walked away.

On the way to my departure gate I stopped at the SCT counter and wrote a telegram to Srta. Melody West c/o Club Acuático in Caracas, Venezuela. I said I loved her, missed her, and hoped she'd come soon to Cozumel. Very soon. Signed, JUAN. The clerk said the message would be delivered at nightfall—but didn't specify which day.

I continued walking to the gate, my thoughts on Melody. Marriage had been her early idea but we were apart now more than we were together, and I wondered if marriage would ever come to pass. Her mother, the much-married, much-divorced Delores Diehl, accepted our living together but considered me one of her daughter's adolescent follies. Her plans for Melody were of a grand scale beyond anything I could offer, but of the two women, the daughter was the stronger and more determined. Whatever Melody decided would, in the end, prevail.

═══════════════════

My plane landed on schedule—two on-time flights the same day comprised a minor miracle—and as the taxi drove me to the Tropical I could see sunlight still gilding the bordering palms.

The room clerk gave me my key and a small sealed envelope. I opened it in the elevator and saw feminine handwriting: CALL ME WHEN YOU GET IN. P.

I'd intended to, but did so only after showering off the dust and grime of Mexico City. I poured a drink, stretched out so that I could view the darkening water, and phoned her suite.

When Nina heard my voice she said, "I'm glad you're back. I was afraid you might stay there overnight. Did you get what you wanted?"

"I did. Miss me?"

"I was so busy I hardly had time—but now I want to see you. May I come?"

"By all means."

"I have exciting news."

"Give me a hint."

Her voice lowered. "You can do whatever you want— tonight."

75

NINE

According to Nina, Ibarra had left his Ixtapa lair in mid-afternoon and flown north to Manzanillo on the Pacific coast. "Why Manzanillo?" I asked.

"He owns a condominium at Las Hadas. His girlfriend Lupita Casillas stays there most of the year. She claims to be a niece of Evita Perón. And even if she isn't, Lupita has a lot of money."

"Does she invest in Ibarra's businesses?"

"She may."

Nina was sitting composedly beside me. I'd ordered dinner in advance of her arrival and we were enjoying drinks together.

I freshened our drinks and said, "You never told me Pedrito is an arms merchant."

"I didn't think you were interested."

"On the contrary. They're as much *fayuca* as narcotics, and very profitable. From the Rio Grande to the Straits of Magellan there's hardly a country without its guerrilla movements. Many cultivate poppy and coca and marijuana to finance their activities—or trade their narcotics for arms and munitions."

"I hadn't thought of that, but I don't take much interest in politics."

"Mao said 'power flows from the barrel of a gun,' which is why clandestine arms trafficking concerns legitimate governments. Many guns equal much power. Who does Ibarra sell or trade his guns to?"

"I've never been interested enough to keep track of his

callers. But once you have his books I'm sure you'll know all there is to know."

"You're sure Ibarra will be in Manzanillo all night?"

"I drove him to the airport, saw him board the plane. It's the opportunity we've been waiting for."

"So the penthouse is empty, uninhabited."

"Ramos was the only one he trusted to stay there, and Ramos is dead. Incidentally, Ibarra is paying for his guard's funeral."

"Ibarra's idea?"

"Well, actually it was my suggestion."

The waiter buzzed and came in pushing a laden warming table.

He set our places, uncorked wine and poured before serving lobster to Nina and lamb chops to me. Undeniably, I was enjoying the good life with Nina, but I was getting increasingly eager to get back to Cozumel, my normally calm life, and Melody. But I pushed those thoughts aside and concentrated on an excellent meal.

After a while Nina said, "I guess you've done break-ins, burglaries, before, so the penthouse safe is routine."

"Not exactly. Every entry is different and safes have their idiosyncrasies. On the up side, a lot of owners write down combinations where they can easily be found, or disguise them as phone numbers in a Rolodex. Professional thieves search for combinations before going through the aggravation of opening a locked safe."

"Aren't you a 'professional thief?' "

"I suppose I'd qualify, except that I only take what's of interest to my government."

"Were you trained to open safes?"

"On-the-job training. Watching and observing specialists."

"How long do you think it will take tonight?"

"Maybe half an hour in and out. Maybe longer. That's a new safe, the tumblers may stick. This is salt air and things get corroded." But I hoped not.

"What if you can't open it?"

"I'll try another time, with explosive." Plastique was on my mind, more powerful than dynamite and a lot more unstable. Too warm, and the puttylike substance leaked nitroglycerine. And it had been a long time since I'd used plastique for anything other than stunning schools of bait-fish.

After refilling our wine glasses I said, "I suppose you insist on going with me?"

"If Ibarra left a watchman I can at least give you a warning."

I didn't like her being there, but I did need her key to transit the back door as we'd done the night before. Besides, in an emergency, two guns are better than one.

We left the table at eleven, took coffee on the balcony for another half hour. Suddenly Nina yawned. Apologetically she said, "My nerves *are* frayed, I've never done this before." She looked up at the clear, starry sky. "When you get what you're after I'd like to duplicate it for the attorney general."

"That's reasonable," I said, "but unsafe in Ixtapa. I'll have it copied for you, give me an excuse to see you again."

"I hope you won't feel you really need an excuse. Visit me whenever you like."

"In Ixtapa?"

"To avoid suspicion I should stay on for a while."

"Makes sense," I agreed, and looked at my watch. I got up and retrieved my Walther from the bedroom mattress-cache. I fitted it under the belt next to my spine and under my *guayabera* shirt. The lock-pick set I slid into a pocket, and got the stethoscope bag from the closet. Then I went back to Nina.

She stood and smoothed her dark pants suit, took her .25 caliber automatic from her purse and dropped it into a pocket. She placed her purse in my carry-bag, and handed me the rear entry key. She drank the last of her coffee, and said, "I'm ready."

So was I.

She drove to the Andaluz and parked her silver Triumph

in a reserved slot. We took the guest elevator to her floor, and went down the empty corridor to the penthouse service door. It opened to her key and we climbed to the top of the staircase. I opened the final door and Nina disarmed the alarm system. I closed and locked the door behind us.

We were in.

She started to walk on, but I held her back. "Call out," I said, "in case there's a stay-behind."

From the kitchen she called, *"Hay alguien? Está aquí Paula."*

Her words echoed through the dark spaces. No response.

After a moment I said, "Let's go," and followed her to the master bedroom door. It was locked by an Alba that looked very much like a Yale. Nina said, "Do you need light?"

"Makes no difference, but I'd rather do without." I fanned out my pick tools, selected tension bar and rake, inserted them in the keyway and began working the spring tumblers from the channel. After about three minutes the last one gave, the keyway cylinder turned and the door opened inward. I withdrew my picks and replaced them in their case. Nina said, "You're very expert."

"It was an easy lock," I said with studied humility—though it was true. Carrying my bag I went to the bedroom wall and swung aside the false panel. "Now we need light," I told her, and she turned on a bedlamp.

I checked the bottom of the bedside telephone, then the front and back of the false panel before examining the safe itself. I was looking for penciled numbers, the lock combination, but the safe's gray paint was pristine.

"Try his office," I said. "Look under the phone, check the desk pad, note paper, drawers—and his Rolodex. Meanwhile I'll get to work."

I unpacked the stethoscope kit, untwined wires, and put on the headset. I fitted one phone to my right ear, leaving the left ear uncovered for ambient sound.

I drew over a chair and sat in front of the big safe. Maybe it only looked locked. I tried turning the bolt handle but it didn't budge. The safe was definitely locked.

The numbered dial had been left on 32. I wet the suction cup and stuck it on the metal facing beside the dial. Listening, I moved the dial right, then left, turned up the volume and repeated. Now I heard clearly the smooth clicking of the pawl, but nothing else. Thirty-two was a random number.

I got out a hotel notepad and pencil, drew a circle and numbered its circumference in intervals of ten. Then I turned the dial to the left very, very slowly. For a time, I heard only the pawl sound, then a muted click on 13. I made a checkmark on my paper dial and printed 13. That was either the set number or close to it, and probably the first in the sequential combination. Safe manufacturers recommend setting combinations with the largest number in the middle, so I laid aside my pencil, and turned the dial knob to the right, passing 13 twice as I listened.

When I realized I was holding my breath, I expelled it and filled my lungs to establish normal breathing. Between my thumb and forefinger the knurled knob turned slowly. If Ibarra followed normal setting instructions the second number would be sizeably larger than 13. The fixed delta-point was at 60, then 70 before my fingers felt a very slight resistance. I wet my lips, flexed knuckles, and turned a millimeter at a time. Finally, at 77 I heard the soft drop-click, marked my replica dial and printed 77. I had an urge to turn back to 13, the first number of the series, but decided to search methodically.

Right, past 77 once, and then I turned an integer at a time, listening for what I hoped would be the final number, my breath fogging the cold steel dial. Sixty again, 55, and the click came at 44. Ibarra's age, perhaps?

I sat back, took some deep breaths and wrote down 44.

13-17-44. My fingers seemed almost painfully stiff as I turned the dial back to zero. I gazed at the gray steel facing. Had I decoded the combination? I gripped the handle and turned.

It didn't move.

I sat back and thought it over. I spun the dial to the right and stopped on 13, two left to 77, one right to 44. Zero, and try again. The safe stayed locked. I looked up, saw that Nina was still searching the office, and checked my wristwatch. Thirty-two minutes past midnight; the way things were going I could be at it all night.

Before beginning a completely new search of the dial I had a thought: maybe this safe didn't open on zero as older models did, but on a factory-set number. Like 10?

I turned from 44 to 10 and gripped the bolt handle again. The lever turned, bolts withdrew, and I tugged the door open.

I had to move back my chair to fully open the safe door, and when I looked inside, I saw what I had come for.

There were four shelves but only two held anything: On one shelf, two ledger books, and on the shelf beneath, two smaller fabric-bound notebooks. On the bottom of the safe lay a large plastic bag stuffed with bundles of currency, most of them Treasury green.

I took out a ledger and opened it, scanning names and figures. The smaller of the two notebooks was a register of Ibarra's distribution network: names, addresses, phone numbers . . . I riffled pages and found a list of clandestine landing sites in Texas and Arizona. The other notebook detailed arms sales and barters, and ports of delivery: Belize, Honduras, Puerto Barrios, Porto Alegre, Cartagena—names, amounts, inventories.

I was staring at them when I heard Nina's footsteps approach the open doorway. Without looking around I said, "It's all here."

"Wonderful." Her footsteps neared. "Congratulations, Juan. You've been a big help."

I was beginning to transfer Ibarra's operational books into my carry-bag when I heard the click of a shell springing into its firing chamber. Before I could react her voice said, "Thanks for everything."

I half-turned, and saw her automatic pointing at me. Her lips were firmly set, her face calm. "*Adiós, Juan*," she said, and fired.

My eyes registered the spurt of red flame from the muzzle but I never heard the report. Pain exploded inside my skull and deafened me. Nina, the room, all vanished in an instantaneous blackout.

Nothingness.

TEN

Pain.

The shark's teeth were imbedded in my skull, my scuba tank was out of air. I struggled to pry his jaws apart, but they were rigid as steel. My fins kicked up sand as I struggled to free myself from the deadly grip, but the effort caused worse pain.

The shark was going to hold me until I drowned. Fifty feet down there was no color, only shades of gray—like the shark's long body. Somewhere I'd lost my knife. I jabbed my thumbs into the shark's eyes and he bit down harder. I screamed and water surged down my throat, filling my lungs.

Pain lessened, but it was too late now. I was dying.

Better fast than slow.

I opened my mouth and sucked in—air.

I was lying on my back, the shark had spat me out.

My right hand clawed for the regulator. Without the regulator in my mouth how could I breathe?

My eyes opened and there was light. I couldn't understand what had happened. The sand bottom was hard and smooth but there was no water. Vision returned and my eyes came to focus on a ceiling.

Where?

My hands felt dry, slacks covered my thighs, also dry. But my face was wet, and my neck. Sticky-wet.

I touched the wetness, smeared it with my fingers and stared at the tips. Blood red.

Wha—?

The pain in my head came over me like a sledgehammer. I suddenly felt stiff and old and helpless. I was a roach pinned under viewing glass.

I heard a long breathy groan, realizing that it came from my throat.

Wherever I was I certainly wasn't drowning. I had to realize that the shark, the water—everything was a dream. My eyes moved and focused on a black hole in the wall. Rectangular.

An open safe.

Like reverse replay, facts reassembled.

I'd opened the safe, she'd shot me. Who? I tried to remember.

Names returned; Paula, Nina. *Thanks for everything.* Even with open eyes I could see flame spurting from her little gun. I shivered. My body was deathly cold.

I turned over and something came off my head. I fingered it, remembered. The headset.

By millimeters I edged my back up against the chair.

Pain ballooned enormously. My skull was a huge boil ready to burst. I couldn't let that happen.

My hands lifted, held my head protectively. The right side was as wet as if paint had been poured on it—paint now drying in the air-conditioned coolness of the bedroom.

My palm was sticky with dark red blood. *My* blood.

How far had the bullet entered?

My fingers found the headset, lifted it. I forced my eyes to focus. The broad, U-shaped band of the stethoscope was deeply dented. Its spring steel had deflected Nina's bullet. A bullshit caliber anyway, the .25. A lot of bark but no bite, ha, ha. Lucky boy!

My gaze lifted to the open safe. Open and empty.

Mother Hubbard's empty cupboard. I couldn't repress a mad giggle. It grew, swelled into hysterical choking laughter that shook my skull and stirred fresh waves of pain.

I'd opened Ibarra's safe and Nina had robbed it, thinking she'd killed me. Good old Nina, very treacherous.

I'd swallowed a big lie.

I managed to get to my knees, gulping deep breaths against the slashing pain. The right side of my head, face and neck were covered with drying blood.

I lifted my wrist and stared: 3:18.

The last time I'd checked was nearly three hours ago. Her bullet had stunned me that long. Thank God for the German-made steel headband, anyway. Lucky indeed.

Slowly I forced myself to do things. Still sitting, I gathered the stethoscope and its case, shoved them into the carry-bag.

As my torso twisted, something prodded my spine. I reached back and felt the grip of my PPK. She hadn't known it was there. Had she phoned the police? No, I'd be discovered by the help, and she needed getaway time.

How far could she run from Ibarra?

She'd told so many lies . . . *was* Pedrito in Manzanillo with his mistress?

Gritting my teeth I got to my knees, gripped the chair and forced myself upright. My knees gave way. I lurched against the safe door. For a time I rested there until the pain and nausea were manageable. Then I used a handkerchief to wipe prints from the metal door, handle and dial. I picked up my bag and dropped notepad and pencil into it.

Time to leave.

She had the books and a fortune in currency.

As long as Ibarra lived, he would hunt her. He had the power, the money, the connections. He'd hired Sid Fertig to rob and kill Eddie Wax; putting out a contract on Nina would be routine.

As long as Ibarra lived . . .

I was halfway to the rear exit door when I knew I couldn't leave. Not just then.

I put down my plastic bag and began searching the penthouse room by room.

The master bedroom was empty, a closet door open. I looked at the blood on my shirt, took it off and put on one of Ibarra's.

Adjoining the master bedroom was a guest room. The

vanity table held cosmetics, a tray of manicure implements. I opened a dresser drawer: underthings. I slid aside the closet door, saw half a dozen dresses and estimated that they would fit Nina.

I was seconds from turning off the light when I noticed the bed pillow. It had a dark, circular mark on it. I picked up the pillow and turned it over. A patch of dried blood. The mark I'd noticed came from the flash of a gun, tiny flakes of black powder peppered the small center hole.

The pillow had been pressed against flesh, the barrel shoved into the pillow, trigger pulled.

I had no difficulty in telling myself what woman had pulled the trigger, but whose flesh had been the target? Whose blood stained the underside?

That the pillow had been used as a silencer suggested the shot had been fired during daylight hours when an unsilenced shot could have been heard by people moving around the hotel. The bloodstain was dry. How long had it dried? Twelve hours? Twelve hours ago I had been in Mexico City. Nina had been here, and Ibarra.

If she'd killed Ibarra, where was his body?

I walked around the end of the bed and looked down.

Lying between the bed and the wall was the body of a naked man. On the upper left quadrant of his chest was a dark contusion. Despite the pain it caused, I leaned over and stared. The dark blue mark was centered by a jet black puncture. Dried blood.

In life he had been a handsome man. White hair, black eyebrows, black mustache. His eyes were open, their surface dull.

His lips were drawn back in a rictus showing perfect white teeth. I lifted the nearest hand and the arm moved limply. Rigor mortis had come and gone. Francisco Pedro Ibarra had been dead a good many hours. Like twelve.

Her final lie, I thought. Ibarra wasn't in the arms of Lupita at Las Hadas—he was lying in the embrace of death, in a room frequented by another mistress: Nina Mendez.

His killer.

I turned off the light and toed the door shut.

Despite concussion my brain was functioning again.

I couldn't restore Ibarra to life, and didn't want to. But I didn't like the way he had died.

As I walked back to the rear door I visualized how it had happened.

Naked, Ibarra had lain on her bed waiting for Nina to join him. She'd come out of the bathroom wearing a robe, playfully shoved a pillow over his chest, kissed his lips, and fired through the pillow. Rolled his corpse off the bed. In complete control.

I wondered if he'd died with an erection.

The pantry door was key-locked from the far side, but I turned the bolt easily and went down the staircase carrying my plastic bag.

At the bottom I disarmed the alarm, opened the door, and stepped into the hall. I reset the alarm and shut the door. The spring bolt slipped into place. I wiped my prints from the door edge and looked around.

Nothing moving, no sign of life.

I went to the window and looked down at the parking area. No silver Triumph, but I hadn't expected it to be there.

I needed a place of refuge, time to get my head together.

I walked to Nina's door and tried the knob. Locked.

The elevator locator panel showed all three cars on the lobby floor. I got out my lock picks and went to work on Nina's door, turned the keyway cylinder in two minutes. Went in.

Through darkness I went into the bedroom, switched on the light. The unmade bed was empty. In both closets there were empty hangers. Shoe racks bare.

Nothing in the bureau drawers. She had cleaned out her suite just as she'd cleaned out Ibarra's safe.

Her vanity table was empty but for powder traces. I turned on the makeup light and noticed fingerprints where she'd tilted the mirror. I broke off that section and carefully placed it next to my lockpicking case.

The bathroom cabinet held a leg razor, some eye shadow,

cosmetic brushes, the stub of a lipstick labeled *Rose d'Amour*, a bottle of tablets for monthly discomfort. *Espasmas.*

I spilled out four tablets and swallowed them with water. Maybe they'd help male discomfort, too.

I stared at the cabinet mirror.

My face was pale. Beard stubble showed. There were circles under my eyes. The right side of my face was stained with dark blood—my own. The hair on that side was matted and stiff with congealed blood. I felt old and sick.

I went back to the suite entrance and set the bolt and chain. Then I ran a cool shower and undressed, placing my pistol on the toilet seat in easy reach. The bitch might come back for some forgotten item.

I was too weak to stand under the shower. I sat on the bottom of the tub and watched dissolved blood trickle down from my scalp to my chest and thighs. After a while I soaped my face and used her leg razor to shave, steadying myself at the washstand with my free hand. I rinsed my face and looked in the mirror.

I looked bad, but not as bad as Ibarra.

I dried off and lay down in her bed, pulled up the covers. Slept.

———————

Light woke me. My head lifted from the pillow and began throbbing. I lurched into the bathroom and swallowed four more *Espasmas.* My watch showed seven-fifteen. I'd had about three hours' rest.

I needed more, much more, but as soon as Ibarra's body was discovered—and that could be happening right now—someone would try to notify his mistress, Srta. Nina Mendez, and she wouldn't be in her suite. Just a stray *gringo* with a bullet wound. And the *policía* wouldn't smile at the irony.

I dressed slowly, pondering my next move. Survival was number one; I had to get away from the scene of the crime. Was it safe to return to the Tropical and get my gear? Not very, and all of it was expendable. My plane was at Cancún.

She didn't know about that, she didn't know my name or where I lived. She couldn't tip the police.

By nightfall, wherever she was, she'd be wondering why my corpse hadn't been found along with Ibarra's. Tomorrow she'd decide that either the police were withholding information, or I'd somehow escaped, despite her efforts.

And it would worry her. It would gnaw at her mind when she realized I had survived. She had expected murder and theft to be her secret alone.

Someone else would know. Me.

In time, if I could get free of Ixtapa, I'd look for her, but not today. Self-preservation was the primary rule of life.

I fitted my stethoscope into its case, wiped off all prints, and put it in her dresser drawer along with the dial I'd drawn. Why not have the cops looking for her, too? I didn't care who found her first though I preferred that satisfaction for myself as the injured party. My pride was wounded as well as my head.

I dumped her wastebasket litter into my plastic bag, tore off the top sheets of her telephone pad, and tucked them into a pocket as I walked to the door. My hand was reaching for the knob when I heard a key slide into the lock.

ELEVEN

I stepped to the hinge side and waited.

The unlocked door moved inward. Six inches.

Stopped.

Snubbed by the night chain.

The door closed. The maid went away.

I expelled breath, timed four minutes and released the snub chain. Ear to the door panel I listened, opened the door a crack and peered out. Four people were standing at the elevators. The maid's cart was three doors down the corridor. The elevator door opened, guests got in, panel lights showed the car descending.

I stepped into the hall, closed the door, and rang for an elevator. The maid came into the hall, took towels from her cart, and reentered the room. Elevator doors opened and I got in. The car stopped at three floors, taking on guests dressed for breakfast or the beach. A boy and girl got on, both handsome and neatly dressed. From their conversation they were brother and sister joining their parents for breakfast.

Finally the lobby.

I left with the group, but angled off to the cab rank and got into the first taxi.

At the airport I studied the departure board and bought a ticket for the next departing flight, leaving for Mexico City in forty minutes. I wasn't hungry, but my weakened body needed nourishment. In the coffee shop I ordered a vanilla shake with three eggs, and the waiter brought it with a bottle of Añejo. I thought the rum might do more for me than the protein. So I drank the health-giving beverage and ordered coffee. After it arrived I laced it with Añejo and sipped pleasurably. The pain in my skull was beginning to ebb.

I trudged to the departure gate and filed out with other passengers. I'd noticed that the metal detector was down, so I didn't have to discard my Walther before boarding the plane.

In my seat I fell asleep even before the DC9 lifted off the runway.

At Mexico City airport I bought a ticket to Cancún, figuring I could manage to fly the Seabee back to Cozumel.

The time was now mid-morning. Nina could be in Europe or South America, planning ways to enhance her holdings. What she probably hadn't yet realized was that she had become a legitimate target for DEA.

And it was to Manny and the Miami office that I had a lot of explaining to do. The bureaucratic mind would instantly suspect that I had made off with a million dollars, plus a hundred and twenty thousand—to say nothing of three million queer. Nina, as far as I knew, had taken it all.

So, they'd say, "Where's Nina?" And I had no answer.

My flight was called. I got up and the effort made my head throb again. I needed something a lot stronger than Nina's female complaint compound. I'd find it in Cancún's airport shop before I tried flying to Cozumel.

At the metal detector I waited until the security guard got involved in an argument with a female passenger. Then I slipped around the archway and boarded the plane.

In my seat I slept an hour, declined a plastic-wrapped luncheon snack, and slept until the plane landed at Cancún.

I signed out my plane and freed the tie-downs. The Lycoming turned over smoothly. I let it warm as I checked controls, oil and fuel level, called the tower, and rolled to the starting line.

Airborne, I cranked up the wheels, swung around and headed south for home.

César and Sheba were wildly joyful to see me. They capered around me like puppies, bumping their sleek hundred-pound bodies against me, licking my arms and face. My house was in good order. I fed my Dobermans, locked them in the yard and lay down, but sleep didn't come. Instead, Ramón's wife, Margarita, arrived and began mopping, sweeping and dusting. I changed clothing, sterilized my head wound with hydrogen peroxide, and drove my jeep into San Miguel.

From the Telmex office I placed a call to Mérida.

When Al Wolcott answered, I said, "I need personal contact ASAP. Cozumel."

"I'll try to get over this afternoon. Bad news?"

"Terrible. Last night everything went blooey."

"Maybe you should report in Miami."

"I'm too beat up for the trip," I said, which was partially true. But I also wanted to avoid U.S. jurisdiction in case some eager bureaucrat decided I should be jailed for absconding with federal funds. No matter that the money was confiscated from Eddie Wax.

"See you later," he said. I paid cash for the call, not wanting Al's office number on my phone bill.

At the post office I opened my box and got out the thick hotel envelope I'd had Valeriano send me. It held forty thousand dollars I'd failed to earn.

Why? Because I'd been using my dick instead of my head. Just like Ibarra.

As I drove home I began thinking that Nina Mendez might not be who she claimed to be. Was she Paula Quiroz or someone else? The mirror prints might establish an identity. Might not.

What she was, whoever she was, she was a classy lay and an astonishingly accomplished liar capable of murdering without compunction. I'd seen her face as she fired at me, and I would forever remember that composed, purposeful expression. She'd seduced me, neutralized (but not killed) me, and flown off with the swag she'd been after all along. And I'd been gullible enough to serve as her accomplice.

The humiliation was worse than the pain.

Each pothole in the coast road sent fresh daggers through my skull, telling me I had become dull-witted and old, unfit for active service. I unlocked my gate, drove in and locked the gate behind me. I swallowed a handful of painkillers and turned in.

———————

Wolcott showed up in time for dinner. I was feeling well enough to mix drinks, make a salad and grill steaks on the patio I'd been planning to enclose as a surprise for Melody. Instead, I handed Al my envelope containing the forty thousand fee, and while we ate—and brushed off mosquitoes—I narrated my tale of deception and death.

Moodily, he thought it over, added *sangría* to his glass, and said, "I'm sure Hagopian will want to hear it from you firsthand."

"Who's Hagopian?"

"Merle Hagopian heads Miami Regional. Valeriano reports to him and so do I."

I said, "Since regaining consciousness some eighteen hours ago I've undergone a period of intensive self-criticism, and I'm not looking for more from some stranger."

"Hagopian's not Phil Corliss, Jack. He's solid, ex-CIA."

"That's solid?" I swallowed a mouthful of Añejo. It suppressed skull pain better than anything I'd tried so far. "Manny Montijo is what I call solid, and I'm in the process of embarrassing him. I'd rather tell the tale to Manny. At least he knows I don't steal Agency funds."

"Manny's in Israel, talking with Mossad about Syrian poppies in the Bekaa valley. If I can persuade Hagopian to see you in some . . . let's say . . . neutral spot, will you meet him?"

"I guess so. Cancún."

I'd wrapped the mirror fragment in tissue, and now I handed it to Al. "Meanwhile, prints might identify her."

"You don't think she's Nina Mendez?"

"I don't think she's anyone she said she is. What I know with certainty is that she's an attractive female, a good lay, smart as a snake, and deadly when armed. Unless I'm very, very wrong—and God knows I've been vastly in error of late—Nina plans to take over Ibarra's operations. All of them, including his arms business. She's got the books, the money, the smarts. She's not some uneducated *bandolero*, but an upscale, highly intelligent and determined young woman who'll flop anytime she thinks it likely to advance her ambitions."

"Quite an evaluation," he remarked.

"Well, I've seen her in action. Horizontally *and* vertically, *amigo*. And I'm disgusted with myself." I managed a sickly smile.

He turned over the envelope in his hand. "I'll put this on hold for now. If we intercept her you'll still get credit." He slid the envelope into an inside jacket pocket. "If I leave now I can catch the last flight to Mérida. Wheels need to be set in motion. Any chance you have a photo of the lady?"

"Not even that. Just a very sore skull, my sole souvenir."

"At least Ibarra's dead."

"I can't even take credit for that," I grunted. I didn't want to tell him I'd set up Chato, or how.

He laid a friendly hand on my shoulder. "I'll probably call tomorrow about a meet with Merle. Okay?"

"Seems unavoidable." I saw him to the gate and watched him drive off in his rental.

Inside, away from the mosquitoes, I cracked a bucket of ice and watched it diminish along with my last bottle of Añejo. The more I drank, the less pain in my head. Finally I lurched off to bed. Too tired—or too drunk—to undress.

In the darkness I could see her face above the gun held at arm's length, pointing at me. Her eyes were cold and deadly. She didn't even hate me, I thought; I was just an obstacle, something inanimate to be gotten rid of.

And I saw the spurt of flame. My body cringed.

My heart pounded. I managed to breathe deeply, then regularly, and after a time I fell asleep.

I slept through the night until morning. Margarita knocked on my door, and when I opened it there was a telegram in her hand.

TWELVE

Over breakfast I reread the telegram. From Caracas it said, "Miss you, love you, want to be with you. Expect me twentieth. Melody."

That was two days off, and I needed the interval for physical and spiritual repair. By then DEA might have located Nina/Paula and I could forget about her.

I walked out to my pier and climbed down the boat ladder into warm water. The feel of it recalled hallucinating beside Ibarra's safe: shark's teeth in my skull, anoxia, panic, bone-deep fear.

Damn her, I thought; damn her in Hell!

But that wasn't solving anything. I paddled around, stretching stiff muscles while avoiding water on my skull scab. Earlier, in the mirror I saw it was big as a half-dollar and black as anthracite. At least it was healing. And I was feeling better.

Dressed, I emptied my carry-bag on the living room table and began going through the residue of Nina's occupancy: lipstick-smeared tissues, strands of hair, a small bottle that had contained nail polish remover, cigarette butts, scraps of Andaluz notepaper that I picked out and set aside, the paper bank binder from a bundle of fifty one hundred dollar bills— tip money for her—three used nail files, and a hotel cash receipt for telephone calls.

Very little to build on, I told myself, unless the paper scraps provided some sort of clue or clues. Painstakingly, I assembled the scraps and found the sheet devoid of writing. I turned them over and examined their reverse. I switched off the ceiling light and slanted a flashlight beam on the assembled scraps. That way I could make out indentations made by a pencil or ballpoint pen as it pressed on a covering sheet.

I was getting interested.

With a paste stick I glued each scrap into position on a sheet of cardboard. While the paste dried I went out to the now cold barbecue grill and scooped half a cupful of black charcoal residue. Very carefully I sifted the dust onto the jigsaw, then blew it off. Enough remained in the depressions to show printed notations:

ZIH-ZLO MX 796 17
ZLO-MTY MX 708
     BOL. MOST.

It looked like a restored palimpsest, parts of the Zimmermann Telegram, or the Japanese Purple Code, but as I stared at the symbols I realized that they concerned air travel. The top line was decipherable as a flight from Zihuatanejo to Manzanillo via Mexicana 796. On the seventeenth.

Yesterday.

The next line was shorthand for a flight segment Manzanillo to Monterrey, Mexicana 708.

So far, so good, but for a time I was stopped by the two final abbreviations. I'd been thinking about them in English, but Spanish was Nina's native tongue, the language she automatically thought in. So the incomplete words were Spanish. And related to air travel. I began recalling common reservation words and phrases until I could complete the abbreviations.

BOL. was *boleto*—ticket. MOST. must be *mostrador*—counter. Her flight ticket or tickets would be ready at the airport's Mexicana counter.

I felt pleased with myself, the first positive accomplishment since I'd escaped the shark. Now I had an idea where Nina had gone: Manzanillo, then Monterrey. She'd lied in telling me Ibarra was visiting Lupita Casillas at his/her

Manzanillo condo, but maybe she was planning to go there herself, taking along the haul from Pedrito's safe. Thus mixing truth and fable.

Monterrey? She claimed to come from Monterrey, of the prominent Mendez family. Mendez Peralta. Brother José Manuel, the architect who designed the Andaluz. Death by suicide she said, but was that, too, part of her fantastic tale? I began making notes to myself.

That done, I slipped the reconstructed note sheet into a plastic envelope and swept the rest of her trash into my bag. I was taking it to the kitchen wastebasket when I stopped and set the bag on the kitchen table. I fished out the hotel's cash receipt and wondered why her phone calls hadn't simply been included in the weekly billing to her suite—whether she or Ibarra paid it was important. Stapled to the receipt was a short computer-printed list of phone numbers, duration, and the cost of each call.

I sat down at the table, stared at the list, and got out my Telmex directory.

Over the past four days ending yesterday, four calls had been made: three minutes, eight minutes, six minutes and eleven minutes, the last as of yesterday afternoon while I was in Mexico City. At a time when Ibarra was probably dead.

Two calls had the long-distance prefix 333, the other two were to an 83 prefix. My finger went down the directory list of long distance dial codes and stopped at 333—that was Manzanillo; 83 was Monterrey.

For the first time I began feeling optimistic. The called numbers were pure gold—if not to me, then to DEA. Now I had something to show Merle Hagopian. Her likely destinations, plus the numbers she'd called before disappearing. Using a computer-reversed phone book, the Monterrey office could identify those phone locations.

If the calls had been social, innocent, Nina would have had them billed to her room extension, but she'd wanted to conceal them, thus cash payment to the hotel. She had carelessly left traces behind, but having put a bullet in

Ibarra, and assuming she'd killed me as well, what had she to fear?

I folded the phone receipt and tucked it into my wallet; now I had to deal with another matter: she had shot me; why hadn't she checked to verify that I was dead?

I dredged the answer from my memory.

She'd refused to cleanse the blood of Chato and Ramos from Ibarra's office floor. Why? Because in her own words: *Blood sickens me.*

And I'd bled a convincing amount.

As she emptied the safe Nina probably avoided even looking at me. The concussion had caused me to breathe shallowly, imperceptibly.

How bizarre are human prejudices, I mused. She'd shot me almost reactively but couldn't stand to look at a bloodied corpse. Which was extremely fortunate for me.

My telephone rang. I went to it, almost convinced I'd hear the voice of Nina. What would she say? Nothing, and hang up? Or it was all a mistake and please forgive me? I really hadn't meant to squeeze the trigger . . . ?

I clenched the receiver. "*Bueno?*"

"That you, Jack?" Melody's mother. What the hell does *she* want?

"Yes, Delores," I said with forced patience. "Are you okay? Everything all right? Where are you?"

"Well, I'm fine, everything is fine, and I'm at home in Miami." She paused. "Melody there?"

"As far as I know she's still in Caracas."

"Well, the tournament is supposed to be over with, and she hasn't come home."

"The event could have been interrupted by strikes, prolonged by labor trouble."

"Well, that's so, it was always happening in Brazil when I lived there with Melody's father—a wonderful man."

Whom you picked clean, you harpy, I thought in silence. I said, "Melody sent a gram from Caracas, saying she'd see me soon. That help?"

"It does. Oh, a great deal. Is she coming to Miami?"

"Short telegram, no details."

"Oh, dear. Do have her phone me when she arrives."

"I promise," I said dutifully, heard expressions of appreciation, and hung up on my future mother-in-law. I wished someone would marry the wealthy widow and carry her off to Tibet and out of our lives.

The trouble was, any eligible male candidate would have to have more money than Delores, which was considerable, and be willing to put up with her eternal bullshit. So far no such suitor had appeared, and I couldn't visualize one who would.

Meanwhile, Delores Diehl lived like a maharanee, involved in every conceivable charity ball, raffle and reception, fundraising cruise, routs and ridottos. She attended fashion openings in New York, Paris and Rome, squired by expensive gigolos, contributed to African Famine, the SPCA, and homes for unwed mothers. A latter-day belle and, in Miami, what passed for a socialite.

Her call had detoured my train of thought. I went outside, played with my dogs, and strolled to the end of my pier. Nearby, my Seabee bobbed invitingly, but I was too played out for a night flight. I liked flying up the channel between Cozumel and mainland Mexico, seeing Cancún's light patterns emerge, watching fishing boats below, big jets taking off from the busy airport . . . but not tonight. I'd wait until Melody could share it with me.

I fed César and Sheba again, gave them fresh water and locked the house from inside.

As I lay in bed my thoughts returned to Nina Mendez. I saw her tawny face beside me on the pillow, eyes closed, lips parted, moonlight pearling her even teeth. And I saw the unmasked face—the true one—rigid, uncompromising, determined, deadly.

She'd seduced me, duped me.

It was a long time before her face left my mind and I let myself sleep.

The telephone woke me at eight-fifteen. Wolcott said Merle would meet me at the Cancún Sheraton for lunch in its Gaviota restaurant. He'd recognize me from my file photo. Noon.

I said that was agreeable. He asked how I was feeling, and I said it was too early to tell. *Adiós*, Al.

My mouth felt lined with moleskin. I rinsed it with white wine, and after I was dressed Margarita arrived and made breakfast for me.

Ramón came over and we worked on the charter books together. He always seemed to do better when I was away for a few days. There was an afternoon fishing party—blue-fish were running—and a full day tomorrow for sail. I paid Ramón his share and, after he departed to fuel *Corsair* and buy bait and ice at the town docks, I socked away the balance in my wall safe.

Opening it reminded me of Ibarra's bedroom again. It wasn't a congenial memory, so for diversion I cleaned weapons and took household inventory. After Margarita left for market I shaved and put on fresh clothing.

At eleven I turned over the Lycoming, ruddered my Seabee into the wind, lifted off, and flew up the slot to Cancún.

━━━━━━━━━

The man who met me in La Gaviota was tall and well built. Tanned face long and lined, topped by a stiff brush of salt-and-pepper hair. His eyes were good, corners crinkled as though accustomed to smiling. He wore a beige embroidered *guayabera* and white slacks. When we shook hands his hand covered mine with nothing at all to spare.

"Appreciate this," he said. "Let's find a table."

The *maître d'* showed us to a side table. I ordered my usual, and Hagopian asked for vermouth on the rocks. "Got used to it in Rome," he remarked. "Can't break the habit and don't want to." He shook out a filter cigarette and lighted it. After exhaling he said, "You've had an active few days, Jack—mind if we're informal? Merle being kind of a sissy name, friends and enemies, even my wife, call me the Hag." I was contemplating asking him which category ap-

101

plied to his wife when he leaned forward and stared at the side of my head. "Damn, you *were* lucky!"

"Luckier she didn't check my pulse." I took a deep breath. "Letting it all hang out I freely admit she was miles ahead of me from the beginning."

He nodded. "I can understand that, and confession is good for the soul. Covering-up, finding excuses is what slows progress, like boulders in a stream." He blew smoke at a fly on the table bouquet. "My idea to substitute three million queer for the good stuff in Eddie's bag . . . I guess that caused you a good deal of grief, eh?"

"More than I wanted," I admitted, "but it got me close to Ibarra."

"So we write off a confiscated million, no big deal."

"Plus that hundred and twenty thousand for four keys of coke."

"Think the transaction will ride?"

"I don't know if Ibarra lived long enough to issue the order."

"Well, we'll tap that phone, make a call for you, see where that takes us. Okay?"

"Okay with me." Our drinks arrived, we lifted glasses and sipped. The waiter left menus and went away.

Hagopian said, "Mind telling me why you're reluctant to see me in Miami?"

"I have negative memories of that office," I said. "Trouble and aggravation."

"I can understand that. I was part of a big organization for a long time and the office could be more stressful than the street." He inhaled cigarette smoke. "Came an era when we spent more time answering congressional queries than fighting the battle I'd signed up to fight. I had enough years to retire and grabbed the chance. Now I'm trying to put into practice what I learned from my former life."

I was going to say lotsa luck, but I didn't want to come off as a smartass. Instead, I said, "I'm getting the feeling DEA could use more men like you."

"Appreciate that. I went over your old file last night. You

did a lot of good work, and thanks to Corliss we lost you."
He eyed me. "Ever consider signing on again?"

"Not really. Manny Montijo still has confidence in me,
though after this caper it could get badly eroded."

"I doubt anyone active in clandestine work hasn't been
led down the garden path at least once."

I smiled. "Not you, too?"

"Especially me. I started off with this idealistic faith in
human nature, the essential goodness of man. After some
monster disillusionments I began to alter my view. We
don't like to be hard and cynical but in our business we
often have to be that way."

I was liking this man, everything he said made sense to
me.

We ordered lunch: turtle soup, grilled bacon-wrapped
shrimp, salad and coffee. After the waiter left Hagopian
said, "So, you had faith in a Mex broad and ended up with
a very sore skull. Hardly unique, but where does that leave
us?"

I handed over Nina's phone bill and flight reservations.
"From her wastebaskets," I told him.

"Manzanillo to Monterrey," he said musingly. "Got a
scenario?"

"Speculative. Nina, let's call her, made a decision to take
over Ibarra's operations, learning what she could week by
week. He appointed her to meet Eddie Wax and pick up
Chato's four million. When she realized I wasn't Wax she
told me a tale calculated to get my sympathy and cooperation, pointed me at Ibarra's safe, killed Ibarra, tried to kill
me, and decamped with what she'd always wanted."

"Why couldn't she have held a gun on Ibarra and made
him turn over his books?"

"Safer to recruit a fall guy like me." I cringed, then went
on. "The sudden death of Ramos, Ibarra's bodyguard, slid
things into place for her. While I was shopping in Mexico
City Nina shot Ibarra, confident that I could open his safe."

"What do you think she'll do now?"

"I think she's already reviewing books and ledgers, getting ready to contact Ibarra's foremen and tell them it's business as usual, except now she's in charge."

"And where will she be doing all this—your guess?"

"Monterrey. Where she has roots, friends, where she knows her way around." I gave him Nina's federal credential, the one showing her name as Paula Quiroz.

After studying it, he said, "Didn't know about this. Think we just maybe ought to turn the case over to the *Procurador General* and back off?"

"If you want it swept under a rug. The attorney general may well be an honest man, but who knows about the people around him?"

"Who indeed." He smiled wryly. "I brought something for you."

From his billfold he extracted a folded paper, smoothed the creases, and passed it to me. The Xerox copy of a U.S. visa application filled out and signed by Nina Victoria Mendez Peralta.

Beneath the small color photograph of the applicant was a thumbprint. I ignored the print because I was staring at the photograph of a young woman with delicate features and light brown hair. She wore rimmed glasses and her dental work left much to be desired. Hagopian said, "Recognize her?"

"I've never seen her before."

"I thought that might be the case, and that narrows things a bit. She's not Nina Mendez but could be Paula Quiroz, right?"

"I guess so."

"So I'll have the name run through *Gobernación* along with those specimen prints you provided. Could be productive and I don't think we'd be giving anything away— the name will be among a dozen sent in for routine check."

I was still staring at the color photograph. "Compared to Paula, this girl is Miss Ugly."

"Well, she's the legitimate daughter of the late governor, and I imagine your Paula knew her. Well enough, I'd say, to adopt her background and identity. Corollary being the real Nina knows the false one—and could identify her."

Our lunch arrived, and Hagopian ordered a bottle of Domecq Chablis to wash things down. After a while he said, "At this point what are your feelings?"

"I'm going to take a few days R & R, then follow up on the phone leads. And I'll need that credential, the photo is all we've got."

He returned it to me.

Over coffee Hagopian said, "I'm no slave to statistics, but close to 90 percent of the coke and heroin entering the U.S. comes from or through Mexico. I don't have to tell you how hard it is to suppress this traffic south of the border. Farmers grow what's profitable, and smugglers smuggle because there's no business, legal or illegal, that yields comparable profits—unless it's armaments, and Ibarra was deep into that, too. So this Paula lady is in a simply splendid position to continue and expand Ibarra's enterprises. You're the only one who's had dealings with her and I'll welcome your continuing involvement."

"*Ni hablar.*" No question.

"Any way we can help?"

"File checks and record search."

He nodded. "Soon as we have anything I'll get it to Wolcott for you. Fair enough?" He stood up, we shook hands and I said, "You make up for a lot of Corlisses."

"Appreciate that. I'm trying." As he left the table I saw a man detach himself from the bar, and casually trail out behind the regional chief. He was as tall as Hagopian and similarly dressed but for the gun bulge at his hip. A hit man spotting Hagopian and his look-alike bodyguard might hesitate just long enough to be neutralized.

Chatting, they crossed the lobby and I looked at my watch. By Gulfstream jet the Hag could be back in his Miami office within two hours, but I wasn't ready to fly home just yet.

A taxi took me to the shopping mall where a pharmacy sold me a roll of masking tape. I used it to cover both sides of Paula's federal ID card except for her photograph, and took the result to a photo shop nearby. I told the proprietor I wanted wallet-size copies of the photo, say ten by sixteen centimeters.

"Much work, *señor*. First I must photograph this small original, make a negative and enlarge the—"

"I understand the process," I told him. "What I want is six glossy prints an hour from now." I laid a twenty dollar bill on the counter. "Another when I come back. Let's not disappoint the lady."

He carried the photo and the twenty into the back of his shop. I stepped out into sunlight and looked around. Most stores and shops were closed for mid-afternoon *siesta*, but the Telmex office was open. At the billing counter I asked for the office supervisor, and the clerk pointed to a desk in the far corner. "*Señora* Asteguí," he said, and let me enter the enclosure.

She was an aging, pinch-faced woman with thick glasses and a broad stripe of white hair that ran back from her hairline. I waited respectfully until she deigned to acknowledge my presence. Only the Russian bureaucracy is more disdainful of common folk than the Mexican. "*Sí?*" she sniffed.

"*Señora,*" I began in confidential tones, "I come to you with a delicate and sensitive matter, knowing that because you are a woman, therefore understanding and discreet, you will comprehend a situation that is both shameful and embarrassing—"

"Shameful? Embarrassing?" Her eyelids blinked rapidly. At least I had her attention.

"It concerns my wife. She—we—have received a series of telephone calls from unknown persons—" I bent toward her. "Obscene in nature. Disgusting."

"Is it not, then, a matter for the police?" Her expression was open, sympathetic. She wanted to help, she needed an excuse.

"The police." I waved a hand distractedly. "Completely unsympathetic, *señora.*"

She nodded quickly. "Brutes, all of them. Go on. Your wife, you say? And these unmentionable calls?"

"Affecting her health, our marital accord. The situation is—" I shook my head sadly. "Intolerable."

"Yes, I understand. What is it I can do?"

I had copied two telephone numbers from Paula's bill and I gave them to her. "Can—will you tell me the location of these telephones, *señora?*"

She grasped the paper and placed it on her desk, bent over and began nodding. "Monterrey and Manzanillo, *señor.*"

"But where? Who?" I tried to look perplexed, desperate.

"Ah, I understand." She looked up and smiled in a strange, astringent way. "A matter of honor, no?"

"Indeed."

"Wait here." She rose, brushed past an approaching clerk, snapped at him, and entered a doorway marked EMPLOYEES ONLY. I sat down and waited. Five minutes later *Señora* Asteguí returned triumphantly. "I believe this will answer your questions, *señor.*" She handed me a torn-off printout sheet.

The Monterrey telephone was located at an address on Avenida Ruiz Cortines, the owner's name: Abela Hakem.

In Manzanillo the telephone was located within the Las Hadas condominium complex and listed to Dario Casillas.

I sighed deeply. "Thank you, thank you, *señora.* You have made it possible for me to deal appropriately with these animals."

"The names—are they familiar to you?"

"Not in the least."

"I admire your respect for your wife, for womanhood, *señor.* But I must ask that you never disclose who gave you this information."

"Never, never, I swear it." I placed a five hundred peso note conveniently near her hand. "For your favorite charity," I said, and stood up. "I thank you, my wife thanks you," I said fervently, folded the printout paper and put it in a pocket. *"Adiós, señora."*

"Que le vaya bien, señor."

When I looked back she was talking to her clerk. The bank note had disappeared. Her favorite charity, indeed.

I strolled back toward the photo shop, stopped at a *café*, drank a chilled Tecate in the cool garden, and watched hummingbirds and golden canaries dart in and out of honeysuckle vines that draped the patio walls.

After an hour I returned to the photo shop and claimed my glossy prints. The enlargements were grainy, but the face recognizable. I gave the photographer the promised twenty dollar incentive, and paid for development and printing. As I left the shop he began rolling down the protective curtains. A window sign advised that the place was closed for the afternoon.

I taxied down the line of beach hotels, around the lagoon to the airport. Tanks topped off, oil checked, I switched on my radio and got tower clearance for takeoff. As the Seabee trundled to the starting line I reviewed the two names Telmex had uncovered for me. Abela Hakem was new and unknown, but Paula had referred to a Lupita Casillas as Ibarra's mistress, the alleged niece of Evita Perón. The Las Hadas phone listed Dario Casillas. Close enough.

I waited while a Mexicana DC-10 landed, and then I richened the mix, advanced the throttle, and with full flaps accelerated down the runway.

Turning south, I flew down the channel toward Cozumel.

By now Paula must realize she had failed to kill me. What she didn't know was that I was coming after her.

Wherever she was.

THIRTEEN

"The whole thing's crazy, lover," Melody said, and jiggled her line in the water. We were at the end of my pier and several fat groupers were cruising below, occasionally nibbling barnacles from the support posts. Melody loved fishing, especially with live shrimp bait. On the way back from the airport I'd stopped at the waterfront to buy a bucket of them. What the fish didn't eat, we would.

When I said nothing, she glanced at me. "Well? What did you expect to get out of it?"

"A screened patio," I said, and gestured at the house.

My avowed fiancée tossed her short dark hair impatiently. "You risked your life just to please me?"

"Any time," I said, "day or night."

"Well, forget it. I'm forever freeloading here, let *me* pay for the work. You know perfectly well I can afford it. Moreover," she continued, after a sidelong glance, "I won't have the children playing on doggy-doo, so the enclosure is essential."

"Children?"

"Of course. Our genes will blend marvelously, and I want to bear children while I'm young and healthy. Then we can devote ourselves to each other and enjoy life before the infirmities of age set in." Melody had everything figured out.

"What larks," I said. "Next you'll be saying our little spread is incomplete without tennis courts and a freshwater pool."

"How else can we entertain properly? With those adjoining five hectares—which we should buy now before the price goes up—the pool and courts can run parallel to each other, dressing *cabañas* between."

I sighed. "I'll get right on it. How is it you're so smart and beautiful when your mother is, well, so sort of average?"

"My real father was a handsome man, and I take after his side of the family. His mother, my grandmother, was a spectacular Southern beauty."

The tip of her rod bent, she set the hook, reeled, and in less than a minute drew out a struggling grouper. It flopped on the pier boards until I whacked its head with my knife handle. "About three pounds," I said, working the hook out of jaw gristle, and I began cleaning her catch. Melody asked, "Is she prettier than me?"

"This fish? No contest." I slit the underside, clawed out entrails and dropped them in the water where they immediately disappeared.

"Jack, you know perfectly well I'm asking about that Paula whoever person. *Is* she?"

"Is she what?"

"So attractive I should worry about her?"

"*Caramba*! She almost killed me, love. How could there be anything between us, ever?"

Melody kissed the side of my face. "If I ever see her I'll kill her without compunction. Endangering my future happiness was what she did. I won't have it."

I drew the bait bucket from the water. "Plenty of shrimp for stuffing this fine grouper. Let's see—onions, green pepper, chilies . . . dinner's practically prepared."

"I'll do the rice." She reeled in her line and caught the hook around the reel bar as I'd taught her. I kissed her small ear, tongued the interior until she shivered.

"Anyway," I said, "I don't even know who this Paula person really is, so relax."

"But you have ways of finding out. Don't deceive me. She tricked you and you feel you have to get even."

"You know I'm not a vengeful person," I lied, "and anyway it's time you phoned your mother."

"I can do that anytime," she sniffed. "Where are your priorities?"

I picked up the grouper by the tail, and with the bait bucket began walking toward the house, Melody following. "Tell you what," I said. "While you're phoning mom I'll mix drinks and take a shower."

"Bargain," she said, "and you'll be startled by the depth of the lust I've worked up for you."

———

I was.

Melody loved all the things I'd taught her, beginning that afternoon in a raunchy Miami Beach motel where she had seduced me. Her petite body was tanned and smoothly muscled. While recycling I administered a mineral oil rubdown, molding her neck and shoulder muscles until she purred with pleasure. Then I massaged her small buns, thighs and calves and she wriggled enjoyably.

"Why don't we," she murmured, "advance our wedding day?"

"I'll endorse that—the very day you have diploma in hand."

"I only lack five credits," she pouted.

"Which you'd have earned long ago if you hadn't been gaining international fame and reputation. What did Delores want?"

"She was frantic to make sure I'd be there for a charity exhibition at the Surf Club."

"When?"

"Day after tomorrow. Come with me."

I wiped oily hands on my thighs. "Next week," I promised, "I'll come over if only to monitor your studies."

"If you fly back with me I'll know you're not pursuing that Paula person." Her head lifted from the pillow and she gazed at me. "Was she a good lay?"

I slapped the nearest bun. "Just average, child, and light years from your accomplishments."

"Bastard!" She grabbed my wrist and bit hard. I began

rubbing the pain away. "Only kidding," I said, gripped her hair and forced her lips to mine. Presently her body relaxed, coiled around mine and we made love. My Melody, all mine again.

Until she left, Melody and I did the things she liked and which made Cozumel living so pleasurable. Lunch in the tropical setting of Morgan's patio, sailfishing (Melody hooked and released a seventy-pounder), night-flying up the channel off Cancún where a lighted buoy marked the hulk of the Parra vessel I'd sunk; diving Palancar Reef, lazing around on the pier—and, of course, imaginative lovemaking.

She didn't want to go to Miami without me, correctly intuiting that I was going to pursue "that Paula person," despite my oaths and denials. But in the end she waved goodbye at the airport, cheered by my vow to join her in a week.

Since meeting Merle Hagopian I'd had no contact from DEA. Lifting Paula's prints from the mirror shard and getting them run through FBI indices was going to take some time, though by now the Monterrey office should have come up with the telephone location. I didn't expect *Gobernación* to report anything tangible on Paula Quiroz, so forget that source. On my own I'd acquired enough to begin the search. That afternoon I flew AeroMexico to Mexico City, where I changed planes for the short hop to Manzanillo.

Las Hadas rose around a croissant-shaped bay, its architecture pure Arab-Moorish fantasy. I telephoned the Casillas residence, but nobody answered. My lock picks opened the door, and I entered a nicely furnished two-bedroom apartment that lacked table photographs and was as impersonal as a Budget Inn. A wastebasket by a dressing table contained crumpled tissues smudged with lipstick that could have been Paula's color, but there was no clothing in the closets or drawers. Apparently whoever stayed there had moved out, and I began to wonder if Casillas was another of Paula's pseudonyms. If so, then she used the condo as a safehouse or staging area. It had been, I was sure, her first stop after killing Ibarra and emptying his safe.

Perhaps she'd left something behind.

Room by room I checked furniture, walls and flooring. Near the bathroom I found a wall safe behind a framed Orozco print. It was unlocked and held only a small package of thermite powder, a substance useful for fast ignition of documents. What sensitive papers had the safe concealed?

The refrigerator contained a hard slab of pita bread, an opened jar of gherkins, sauces and spices, bottles of mineral water and white wine. The freezer section was stocked with cuts of lamb, breast, shoulder and leg. I took them out and found behind the frozen meat a Beretta automatic enclosed in a condom. I didn't need the Beretta because I was carrying my personal Walther, a heavier, more powerful piece.

I put everything back into the freezer, feeling that this trip to Manzanillo was a wasted effort, so far. Daylight was fading fast. Too late to take a flight to Monterrey or even Mexico City. I was stuck in Las Hadas for the night and I might as well make the best of it. The hour was early for dining fashionably in the capital, but I was at a resort and I ate at stomach-time. Demand feeding.

There was nothing in the kitchen I wanted to fool with, such as roasting a leg of lamb and eating it with dry Syrian bread, so I wedged the door lock to avoid having to use my picks again, drew the door shut, and went down four floors to the nearest restaurant.

I was tired and disappointed. The Casillas condo had been unproductive and I was stuck there for the night. On the restaurant patio festooned with Japanese lanterns I ate a small undistinguished steak advertised (falsely) as Sonora beef, potatoes, *bolillos*, and downed three mugs of Tecate beer.

The arrival of several customers invigorated drowsing bus boys and waiters. The *maître d'* clicked his heels smartly, ran a hand through oiled hair, and began making dinner suggestions. The party was German or Austrian, over-dressed for seaside relaxation, sunburned and overweight. As I finished my coffee I listened to them gurgle and grunt and watched the last trace of sunset leave the Pacific horizon.

I bought a newspaper and carried it back to my borrowed lodging and locked the door. I read the paper, watched television for a while—the cabinet was set into bookshelf-style furniture that also held a large stereo rig. At ten o'clock I turned off the dubbed *M*A*S*H* rerun and went to the kitchen. Outside the service door on a staircase landing I found the customary five-gallon *garrafón* of purified water, and poured myself a bedtime drink. Then I turned out all lights behind me and went into the bedroom nearest the kitchen.

After taking off my shoes I lay back on the quilt and thought of Melody for a while. In their big house on Bay Harbor, Island Mama would be making a big welcoming fuss over her daughter, and finding opportunities to slander and downgrade me. Hell with her. Whatever Melody and I did was beyond her influence.

From somewhere in the building came a long hilarious burst of party-type laughter. A dog barked at the moon. Then it was quiet.

=============

The sound of a key grating in the front-door lock woke me and I heard the scrape of entering feet—more than two.

I grabbed up my shoes and went quickly through the dark kitchen while lights brightened the living and dining rooms. I barely made it to the service stairway and closed the door before the kitchen lights went on. The top half of the door was etched glass, translucent but not transparent. Above it was a ventilator fan. Very quietly I laced my shoes and perched on the top step.

Two men came into the kitchen. I could hear them through the fan hole. The refrigerator door opened, then the freezer compartment. Ice cubes rattled.

114

In Spanish a voice said, "Where's the water, Dario?"
"Out there. A big bottle."

As I crouched in the stairwell's dimness I realized that within seconds the door would open.

I got out my gun.

FOURTEEN

Before the door opened I managed to slip downward into deep shadow. The man tilting the *garrafón*'s iron frame made enough noise to cover any sound I made, and from the floor below I could hear water gurgling and bubbling as it poured. Finally, he righted the *garrafón*, recorked it, and went back into the kitchen, closing the service door.

I slid the Walther under my belt and climbed partway back to kitchen level. From the closeness of their voices they were sitting at the kitchen table. "Wine's not bad," said one. "You should try it."

"You know I don't drink alcohol."

"All the more for me." Clink of bottleneck against glass.

In the silence that followed I realized that the abstainer spoke a curiously accented Spanish, totally fluent, but in an accent I'd never heard. The wine-drinker's Spanish was Mexican, not the lilting singsong rhythm of peasant Mexico, but the flatter, more precise enunciation of *chilangos*, or north Mexico. I shrank into stairwell shadows and listened.

The drinker said, "I haven't decided how I feel about it. Have you?"

"She's done very well. I have confidence in her."

"Still, I don't like the idea of taking orders from a woman."

"I don't know that you have a choice."

"Since my mother I don't listen to women." Wine poured into his glass. "Women are useful for their loins and breasts, for bearing children. Men do the hard work, they're entitled to make decisions."

116

After a silence the accented voice said, "In our cause it is seen differently. Ability and accomplishment are the essential things, not whether *pinga* or *fica* is between one's legs."

Cause? *What* cause, I wondered as the speaker continued. "Many of our best people are women, fully dedicated, selfless, sacrificial. You've seen what this one can do."

After a while the drinker said, "It's true she did well in Ixtapa, but as for the rest—"

"Suspend judgment, Dario. She organizes well, and it will be to the benefit of all. Did she not keep her promise? Admit it."

Grudgingly he said, "It is true."

"And you'll come to the meeting?"

"If I must. Yes, I want to hear her proposals, her plans." He paused. "Did she admit she killed Ramos?"

"She said she did not. It was provoked by the American."

"*What* American? They found no American. I think she made him up."

"He used a false name and left the hotel without paying his bill. Left a travel bag in his room."

Dario grunted. "Still it sounds fishy to me. If he exists why can't the police find him?"

"Your police are not, let us say, awesomely efficient. What are they? Poor, illiterate farm boys in uniform, good only for traffic directing and petty theft. If Furlong didn't open the safe for her, who did?"

"I think she forced Pedrito to open his safe then shot him. That is logical so that is what must have taken place. Killing Ramos gave her the opportunity."

"I have never found her to be untruthful, Dario. Besides, she succeeded and I for one don't question success."

"Still, I'd like to know." A bottle thunked heavily into a trash basket. "I'm hungry and we have time to eat. I'll take you to a new Oriental restaurant, you'll like it." Chairs scraped, feet moved and the kitchen light went out. I could hear them talking as they moved away.

A toilet flushed.

A minute or so later the front door creaked open and

closed. I timed five minutes before quietly opening the service door and entering the kitchen. Pistol in hand, I tiptoed through the apartment checking each room, but the visitors had gone. One was Dario Casillas, the presumed owner. For the other man I had no name.

Clearly, they had been discussing Paula's takeover, but what "cause" had the nameless man referred to? The cause of making money? No, that made no sense. These days a "cause" connoted revolution, but I'd never seriously entertained the idea of a revolution in Mexico. So long as the government continued taking from the rich and giving to the poor, as was its wont, there would be no revolution. Anyway, there were too few rich to make a revolution. Everyone was being accommodated in the Mexican way.

I returned to the bed where I'd been sleeping and took off my shoes. I didn't think I'd be bothered again, because the eavesdropped conversations gave me a feeling of imminent departure, after an Oriental meal.

I could use some tempura and rice myself, I reflected, but under the circumstances I was going to do without.

Tomorrow would be another day . . . in Monterrey. I hummed to myself and turned off the light.

FIFTEEN

The capital of the state of Nuevo León is large, sprawling, and unlovely. The air is a choking combination of smoke from Pemex refineries, steel-mill soot, cement dust, fumes from diesel buses and locomotives. Monterrey dominates the industrial north as Mexico City dominates the rest of the country. Monterrey produces, Mexico City spends. Hostility between them is as old as it is intense. You can feel it when their soccer teams face off.

My taxi driver let me off at the corner of Guerrero and Ruiz Cortines, not far from the *plaza de toros*. On foot I made my way to the address given me by *Sra.* Asteguí and passed it on the far side of the street.

Abela Hakem's two-story house was unimpressive. The walls needed whitewashing, and the iron gate and window grills showed rust patches and flaking paint. At the end of the block I crossed over and walked back for a closer look. A tall iron-faced door blocked the entrance to the driveway. It was mid-morning, but all the windows showed closed blinds. From the gate angle I could see a car in the driveway, a dark green Chevrolet sedan about five years old. There was a ten-foot garden wall topped with broken bottles and glass shards set in cement. I strolled to the end of the block, walked toward the bullring and found a taxi *sitio*.

The home of Nina Victoria Mendez Peralta was on Madero near the medical center. I read the address on her visa application to the driver, and settled back for a ten-minute drive.

The house—a mansion, really—was of Victorian design:

brown brick, corner turrets, mansard roof, rising from a setting of pine, *nogal* and *galeana* trees. About two acres, I estimated, surrounded by high brick walls.

An Indian maid answered my ring, and I asked to see *Señorita* Mendez, giving my name as Paul Mahan, the first alias that popped into my mind. The maid unlocked the gate and ushered me into a dark, tapestry-hung sitting room. It was a fussy room with gilded furniture and needlepoint antimacassars, photographs on marble-top tables, some old, some new, an ormolu clock, and a life-size oil portrait of a white-mustached man in Knights of Malta uniform, sword and all. He resembled King George V but was probably the late governor, Nina's father. I was viewing the family photos when Nina glided in, so quietly I wasn't aware of her until she spoke. "Mr. Mahan? I'm Nina Mendez."

She was Paula's height, but her figure was emaciated and her face thin, dark circles under her eyes. Anorexic? She gave me a delicate clawlike hand. "What can I do for you?"

"I'm from the personnel office at Rice," I told her, "and if no one's yet notified you, someone has been impersonating you for perhaps as long as a year."

"Impersonating *me*? Why would anyone do that?"

"The university thought you might be able to tell me."

Her mouth twitched. Thick lenses magnified her eyes enormously. She seemed to shrink into the gilded chair.

I got out an enlarged photo of Paula and gave it to her. "This is the impersonator," I said. "Do you know her?"

She lifted the photo close to her face and stared at it. "Has she done something wrong?"

"I'm not prepared to say—but inquiries have been made to the university and we'd prefer to avoid any possible embarrassment."

She placed the photo on the side table. "Who—what kind of inquiries?"

"The Department of State, for one. Apparently this woman applied for a visa using your name and personal data. It would be helpful to everyone if we knew who she is.

Otherwise, it could cause confusion and slowdown the next time you want a visa to visit the States."

"I have no plans to leave Mexico."

"Even so, false application for a visa is a federal crime, and—"

"Anyone can cross a bridge, the river, and enter the U.S."

I was tiring of evasive banter. "Do you recognize the woman in that photograph?"

Her hands balled into small fists. "No." It was almost a squeak.

"If you knew her name would you tell me?"

She gazed at me defiantly. "No."

"What can you tell me about Abela Hakem?"

Her eyes widened. She swallowed. "Nothing. I don't know him."

"Dario Casillas?"

She shook her head. I said, "What are you hiding—or protecting, Miss Mendez?"

"I've answered your questions, Mr. Mahan, if that's your name. Please go."

"Sure," I said, "but until this impersonation is resolved don't expect to be granted further visas to the U.S."

She stood up and faced me. "I wasn't happy at Rice. I have no desire to return to the States."

I pointed at a table photograph of her standing beside a taller young male. "Does José Manuel feel the same?"

"Pepe is content to work in Mexico—for Mexicans."

A miraculous resurrection from the suicide Paula had so touchingly described. "Commendable," I said, and left as I had come. The maid let me out through the front gate and locked it behind me. I looked up at the old mansion's turrets and gables. *Señorita* Mendez had worn a dark crepe dress with long sleeves, almost mourning garb. A half-starved, embittered woman. I wondered what her problem was.

I found a taxi and rode to the U.S. consulate on Constitución, a broad avenue that bordered the channel of the Santa Catarina river. Normally the channel was dry, allowing kids to play soccer on its flat surface. But the last hurricane and its heavy rains had sent down a torrent that ripped squatters' huts from the far bank and destroyed large sections of the avenue. For months traffic had been dislocated, but repairs were finally made and the avenue's bank reinforced. Among the squatters loss of life had been heavy, but I could see new tin-and-cardboard huts beyond the channel and a pair of soccer goal nets just below. Maybe the next hurricane wouldn't cross the Sierra and tear everything away.

To avoid a long line of visa applicants, I walked around to the entrance for U.S. citizens who had business at the consulate.

The Marine guard frisked me and took my Walther for safekeeping. He called the DEA office, and after a while a secretary appeared and escorted me down the hall.

I'd never met Sean Murphy, but I found him on the short side of forty, red-haired with heavily freckled pink skin. He said he knew my name. I told him I was doing a short-term job for Manny Montijo and had been cleared by Merle Hagopian.

"That explains a message I have for you." He shuffled through desk papers and came up with a Telex. From the Miami office it said the FBI had determined the mirror-prints were not identifiable with any Mexican national of record. I wrote down two names and showed them to Murphy.

"Never heard of Casillas, but Hakem does occasional business with the consulate.

"In what connection?"

"Claims to have an import-export business. Mexican national of Lebanese or Syrian descent, maybe Iraqi. Ships to the Middle East."

"Drugs?"

"If so, we don't know about it." He went over to a computer console and punched the keyboard for a while, sat back and read the screen. "Office in his house on Ruiz Cortines. Clean as far as we know. Visa-eligible."

"That category is subject to change." I gave him one of my glossy prints and said, "This character uses a variety of names. She's usually armed, and deadly. Right now she's busily taking over Pedrito Ibarra's interests, having killed Ibarra."

"No kidding!"

"No kidding. Putting a true name under the photo would be extremely useful."

"I'll pass it around, see if she's recognized."

I gave him a spare print. "There is, or was, a connection among Ibarra, Casillas and Hakem. Drugs principally, but more than a whiff of arms dealing. Hakem does Mid-East business. Normally narcotics come from the Middle East, thanks to the Syrians and Iranians, people who could be looking for armaments in return. If a man wanted to send arms to the Middle East from Mexico, where would he acquire them?"

He scratched the side of his neck. "A triangular deal with Belgium, France or Italy. Even Germany, if it's offshore. Otherwise—"

"Czechoslovakia? Those big factories keep plenty busy."

"Yeah. But if not from abroad the weapons would have to come from Mexican government stocks and be shipped out under false invoices."

"Army stocks—that a problem?"

"Not if the payoff was big enough." He grunted. "Pemex can't account for about a quarter of its annual oil production, meaning it's exported for the enormous profit of a few insiders. Can't expect the mere Army to know how many cases of rifles, grenades and bazookas it has in its warehouses."

"Hardly."

"Be around long?"

"Only as long as absolutely necessary. This so-called air burns my lungs."

"Almost as bad as Mexico City," he agreed.

On the desk I unfolded and smoothed out the visa application once made by the real Nina Victoria Mendez. Using a marker pen I printed across it diagonally: EMBARGOED, recapped the pen and shoved the sheet between his hands. "Stick this in her file," I said, "and do everyone a favor. She's uncooperative and she hates America."

Sean Murphy nodded. "Fuck her," he said, "she looks like Death."

"She's involved, but I don't quite know how. Mind letting Miami know I dropped in?"

"I'll get off a Telex." We shook hands and I left the DEA area. The Marine guard who returned my Walther was young, clean shaven and concerned. "Sir, in Mexico it's illegal to carry a concealed weapon," he informed me.

"I know that, son," I said, tucking my piece out of sight, "but because I went to the Naval Academy it's okay."

"Is that so? I never knew that."

"Have a good day," I said, and went out to the street.

Lunch time. I strolled down to a restaurant named J.J. Charlie's, attracted by a horse on the roof. The building's green paint was a loathsome shade, but perhaps it served to repel hungry crowds. Inside, the décor was early twentieth century graffiti—not too easy on the eyes, but the menu was inviting. I ordered a stein of Tecate beer, Oysters 444— the house special—and a plate of barbecued spareribs. After that I checked into a one-star downtown hotel unaccountably named the Sorpresa, and slept undisturbed until nightfall.

Then I went hunting.

SIXTEEN

The little *tienda* was lighted by a single overhead bulb. Its bins offered unculled vegetables, unrefrigerated eggs, and jumbled *bolillos*. Crates of Pepsi and Coca-Cola, Peñafiel water, and Dos Equis beer were stacked around the walls. I bought a packet of violet Chiclets and chewed for effect.

A *chamaco* came in with an empty Nehi bottle, exchanged it for a full one and scampered away. I was alone now with the elderly storekeeper, a whitehaired Indian woman with a fine Aztec profile. I got out one of my remaining glossy prints and exposed it to her gaze. "*Abuela*," I said, "I was happily married until the rat of suspicion began to gnaw my heartstrings. This woman—have you seen her pass by?"

She bent over to focus old eyes. After a few moments she said, "Yes, I have seen her. Your wife?"

"Where? Over there?" I gestured at the house across the street. Abela Hakem's residence.

"She buys mineral water here. Where she comes from or goes to I cannot say."

I put away the photo, let my shoulders slump. "Nevertheless, the horns are growing." I tapped my head significantly. "Friends laughed and called me *cabrón*. I thought they were slandering my Manuela. Alas, their words were true."

"My regrets, *señor*. Yet there are faithful women in the world."

"Where?" I said, as I shuffled out dejectedly. "But where?"

125

The block streetlight was out. I walked slowly past Hakem's gate and saw that the green Chevy was not in the driveway. Any lights in the house would be screened by the still-closed blinds. If this was where Paula had gone to ground, getting inside was worth the risk.

I went back to the *tienda* and found the storekeeper closing up. Handing her the peso equivalent of a dollar I said, "How long ago did the green car drive away, *señora*?"

Her leathery face wrinkled. "*Pos'*, it was before dusk."

"How do you know?"

Her eyelids became slits. "The headlights were not on."

I gave her more pesos and walked away. Never ask a cop for neighborhood information was a rule to work by; always ask neighbors. While cops are looking for stolen cars and thieves, neighbors are watching each other. They know everything.

I hadn't asked her who was driving the Chevy, but perhaps her weak eyes couldn't have seen.

Waiting until the street was clear, the *tienda* shuttered for the night, I went to the grill gate, lockpicks in hand, but the gate wasn't locked. I went in, closed the gate and went up the short walk to the front door.

Listened.

The lock was an Alba, and I defeated it in two minutes' time. I opened the door far enough to slide myself in and closed it. The room was utterly dark.

But there was something, someone, in it. My neck hairs prickled. I'd expected to be alone but I wasn't, something was there. I heard its low growl, the scrape of claws, and ducked. A hundred and thirty pounds of snarling Alsatian launched itself at me, and slammed me against the door.

Before I could draw my pistol its jaws snapped around my left forearm.

I remembered SEAL training: give a little, take the rest. I gave him my arm to chew and slammed his belly with my knee. He growled more fiercely and tried to bite off my arm. I kicked his testicles and that made his jaws open. He dropped back and began whirling around in frantic pain. I clobbered his head with my pistol, and he dropped with a drawn-out whimper. My left arm was oozing blood from every tooth imprint, and I hoped the Alsatian had had the full series of rabies shots.

The kitchen was where one ought to be. I turned on a light above the gas stove and bared my arm over the metal sink. Bleeding would cleanse the wounds. I let them bleed. Drops discolored the sink's stainless steel. I turned on the hot water faucet and looked around.

Hanging beside the back door were a chain leash and a wire muzzle. I squeezed more blood from my arm and rinsed it under the faucet. Then I tore a kitchen towel into strips and bound up my injured arm. In a hard, painful way I was earning my pay.

Aftershock was setting in. I lurched back to the living room where the guard dog lay, turned on a table lamp, and strapped on his muzzle, then leashed him to a sofa leg. It would have been far easier to put a bullet through his head, but he was a fine and faithful dog. I couldn't blame him just because he worked for villains.

I turned off the downstairs lights and went up to the second floor. There were two bedrooms, one bathroom, and a sparsely furnished office containing a desk and chair, Olympia manual typewriter on a pressed-steel table, a scarred leather chair, and a four-drawer steel cabinet closed by a small spring lock, the kind that closes flush with the surface. The only obstacle to opening it was the pain and stiffness in my left arm. The lock stood at the level of my chin, difficult to work on from that angle, so I stepped on a chair, selected a thin tension bar from my set and a narrow rake. The lock surrendered in about a minute.

I stepped down from the chair and pulled out the top drawer. It held maybe thirty file folders, each captioned in Arabic. I opened the first one and found it contained shipping invoices for Mexican wrought-iron artwork. POE, Veracruz. Destination, Cyprus.

I sampled other folders; same stuff, destinations Gibraltar, Alexandria, Piraeus, Naples, all Mediterranean ports. How much Mexican wrought-iron could those merchants absorb? I wondered. Especially when their local artisans turned out exceptional wrought-iron work themselves.

I replaced the folders, closed that drawer and opened the second. Inside was a thick attaché case. The unlocked lid raised to reveal a compact shortwave transmitter that worked on rechargeable batteries or house current. There was a one-phone headset, and a transmit/receive schedule pasted on the inside of the lid. I couldn't get it off without tearing it apart so I left it and closed the drawer.

The third rattled as it rolled out. The rattles came from eight hand grenades: three AP, two fragmentation, three stun. Each was labeled in Arabic, with a price in pounds. There was a small gray bar of a puttylike substance that I recognized as C-4. Its principle ingredient is RDX—next to a nuclear warhead, mankind's most powerful explosive. A sealed plastic box separated binary components of Triex—another bad-news explosive—and a cardboard box contained assorted blasting caps, time fuses, and primers.

Very carefully I closed the sample drawer lest the place atomize like Trinity. Kneeling, I opened the bottom drawer, adjusted the desk light so I could see inside.

Except for one item the drawer was empty, and I'd seen that item before. It was Pedrito's notebook, recording details of his arms transactions, quantities and ports of delivery. Payment sums in dollars and/or keys.

I'd been scanning it when Paula drew down on me seconds before she fired. The memory made my head ache. But this time there was no killer behind me with a pointed gun. So, as I'd intended to do at Ibarra's safe, I put the fabric-bound notebook in my pocket. Then I closed the final drawer and relocked the file cabinet.

I was turning off the desk light when I heard the driveway gate creak open; moments later a car drove in.

My heart pounded and my arm began to throb.

I got out my gun and waited in the dark.

If I were Abela Hakem, I thought, I would release my dog to search for the intruder.

The front door opened, but the dog didn't whimper or bark. It was either unconscious or dead.

Downstairs lights went on. One person. Hakem?

He must have taken off his shoes to climb the stairs because if I hadn't been listening intently I wouldn't have heard him come. A hall light went on. I shrank against the wall.

The searcher checked each bedroom, came out. Footsteps neared the office door. Stopped.

He started in.

Gun arm first.

I slammed the door on it. He screamed and the gun discharged, bullet splintering the floor close to my feet. I kicked his gun away and jerked him in. He scrabbled for his revolver but I stamped on his hand, pressed my pistol against his cheek. He looked up at me, fear bright in his eyes. In Spanish I said, "On your back."

He turned over, clutched his damaged arm and moaned.

I moved back and stared at him.

A small, compact man in a dark three-piece suit. Most of his head was entirely bald—not shaven, mind you. What hair remained was a dark fringe that dribbled down into compensatory sideburns. He wore a bristly Hitler-style mustache. Four stubby fingers had gold-and-diamond rings. A thick gold wristwatch circled his left wrist. I shoved the Walther at his face. "Who are you?"

"Who are *you*?" he said, and in those words I recognized the voice I'd heard last night in Casillas' kitchen. The vaguely accented voice, the voice of the one who didn't use alcohol.

"Don't fuck with me," I snapped, and lowered the gun just over his crotch. "Who are you?" I repeated.

"This is my house. I am Hakem—Abela Hakem." He bit his lips against arm pain. He was suffering. I liked that.

129

"Where is she, Abe?"

"Who—who do you mean?"

"The woman you and Dario were discussing last night."
His eyes widened in sudden fear. "How—"

"Who is she? And don't say Nina Mendez or Paula Ortiz,
if you value your little friend." I moved the muzzle closer to
his crotch and fanned a glossy print in front of his eyes. Even
that pained my left arm; it was stiffening fast. "Her name."

"I don't know, I never saw her."

"Abe," I said wearily, "I've come a long way for answers.
Your dog tried to chew off my arm, and . . ."

"You killed him!" he squealed. "You killed my Fritz!"

"He'll survive, old man. But I'm in pain and I don't want
lies. Tell me the truth or I'll shoot off your *cojones* and drill
your kneecaps. Is the woman here?"

"She was." Abe was frothing at the mouth, and his words
squeezed out like caked paste from a tube. No doubt he was
thinking how horrible his existence would be *sans acces-
soire.*

"When did she leave?"

"An hour ago. I drove her to the airport."

"Flying where?"

"Mexico—the capital."

"With Ibarra's ledgers?"

"Everything. She took everything with her." He wet his
lips. His eyes were glassy.

"Except for what she left you, the arms transactions.
That's your real business, exporting weapons. What's the
'cause' you share with her?"

"Freeing Lebanon of foreign occupiers."

"Meaning—"

"Syrians, Israelis, Iranians." He paused. "French . . .
Americans . . ."

"So you're all dedicated, patriotic resistance fighters."

"*Yes,*" he hissed.

"Selling narcotics to buy arms for your cause."

"A dirty business but there is no other way to equip our
fighters."

"How does Nina Mendez fit in?"

"A sympathizer. A friend of—" He stopped abruptly.

"Go on, her name." I dug the muzzle into his crotch.

"Shari." He tried to twist away.

"*Nom de guerre,* or birth name?"

"It is the name by which she is known among us."

"Did Casillas go with her to Mexico City?"

"Yes, to meet with others from Ibarra's organization."

"Where can you reach her?"

"I don't know. Shari is very careful, secretive."

"She's all that," I said, "and much more. Is she returning here?"

"She didn't say."

Knowing the lady as I did, I believed him. Squeezing more out of Hakem could only be accomplished during serious torture, and I didn't think he had enough clout to make the effort worthwhile. Besides, my arm pained badly and needed medical attention. I left Hakem on the floor, went through his desk drawers and came up with a roll of heavy twine. I bound his ankles and wrists, cut the telephone cord. Then I stood over him, pistol in hand, and said, "I'm not concerned with political conspiracies—your 'cause'—so my advice to you is to say nothing of this visit—not to Shari, not to Dario, not to the police. You can't find me, but I know where to find you, Abe. Leave it at that."

I went down the staircase to the living room. Fritz was on his belly trying to claw off the wire muzzle. He growled at me. I pointed the pistol at his head, said, "*Boom,* you're dead," and let myself out.

It ought to take Hakem no more than ten minutes to free himself, a little longer to warn Shari, if he knew how to contact her. Meanwhile, my arm needed attention. At the corner I waited for a bus and rode it until I saw the lighted green cross of an all-night clinic. The doctor was a young woman doing her obligatory two years of social service in return for her free medical education. Thick lenses reminded me of Nina Mendez. Very carefully *la doctora* cleansed the teeth punctures in my forearm, applied hydrogen peroxide soaks, and injected antibiotics in my right arm. She bandaged my arm and charged me the peso equivalent of two dollars. I thanked her and took a taxi back to the Sorpresa. It had been a full day and an active night. The case was expanding in unexpected directions, ballooning far beyond Chato, Eddie Wax, and Pedrito Ibarra. I needed to consult DEA, but that would be tomorrow's *chamba.*

The *doctora* hadn't told me not to drink alcohol. I downed a good slug of Añejo, switched on the air conditioner, which somewhat filtered the air I was going to breathe, and turned in.

═══════════════

I was at the consulate when it opened in the morning, a draft Telex message in hand. Sean Murphy sent it off Priority, and while waiting for a reply we had coffee and *pan dulce* together. He had been a Border Patrolman for five years, he told me. The only thing it taught him was the impossibility of containing the wetback invasion, and after his kid brother got hooked on drugs, he decided to join DEA.

I said, "You think it's possible to end the traffic from Mexico?"

"Not without a lot more help from the Mexicans. But I'm optimistic by nature. Maybe we can reduce the flow, save a few lives. That's worth the effort. Isn't that why you're involved?"

I said it was.

"If we can ever get Ibarra's organizational books that would give us a lot to work on."

I had another cup of coffee while he cleared his In box, and then Hagopian's reply came in. Murphy read it first and handed it to me. "The Hag wants you in Miami ASAP. He's sending a plane."

SEVENTEEN

I scanned the message. "I could have flown commercial."

"The day's only flight left Monterrey about three hours ago," Murphy said. "Change in Mexico City, and you wouldn't reach the office until closing time. The Gulfstream does it in about two hours. Give me half an hour and I'll drive you to the airport." He handed me a sheaf of newspaper clippings.

I took a corner chair and began going through the clips. From Ixtapa and Mexico City newspapers, they covered the murder of entrepreneur developer Francisco Ibarra. The level of investigative reporting was abysmally low, the stories merely repeating police handouts: Chato had killed Ibarra while robbing him, and shot bodyguard Ramos, who succeeded in killing the burglar before expiring.

Nothing about the woman who lived with Ibarra. Nothing about a vanished American. I set the clippings aside. If that was how the cops wrapped it, fine with me. No narcotics angle, of course, nothing about Ibarra's arms dealing. Any such revelations would embarrass his political cronies. Newspapers depended on government newsprint allotments, and raising waves automatically cut off paper supplies, making the print media subject to government control. No one was going to be embarrassed by Ibarra's murder; everything was resolved. No one was wondering how Chato could have killed Ibarra when Chato was already dead. Murder by ghost. In Mexico even stranger things had happened.

Valeriano came over on the jet, looking tan and healthy and, mercifully for him, he wasn't wearing a straw hat. I had a beer with him while the Gulfstream refueled, and then we were airborne for Miami, ground time twenty minutes.

Pete said, "It's a big interagency meeting, Jack."

"Meeting? I expected a debriefing. Mine, I mean."

"What I should say is that a lot of people are interested in what you have to say. Manny's flying down from Washington. There'll be reps from the U.S. Attorney's office, BATF, FBI, State, and maybe CIA."

"Show-and-tell, eh? Do I get a slide projector and pointer?"

"You got anything better to do?"

"Well, I was planning a Mexico City visit and a chat with the resurrected architect José Manuel Mendez, whose name Shari so freely used."

"Maybe that won't be necessary."

I looked out the small oval window: nothing but white clouds. I went up to the cockpit and relieved the copilot for a half-hour's refresher time. Compared to piloting my Seabee, flying a jet was as exciting as riding an elevator, but it kept my mind off Shari, whose successes rankled me.

Over the Everglades I relinquished my seat to the copilot, thanked him, and buckled in beside Valeriano. The pilot set the Gulfstream down as gently as a swallow, a black limousine glided alongside, and within twenty minutes we were walking into the Federal Building.

I entered Hagopian's office; I'd been there before, under less congenial circumstances. There was a pile of sandwiches and coffee on a table. I bit into rare roast beef on rye, and sipped coffee. The Hag said, "Feathers have been ruffled, Jack. Mid-East politics strikes a sensitive nerve in Washington."

"Ruffled? Why? Because I came up with information they couldn't produce?"

"Something like that. Washington isn't the smooth-functioning apparatus it pretends to be; it's a nest of bitter rivalries." The telephone rang, he answered and said, "We'll be right there."

He stood up and said, "Showtime, Jack." I swallowed the rest of my sandwich, carrying my styrofoam coffee cup as we rode a private elevator to the office of the U.S. Attorney for the Southern District of Florida.

Manny gave me a big *abrazo* and began introducing me around. His boss was Ray Maguire, a fat-faced ex-cop from San Diego, who gave me a hard, hostile stare, and a limp handshake.

McInerny was the local FBI's assistant special agent in charge, tall, lean and intelligent-looking. The BATF rep was Stan Franciscus. State's Mid-East desk was represented by an uptight FSO, who gave his name as Stanton. A short, dark-skinned man told me his name was Issar Levi without further identification. Hagopian whispered, "Israeli intelligence—Mossad," and then the U.S. Attorney came in with two bag-carriers and note-takers. One placed a nameplate at the head of the table. It read MORRIS J. STONE. "From Dallas," the Hag whispered. We took seats around the long, canoe-shaped table, and Stone said, "Perhaps you'd better sit at the far end, Mr. Novak." He looked at his watch through rimless lenses. "In forty minutes I have a conference with the senior circuit judge. It can't be postponed, so let's get to it. Everyone know everyone?" He sat down and gazed at me. "Mr. Novak, I understand that DEA maintains an informal relationship with you as independent contractor. Correct?"

"If it needs defining," I said, "I'll accept that definition."

"Very well, suppose you begin at the beginning. Mr. Montijo brought you into this—how shall I describe it—this ill-defined activity."

"I did," Manny confirmed. "Jack, let's hear what you've accomplished."

I stayed seated as I spoke, but I was reminded of Academy classes where you stand beside your desk and recite every day on every subject. I wondered what today's grade would be.

Beginning with my Eddie Wax impersonation, I took them through Shari, Ibarra, Chato, Ramos, and the overheard conversation between Casillas and Abela Hakem. I described how I'd obtained names and addresses from Telmex, and last night's interrogation of Hakem. I unbuttoned my left sleeve and let the bandage show. There were a few murmurs of sympathy. U.S. Attorney Stone said, "I suppose you realize that much of what you've done would be prosecutable under U.S. codes."

"Not to mention Mexican law," I replied, "which can be circumvented. No U.S. laws have been violated."

Stan Franciscus of BATF said, "How about the Ibarra notebook you got from Hakem?"

I slid it down the table to him. "My theory," I said, "is that Shari gave Hakem the notebook so he could exploit Ibarra's arms sources and purchasers for the benefit of whatever organization they belong to."

"Duly noted," said Stanton, of State. Morris J. Stone said, "I've heard nothing to indicate that any arms have been purchased in or transshipped through U.S. jurisdictions."

"And I haven't suggested that. What's clear, though, is that Ibarra acquired arms using the proceeds of narcotics sales in the U.S."

Stone said sharply, "Can you prove that?"

"Can you plausibly deny it?"

His sallow face got red. His note-taker overlined our exchange. Stanton said, "Mr. Novak, you said Hakem's shipments were sent to such Mediterranean destinations as Piraeus, Cyprus—"

"Naples, Gibraltar and Alexandria," I finished. "Those are the names I saw."

Stone shrugged. "Manifested as wrought-iron work. The ports you named are not in countries hostile to U.S. interests. Sounds to me like a series of normal commercial transactions."

Issar Levi sat forward. "Unless the materials move on-ward to, let us say, hostile countries."

Irritably, Stanton said, "Meaning Arab nations? Not even Beirut was among the ports Novak mentioned."

"I didn't see all the folders," I told him, "I had time only for a sampling."

Stanton smiled thinly. "A selective sampling?"

"Random."

"Even so, how does one know Hakem's shipments con-tained munitions rather than wrought-iron as mani-fested?"

"One doesn't," I replied. "Unless one gets busy with a crowbar and opens the suspect crates." Someone snickered and Stanton flushed. I said, "Besides, there was a drawer filled with grenades, blasting caps, timers, fuses, C-4 and Triex. Hardly an innocent assortment."

Morris J. Stone said, "That's properly a matter for Mexi-can concern, seems to me. The Department of State might want to mention it to the Mexican ambassador."

"That would certainly take care of everything," I said, and smiled engagingly.

"Or," Stone continued, "FBI liaison could take it up with the Mexican federal police."

Staring at folded hands, McInerny said, "That could be done." As long as assignments were being parceled around, I turned to Ray Maguire. "With the arms shipments under control—"

"The *alleged* arms shipments," Stanton interjected.

"Thank you. It pays to be precise. With the *alleged* arms shipments disposed of, there remains the matter of Ibarra's narcotics sources in Mexico and South America, his plan-tations, delivery systems and U.S. contacts."

Maguire snapped, "We're working on all that; I already sent out orders."

I looked at Manny Montijo. His face was stolid as an ivory mask. "Finally," I said, "there's the fulcrum of it all, the lady of many names—Shari is her latest, could even be the true one. She's got Ibarra's organization books, minus the one I brought in. She's got a million in U.S. currency, three million queer, and a large sack of Ibarra's cash. So—"

The Hag had been silent until now. "That million of Chato's never passed through our books, and Treasury was going to destroy the three million queer. As it stands, we're three million to the good, thanks to Eddie Wax's demise."

Over congratulatory murmurs around the table, I said, "Under Shari, Ibarra's organization will be resuming business in very short order. That means more narcotics to Ibarra's usual distributors in the U.S. The only difference, if we're to believe Hakem, is that the profits will arm, vitalize and maintain some guerrilla faction."

"Militia," Issar Levi said. "Entirely correct, Mr. Novak. Israel would maintain a hands-off policy if the Lebanese merely slaughtered each other. Unfortunately, all too frequently they turn their guns on Israel. Accordingly, our policy is to prevent *any* munitions from reaching Israel's enemies."

Stanton said, "They have rights, too, you all live in the same area. You have to sit down with them, talk things out, come to an agreement."

"Thank you, Mr. Stanton," Levi said acidly, "for your illuminating insight into what the department persists in calling 'the Palestine problem.'" He glanced around the table. "There is no such entity as Palestine, never was. To treat with one's enemies is to accept at least partial surrender. But what you have said clearly confirms the trend of State Department thinking." He said it all very cooly, hands never moving, as though explaining the obvious to a backward schoolboy. Stanton did not look at him.

"Well, now," Morris J. Stone intoned in his best summation voice, "no need to dissect the Arab-Israeli conflict at this gathering. Everything seems to be in appropriate hands, and I believe we owe the government's thanks to Mr. Novak for having brought these affairs to light." He looked at his watch. The allotted forty minutes hadn't expired, but he was moving on. Onward and upward. A bright young attorney, model rapporteur, and upwardly mobile as they come.

If he'd had a gavel he would have used it to close the meeting. Instead, he said, "Thank you, gentlemen," and left through a side door, gofers following with satchel and papers.

Stanton and McInerny left the conference room. Stan Franciscus came over and said BATF would be grateful for Ibarra's notebook. Hagopian and Manny were still in their seats when Maguire waddled around the table to me. "I heard of you," he said, "but I never seen you in action before. Very smooth."

I said, "Does articulate presentation offend you?"

His face seemed to swell. "I heard about you from Corliss. Phil Corliss, a close friend of mine."

"You ought to pull him back from Toronto," I suggested. "Have him do something useful like polishing your shoes."

He leaned close to my face and his acid breath fouled my nostrils. "One of these days someone's gonna break your fuckin' back, Novak. You got it comin'. And y'know what? I wouldn' lift a hand."

"I know that," I told him, "because you could barely lift out of that chair." I felt in my pocket, fished out a bill and tucked it in his coat pocket. "Get your pants cleaned, Ray. Yellow stains all over the fly."

He looked down quickly, then slowly up at me. A purple vein quivered in his forehead. He would have liked nothing better than to shove his Police Special in my belly and pull the trigger—nice boys, Phil's friends—only there were witnesses and one was *my* very close friend.

With a surge of effort he pulled himself upright, looked at Manny and pushed his shoulder. "C'mon, *taco*, let's get outa here."

Icily, Manny said, "Mr. Maguire, I have informant contacts to renew. I'll be in the office tomorrow."

"Make it on time for a change," Maguire snapped, and waddled off, paunch first.

I turned to the Hag. "This is like the old days. Nothing's changed."

Hagopian's face seemed to have aged. A thumb rubbed

against index finger. "In my long experience, nine out of ten interagency meetings accomplish nothing but move chairs around."

"Why," I said, "I thought it was a jolly get-together. Didn't everyone have fun?" I saw Manny begin to smile. "Scant hospitality, though. I'd counted on gin and little cakes."

Hagopian had been a civil servant too long to criticize his seniors. He mumbled something, then cleared his throat and said, "My solid impression, Jack, is that the assembled gentlemen have no interest in your carrying on."

"Mine, too," I said, and looked at Manny, who nodded.

The Hag looked relieved. "Then we're in agreement."

"Sure," I said. "We agree that the interagency group wants me to lay off the villains. It perplexes me somewhat, but then I haven't enjoyed your long exposure to the complexities of foreign affairs."

He frowned slightly, not sure I wasn't needling him. "And they *can* be complex," he rumbled. "I remember this pal of mine, Sasha, ran a clandestine radio station out of Vienna at the time of the Hungarian uprising, oh, thirty-some years ago. He broadcast words of encouragement to the Hungarians, and pretty soon they were stampeding across the Austrian border." He looked up at me with sad beagle eyes. "Poor Sasha, that was the last paycheck he ever drew from the USG."

Montijo said, "I thought that whole radio setup was to encourage dissidence behind the Curtain."

"Well, yes and no. Nobody ever thought there'd *be* an uprising. The Austrians barked at us, the Commies ranted about American provocations, and a lot of people were in hot water." His lips set reprovingly. "Very hot water."

"Well," I said, "that's the way it goes. Commendations one day, pink slips the next." I glanced around the empty table. "An illuminating experience," I said, "that brings to mind the Bishop of Chichester's remark that truth is unwelcome in the ears of princes."

Manny said, "It was the Bishop of Gloucester, Jack,

and as I remember it he said, 'Avoid telling the truth to princes.' "

"Uh-uh, we're both wrong," I corrected. "It was Canterbury, and I recall he said rather notably that truth lies heavy in the ears of princes."

Hagopian had been looking from one to another as we bantered. Finally he pulled himself upright, cleared his throat again, and enclosed my hand in a big fraternal grip. "So it's back to Cozumel, eh?" he said hopefully.

"Right now I'm going to look in on my fiancée," I said. "Manny, come along and make Delores's day, while I make out with Melody. If the folks are home we'll have dinner."

"I'd like that," Manny said and got up. "See you, Merle."

We left the Hag alone with his thoughts in the conference room and took an elevator to the lobby. Just by the guard desk a man was waiting. He walked over to me and said, "Mr. Novak, could I have a moment of your time?" Issar Levi.

"Why not?" I said. "Of the whole platoon you were the only one who made any sense." Manny said, "I'll get an office car," and went off to the federal motor pool. Levi drew me away from the guard desk and opened by saying, "You've done extraordinary things, Mr. Novak. My organization was only superficially aware of Hakem's activity, and I'm glad to have him more clearly identified. As for Shari, we have a rather complete dossier on her. I wonder if you'd care to review it?"

"You heard how the meeting went, the whole thing's dead and buried. I'm not working the case because there's supposedly no case left."

"Nevertheless, I sensed that the decision, if it was so formalized, was unilateral."

"I wasn't asked to vote."

Issar Levi smiled. "I sensed also—forgive my presumption—that their joint views were unimportant to you and that you intended to pursue Shari despite the tacit ban on further action."

I shrugged. "At the moment I'm on the way to visit my fiancée."

"And when will you be returning to your, ah, operational base?"

"My little vine-draped cottage on Cozumel? Oh, in a day or so."

"Would you resent receiving a copy of Shari's dossier?"

"Not if you want to go to the trouble."

"Consider it a souvenir. I believe it will make interesting reading." He handed me a card, said, "Good luck," and I said, "*Shalom.*" He went away quickly, and Manny drove up to the curb in a black Ford sedan with USG plates.

As we headed north on I-95 I looked at Levi's card. It was engraved on good quality cream parchment, and identified him as assistant commercial attaché, embassy of Israel, Washington.

Manny braked and swerved to avoid a white-haired woman driver whose car was drifting across traffic lanes, no signal, *nada.*

When my heart stopped thumping, he said, "These senior citizens are something, Jack. She doesn't have the least idea what she's doing."

"Disoriented, thinks she's back in Coopers Corners, 1924. This highway is Death Row."

"Where executions come quick." He avoided a high-axle swamp buggy bearing down on us from the starboard quarter, deer antlers, Confederate flag sticker, and busted muffler. That menace past, Manny said, "I'd apologize, Jack, if I could figure out how."

"Hell, forget it, the party's over."

"In Hag's defense I have to say it wasn't his fault, he's a decent guy."

"Decent doesn't equal stalwart," I remarked, "and he crumbled fast."

"He was heavily outranked," Manny said, "just as I was. He meant well, give him that much credit."

"Good intentions . . ." I began, and let the cliché die.

From an inside pocket Manny drew out an envelope and

passed it to me. I'd addressed it to my PO box and Valeriano
had sent it from the airport. I'd returned it to Wolcott, and
now Manny was handing it back to me.

Forty thousand dollars.

"Well, well," I said. "Never expected to see this again.
Isn't payment premature?"

"How so? You heard the group verdict. Your participation
is over with, and Stone voiced government thanks. I con-
tracted with you and agreed to your fee. Here it is." He
chuckled. "The Hag felt under the circumstances you
hadn't really earned it, but I said different. Enjoy it in good
health."

"We will," I said, thinking of Melody.

After a while, Manny said, "That Mossad fellow—Levi—
what did he want?"

"Expressed appreciation for my clever work. Now I've got
a friend in Israel. How's the family?"

"Hmm. Splendid." He couldn't repress a smile. "But
Washington's too cold for the kids."

"I gather you don't see Maguire socially."

"No one does."

"Well," I said, "he can always commiserate with Corliss
on the Wats line."

"And he does, the prick."

At 125th Street Manny turned off the interstate and
paid the Broad Causeway toll across Biscayne Bay. A
chunk of concrete railing hadn't yet weathered in with the
rest of the stretch. It marked where I'd crashed a car into
the bay. Melody and I came out alive, but Luis Parra
hadn't. Everyone had been pleased except Phil Corliss
who accused me of killing a federal fugitive by vehicular
homicide. I denied it for the record, but it was perfectly
true. That night it had been either Parra or Melody, and I
wasn't in love with Parra.

So screw Corliss, I thought. In Toronto he could do only
minimal damage to DEA's liaison with the Canadians. No
one bothered about Canadians anyway, which was why
Corliss had been sent there to annoy them.

We turned into the spacious grounds of the big bayfront house Delores had inherited from her late husband, a prominent drug mouthpiece and bagman named Paul Diehl. The then U.S. Attorney couldn't prove Diehl had acquired it with tainted proceeds, so the place wasn't confiscated and Delores continued enjoying its considerable amenities.

Thomas the houseman let us in, and in a few moments Melody came squealing into my arms. Delores was less enthusiastic. We brushed cheeks and she extended a hand to Manny, whom she had met before. I'd given up explaining to her that Manny was of Spanish heritage, educated in Europe and at UCLA, but she treated him with the same condescension she would have a peasant on a mangy burro. In her world all Latinos were the same, except for the Italian gigolos she paid to escort her here and there. They were young, handsome, intellectual, and okay.

We extended cocktail hour while the cook expanded the menu to include two unexpected guests, and by the time Delores had quaffed six stingers her mood was mellow and she was gazing covetously at Manny. As a token of esteem she asked him to select our wines, remarking that we would be having stone crabs followed by lamb chops. After conferring with Thomas, Manny chose a '59 *premier cru* Haut-Brion, followed by a Musigny burgundy '61.

Delores clapped her hands delightedly, and Manny modestly remarked that her late husband had laid down an excellent cellar of choice vintages. Thomas announced dinner, and we went in.

Dining proceeded reasonably well, though Delores's coltishness distressed us all. It was one thing for her daughter to act immaturely, having barely achieved legal drinking age in Florida, but for the Old Campaigner to hang on Manny's every word and press his hand possessively was noticeably out of place.

Eventually dinner ended. As we walked into the lounge for coffee I said to Manny, "I don't see much chance of you

144

making Washington tonight, plenty of beds here. But how about Maguire's parting injunction?"

Manny grunted. "Think I live my life according to his wishes? Forget it."

Melody selected a favorite movie and started the VCR. *White Nights.* We particularly liked the Ritchie music and the phenomenal *pas de deux* performed by Baryshnikov and Gregory Hines.

When the film ended Melody turned up the lights, and there was Delores snoozing on the wicker sofa in an unladylike pose. Rearranging her mother, Melody said, "Well, that solves one problem, gentlemen. I was concerned for Manny's virtue."

We three laughed. Never had there been a more faithful, adoring husband and father than Manuel Montijo. "C'mon, Manny," she said. "I'll show you your room."

"What about your mother?"

"She likes it here."

I looked down on the fallen chatelaine. "Yep, mom's a real card, eccentric in some ways but basically solid as brass."

Melody crinkled her nose. "Solid as *brass*? Sure that's what you meant?"

"I'm sure," I told her, "because today I had a grammar lesson from a high official in State, the ultimate arbiter of precise wordings."

"You mean diplomatic bullshit," Melody shot and started up the stairs. She got overnight supplies for Manny, we said goodnight, and then she took my hand and walked me down the long corridor to her ultrafeminine room whose shelves were bulging with childhood dolls and stuffed bears. "One day," I said, sitting on the bed to pull off my shoes, "you'll have to put away all these wonderful memories."

"Why?" She kicked off sandals and undid her halter.

"Because you've often said that life began with me."

"I did? Funny how I can't remember."

I yanked her across my knees and slapped her buns smartly. She gave the expected yelp, then twisted around for a long, luxurious kiss. We showered together, toweled semidry and got under the covers.

"Isn't it nice," Melody murmured, "when mom zonks out and we don't have to pretend we're sleeping apart."

"It's regal," I said, and that was my last word for a while because she began nuzzling my throat, kissing eyelids and fluttering her tongue in my ears. A woodie rose between us, and very promptly I shared it with my bride-to-be.

After a morning swim in the family pool, Manny, Melody and I had breakfast at a canopied table near her diving board. We had crepes and small Jones sausages, orange-blossom honey, warm croissants from the Bay Harbor Boulangerie, and ultrastrong coffee.

Manny said, "This is better than a weekend at Atlantic City, *mes amis.*"

"Lacking gaming tables and broads," I observed, "but very easy to take."

He looked at his watch and sighed. "Much as I hate to tear away from never-never-land, I've got to get back to D.C. Otherwise, Raymond may dock my pay." He grinned and I knew what he was thinking. Melody said, "Well, if you must. Thomas will take you to the airport."

"Thanks, but I have an office car."

"Manny, I'm so glad you came. When you're not around, I worry."

I said, "Worry?"

"Yes. Manny is a restraining influence on you."

Manny and I exchanged glances. Melody said, "I'm also grateful that you got Jack his full pay envelope, though I'll probably never know all he did to earn it."

"Sometimes," Manny said, "it's better that way. Or so I tell my wife." He kissed her cheek, thanked her for her hospitality to a wayfarer, and walked into the house. Melody had begun licking honey traces from my mouth when Thomas appeared, carrying a large Federal Express envelope. "For you, sir," he said, and handed it to me.

"Now who would that be from?" Melody asked, peering curiously at the return address. "Embassy of Israel? How now?"

"Bond solicitation, I guess," I said without opening it. I'd forgotten about Issar Levi, but he hadn't forgotten me. How he knew where to find me was something I was tactful enough never to inquire, though it made me shiver a little.

Melody looked up at the houseman. "Is mother going to join us?"

"I doubt it, Miss Melody. A little while ago she sent out for the masseuse and is under her ministrations now." He walked back toward the house. Melody said, "God, mom must be feeling cremated this morning."

"Stingers are not for the casual social drinker," I said. "The drink was developed to ward off Malayan crud, dengue fever, and tertian malaria."

"You know so many exotic things, dear," she cooed, "and I think you make up half of them."

"At least half."

"So, why don't you open your envelope and find out what the Israelis want?"

"Because it's too early to cope with reality." I touched the wet bandages on my arm. "Reality is getting these changed this morning."

That made her all concerned. "Does it hurt dreadfully? I saw you favored the arm while swimming. I'll phone Dr. Medaris right now and make an appointment.

"Isn't Medaris your gynecologist?" I objected.

"Of course, but I assume a skilled pussy-poker is capable of changing an arm bandage." She picked up her towel, stepped into sandals, and ran off to the house. I followed, and while Melody was arguing with the GYN's appointment secretary I took refuge in the bathroom and opened what Federal Express had brought me.

Inside, on embassy letterhead a short note read:

IF AFTER NOTING THE CONTENTS YOU ARE INTERESTED IN PURSUING THE MATTER, PLEASE CALL ME.

A 202 number followed, then the initials I.L.

I opened a large white envelope and pulled out a file filled with Xeroxed pages. The file was captioned:

VALOUR, SHARI NÉE VALORIN

I began to read.

EIGHTEEN

The top two pages were a single-spaced summary of the dossier's contents. The file itself was composed of reports from MI6, France's DGSE and DST, Italy's SISMI, INTER-POL, school and university transcripts, photos of Subject, copies of visaed pages in several passports. In addition to the three Hispanic names I was familiar with, Subject had at different times gone by Salamon and Chandos.

Her father had been a French-Lebanese banker of considerable fortune, her mother was Greek-Lebanese. Both were Maronite Christians.

Under the name Shari Valorin, Subject had attended the French lycée in Beirut. Later studies at Beirut's American University had been interrupted by the increasing presence and bellicosity of Palestine Liberation Organization guerrillas, hence her transfer to the Sorbonne in Paris, studying modern languages. Then the University of Madrid, and a final year at the National Autonomous University in Mexico City, acronymed UNAM.

By the time Shari returned to Beirut her father's bank had been shelled to rubble, and his two apartment buildings and the family home had been occupied by the PLO. At a roadblock her parents and chauffeur had been dragged from their Mercedes and machine-gunned to death.

Shari's conspiratorial education began under the wing of a militia faction allied to the Gemayel family. She was trained in small arms and explosives, secret writing, surveillance techniques, and physical disguise. Twice she had been captured by the PLO but managed to escape. After that she was dispatched abroad to gather funds for the militia by all possible means. She robbed an exchange office at Rome's Da Vinci Airport, an armored truck in Lyon, a bank in Manchester. In Damascus she assassinated the deputy chief of Syrian military intelligence, and badly wounded the Iranian ambassador in London.

The final entry noted that she was believed to be in Mexico, where her contacts included members of the Mendez family, particularly Nina Victoria Mendez, who was said to have had a crush on Shari when they were students at UNAM.

I scanned the dossier again before fitting it into the white envelope, wondering why Mossad maintained a file on Shari Valour; independently she was doing their work for them. Maybe the Israelis had co-opted her at some point. The file didn't say, but I expected that it would. Nothing I had read suggested that her operations were inimical to Israeli interests, and I understood now why she had been able to manipulate me so easily. She was intelligent, resourceful, well trained and completely ruthless. Compared to Shari, I was Clyde the country bumpkin.

Melody rapped on the door. "Honey, Dr. Medaris can fit you in now. Let's go."

"Coming, dear," I called, opened a cabinet, and tucked the dossier under a stack of towels.

———————————

The doctor's waiting room was filled with female patients who regarded me with curiosity. I suppose they thought I wanted a sex-change operation. As I reported to the nurse-receptionist, I noticed a sign on the window-counter: PAYMENT IS EXPECTED WHEN SERVICES ARE RENDERED. MEDICARE ASSIGNMENTS NOT TAKEN. WE DO NOT PROCESS INSURANCE CLAIMS.

That's laying it on the line, I thought, up front. Needy need not apply. I didn't see any needy-looking females waiting for their five minutes with Dr. Armand Medaris.

A nurse showed me into the dispensary and I rolled up

my left sleeve. Medaris bustled in, a short fortyish man with wave-cut hair and a trim Vandyke beard. The nurse scissored off my damp Mexican bandages. Medaris said, "It's not my usual custom to do this sort of thing, you understand, but Mrs. Diehl and her daughter are valued patients." Translated: they pay good money so I'll treat you as a favor to them.

Under a strong light he scanned my healing wounds, shrugged and said, "Allergic to penicillin?"

"No."

"Nurse, two million units *s'il vous plaît*." He managed a modest smile over his superior grasp of foreign tongues, and said, "Keep the bandage on for another two days. *Ciao*."

"*Adiós*," I said. He blinked and went out, closing the door.

The nurse said, "Which cheek?"

"Left." I dropped my pants and bent over the examining table. She stuck me expertly, massaged the area, then dusted my arm with antibiotic powder, and wrapped it with flesh-colored gauze and tape. "You'll live," she said cheerfully.

I rolled down my sleeve. "Pay on the way out?"

"Please."

The cashier took fifty dollars and was miffed that I asked for a receipt. Not that I had any use for it; I just wanted it to show on the office books. Then Medaris would have to pay tax on the money, and I wanted to reduce his unreported cash income.

As we left the waiting room Melody said, "How did it go?"

"Fast," I said. "A one-minute consultation and three bucks' worth of medication and bandage."

"You don't sound appreciative. You don't like Dr. Medaris?"

"I don't like his type."

"Oh, Jack, you're always so critical of everyone."

"I know, everyone says so."

We got into her Porsche 940 and drove back to the Diehl manse, pulling into the drive as the masseuse was leaving.

For a half hour I watched Melody practice her dives. Delores came to poolside looking listless and asked what I thought would make her feel good. "Lots of things, some illegal, but my prescription is a brace of margaritas."

"Would you?" she asked plaintively, eyes following her daughter's clean trajectory into the water.

At the poolside bar I got busy with Cuervo *Especial*, triple sec, lime juice, and ice. The blender whipped it into a frosty mix that Delores pronounced delicious and invigorating. "I can understand why Mexicans are so slothful," she said, swallowing. "Drinking this wonderful beverage every day I'd *never* get any work accomplished."

Without inquiring what work she referred to, I drew Melody out of the pool and draped her with a towel. Delores crunched ice and said, "I'll be so relieved when Melody is happily married."

"That makes three of us," I said, with a pleased smile. "Your daughter and I often remark that you'll be a doting grandmother."

Her eyes narrowed and she looked away. Two jays were chasing a blackbird from their nest in a large banyan tree. I watched the jays' successful defense and decided it was an omen, symbolic.

Thomas came out and said I was wanted on the telephone. I activated the bar phone and heard the voice of Issar Levi. After asking pardon for interrupting my tranquility he said, "Did you receive the package?"

"And perused the contents."

"Did the dossier interest you?"

"It did, though perhaps not in the way you intended."

For a moment the wire was silent. "I would be interested to learn how you interpret my intentions, Mr. Novak, but perhaps you'll tell me another time."

"That's possible," I said, and glanced at Melody who was talking to her mother.

"On the chance you decided not to telephone me I thought I would try to reach you before you left Miami."

"I hadn't made a decision," I told him, "but since we're conversing, what's your interest in me?"

"That's not a subject I care to confide to telephone lines. Could you spare an hour of your time this evening?"

"Where?"

"On Miami Beach across from the Carriage House there is a condominium building, Le Manoir. Ask the doorman for Mr. Sampson. Eight o'clock?"

"Eight o'clock," I repeated, and switched off the phone. I set it down and dived into the cool water, swam a few laps with my sweetest love.

As Melody entered the house with me she said, "I'll bet that call had to do with your Federal Express package."

"You're a whiz at adding one and one, always have been."

"And you're meeting someone or doing something at eight."

"We'll combine it with dinner."

She put on her little-girl face. "You mean I can actually go along with big wunnaful man?"

"If you don't ask questions."

At Alberto's 51 we enjoyed a scrumptious and expensive dinner. Melody and her mother had known Alberto at Dominique's when he was *maître d'*, so he came to our table and fussed over my girl and complimented her until she blushed becomingly. The sommelier didn't dare request her proof of age, so I ordered a bottle of red Bordeaux, Château Latour '81, sure that Manny would commend my choice. It enhanced the flavor of our prime steaks, and after Melody put aside knife and fork she said, "Treat all your broads this good?"

"Only you, presh. The bawds and doxies know full well how you are Numbah One."

She toed my shin. "I better be. You have no idea how many proposals I turn down in a week."

"Three?"

"Minimum. How long will your meeting take?"

"Less than an hour. Where will I meet you?"

"I thought I'd go on to the Surf, see if I can stir up some trouble."

"That's why I won't be late."

Walking down Collins Avenue I felt the sidewalk's retained heat through my soles. The concrete took a long time to cool even though it wasn't yet summer. As a resort destination Miami Beach had long since been bypassed in favor of the Caribbean isles, but Latinos still liked it and the high-rise zone I was walking toward had a large percentage of wealthy Central and South American condominium owners. Some were legitimate, others drug traffickers, and a scatter of defenestrated politicos. The really well-off ones maintained mistresses in the same building as their families, an efficient arrangement beneficial to all concerned.

Le Manoir was a handsomely designed high-rise faced with light brown stone and wide, ornate balconies. Passing the uniformed doorman I entered a marble-and-brass lobby and angled over to the security guard who was scanning a bank of closed-TV monitors. The guard was paunchy, with the veined face and slit eyes of the ex-cop. He had a look of latent brutality that reminded me of Ray Maguire. "To see Mr. Sampson," I said, and drummed my fingers on the barrier.

"Who wants him?"

"His wife and children," I said, "but I'm Shalom Aleichem." I smiled agreeably and he had me repeat the name. Turning away he placed a call, spoke, nodded, and turned back to me. "Five-B," he said, and gestured at the elevator. I entered it and rode to the fifth floor.

The door of 5-B was carved walnut, no vulgar nameplate to mar its oiled perfection. A button was set discreetly into the wall and I pressed it. The door opened on Issar Levi wearing a white short-sleeved shirt and a smile. "Thank you for coming," he said. "Please come in."

The apartment was spacious and luxuriously appointed with modern furniture covered in brown, beige and tan leathers. The carpeting looked like hand-woven tapestry, and the lamps were of turned brass, mahogany and fired ceramic. I followed Levi to the inset bar where he poured

Hine cognac into two crystal balloons, warmed them over an alcohol flame. We settled ourselves in a large sofa overlooking the boulevard and Levi said, "Unfortunately, Abela Hakem cleared out. Your encounter with him apparently had a frightening effect."

"That was my intention at the time," I said.

"Too bad you didn't take along his files."

"I see that now, but my principal interest was getting a line on the woman I now know as Shari Valour."

Levi inhaled the cognac's bouquet and sipped delicately. "An interesting personality, don't you think?"

"All that, yeah. Fact is, I was like a kid trying to match wits with Jezebel. I came out a distant second."

"Still, you recovered rather well—you managed to learn her name, identify some of her associates. It wasn't a total loss, Mr. Novak. And by no means are you the first intelligent man she's deceived."

"So I've read." I tasted the warm liqueur. "What position do you take regarding her?"

He spread his hands. "While approving her aims, I must nevertheless lament her methods. They too much resemble those of our enemies."

"Then she doesn't work for you?"

"You thought she might?"

"It seemed a possibility."

"Mademoiselle Valour is uncontrolled, perhaps uncontrollable. My immediate concern is that she may be going into business for herself." His gaze found my eyes. "Is that not a possibility?"

"So far she seems to have been trying to help her people against Palestinian occupiers."

He nodded thoughtfully. "So far—but the narcotics business is something new, different. And it involves so much money. She's proved her competence as an organizer. I suspect she will try to squeeze every possible dollar from narcotics trafficking in order to escalate Hakem's arms shipments to the Middle East." He sat forward, elbows on his thighs. "For the enemies of Israel, Lebanon

155

has become the cockpit of the Middle East; many interests vie for control—Syria, Iraq, Iran, Moslem extremists, Lebanese Druze, Phalangist Christians, and a variety of private so-called militia, some of which are no more than marauding bands of pillagers and robbers. There was a time when Israel gave discreet support to a faction here, a faction there, most notably the South Lebanon Army. After '85, that support became untenable. I won't go into the reasons, but to our present satisfaction a *de facto* stalemate has taken hold. The armed supremacy of one faction would result in a mad rush by supporters of rival factions to arm and bolster them, escalating internecine carnage and posing fresh dangers to Israel . . . patience Mr. Novak, I'm coming to my point."

I sipped and said nothing.

"What Israel does not want to see occur is an imbalance among the warring groups."

"In short, you don't want Hakem's arms to reach Shari's people—do they have a name, by the way?"

"They call themselves the Lebanese Patriotic Army, in keeping with the Mid-Eastern tendency to exaggeration. Actually, the LPA's strength is never more than two thousand combatants, and sometimes it drops to half that when there are no funds for families, food and ammunition. But they are courageous fighters, resolved to driving out all foreigners from what used to be their country."

"That seems reasonable," I said.

"Indeed. At our interagency meeting—" he smiled sardonically "—you named a number of Mediterranean ports as the supposed destinations of Hakem's cargoes. This is well and good, so long as those munitions actually reach their intended end-users, the LPA. But what if a portion—a large portion—is diverted elsewhere—into hands hostile both to the LPA and to Israel? Then we have an undesirable situation." His eyes narrowed.

"You're suggesting Abela Hakem is not the completely loyal ally Shari believes him to be?"

"Let me put it in these terms: there is evidence that not

everything paid for with LPA funds via Hakem reaches the LPA."

"So he's diverting arms to another group or groups."

"A sound premise." Levi drained his glass. "You came across radio equipment in his locked cabinet. I suggest that he uses it to arrange the diversions."

I looked at my watch. "I'm average bright," I said, "but I don't understand why you're telling me all this."

"First, because you became involved in the situation without understanding its ramifications. Second, because if you are able to stop Shari's narcotics business you will have deprived Hakem of the funds he has been misusing."

I smiled. "You think I can persuade Shari to be a good girl after all she's done?"

"Persuasion was not my thought. From what I have gleaned of you I understand that you tend to more direct methods."

"I've been known to favor them," I admitted. "And so you'd like me to close out Shari's new business career."

"Very much so. And to that end my organization is prepared to, ah, cooperate with you."

I nodded. "I have a great deal of respect for your organization, Mr. Levi, but the last American detected cooperating with Mossad is serving a life sentence. I have plans for my life and they don't include prison."

"Believe me, I understand your concern, but have I made the slightest attempt to recruit you? No, Mr. Novak, in no way. But as a participant in that unfortunate gathering, I could hardly fail to understand that whatever you might plan to do with regard to Shari Valour you will have to undertake without the support of your government. The purpose of my inviting you here was to let you know that you are not without friends." He paused. "Interested friends."

"That's always welcome to hear, seldom as it is." I got up and glanced down at the lighted boulevard. Clean, antiseptic, no bums, no beggars; they were forty blocks to the south in an area that was itself getting to resemble a Lebanese refugee camp.

157

Issar Levi rose. "You have my card. If I can be of help, let me know."

We shook hands and I went down the elevator, past the surly cop. He was eating corn chips from a big bag, fragments on his desk and floor. His face was turned toward the monitor screens, but his eyes were only partly open. I wondered about his law enforcement career as I walked down the wide steps to the street.

Strolling north along Collins I thought over all that Levi had to say, and I concluded that there was a good deal left unsaid. By the time I entered the Surf Club's portals I'd developed a strong feeling that his goals and mine would best prosper along separate lines. Geopolitics were his bag, not mine. I wished him well.

I found Melody by the club pool watching a chain of preteens diving and jumping from the one-meter board. I kissed her tenderly and took her home.

Two days later Melody dropped me off at Miami International, but instead of buying a ticket to Cozumel as she had expected, I bought a ticket for another destination—Mexico City, where I had further work to do.

NINETEEN

From the airport I phoned the architectural firm of Vega, Galindo, Ferro y Mendez, and learned that *arquitecto* Mendez was occupied with a client. I said I'd phone later and went over to the Five Star Auto Rental counter, filled out the forms and began counting out a large deposit for a two-door Ford Topaz.

Peripherally I became aware of a small man about ten yards away. Leaning against a pillar, holding a newspaper, he was getting a shoeshine. He wore a frayed Panama hat and blue *guayabera*, and when he realized I was looking at him he got very interested in his newspaper. I went back to my counting, got the receipt, car papers, and directions to the *Cinco Estrellas* lot. As I boarded the courtesy bus I looked back but didn't see blue *guayabera*. Maybe a plainclothes airport cop. I couldn't think of anyone else who might be interested in my arrival.

On the chance he'd passed me on to mobile surveillance, I didn't enter the capital by Zaragoza, but continued on, turning west onto Mier. I looked back from time to time but saw no obvious tail. I kept going to San Juan de Letrán and eased into the Pink Zone. The Ford's air conditioning blew hot air, and failed to filter out sulphurous black fumes as buses shouldered past me.

The firm's offices were located in a tall, modernistic building that rose from a dozen cylindrical columns. The pylons thrust down to the earth's subsoil and immunized the structure from earthquake shock, a construction technique found in the capital's more recent buildings.

Building occupants had reserved parking spaces among the support pylons. Mendez's was occupied by a white BMW, and as two o'clock approached I watched it carefully, expecting him to leave for the customary *comida/siesta*. At two-fifteen he got into his convertible and turned out the Paseo de la Reforma. For an alleged suicide, José Manuel appeared in downright normal health, and walked with a confident stride. Even without his name-marked parking slot I would have recognized him from the photo I'd seen with his sister, the neurotic Nina.

Traffic was so slow I had no difficulty tailing him out Reforma and up into the residential Lomas de Chapultepec, from where I could look back on the smog-covered city. The street led along a deep ravine, on the far side of which destitute squatters had dug shelter holes into the *barranca*'s wall. We passed substantial homes, then turned onto Calle Tehuantepec, where Mendez parked his car and unlocked an entrance gate.

I drove slowly past, glimpsed an attractive two-story house before the gate closed, drove around the block and found the block's *sereno*—watchman—drowsing under a jacaranda tree, a half-liter bottle of *pulque* propped between his knees.

His eyes opened on a 50 peso note in my hand, focused. He stared, licked his cracked lips and looked up at me. "*Sí, señor, a sus órdenes.*"

"*Poca cosa*," I assured him, and showed him a photo of Nina Mendez. "Have you seen her around here?"

He shook his head, reached for the bill but I drew it back. I showed him an enlarged glossy of Shari Valour. "This one?" I asked.

The *sereno* thought it over. "Why?"

"She applied for insurance and gave an address nearby. I have to verify her residence."

His head turned and his gaze was in the direction of José Manuel's house. "I have seen her come and go with the *arquitecto*."

"When?"

"In these days."

"When did you last see her?"

"Yesterday. Perhaps the day before." He looked down at the *pulque* bottle and shrugged. "It is difficult to be precise."

"Today. Have you seen her today?"

"*No, señor.* She is the wife of Don Pepe?"

"Is that what he says?"

"He told me nothing."

"What makes you think she is his *señora*?"

"A servant." He licked his lips. One hand closed around the bottle's neck. "She said they share the same bed."

"Then," I said, "she must definitely be his wife." I passed him the bill. "*Gracias*," he said, lifted and tilted the bottle. I got into my Ford and drove down into the smog-hung city.

═══════════════

An embassy receptionist took my name and agreed to call the office of the naval attaché, then handed me the phone. When an enlisted man answered I asked for Lt. Comdr. Ernest Gilray. We'd been at Pensy together, Ernie and I, but he had washed out of the flight program while I managed to get my golden wings and go on to fighter jets. Over the years I'd kept track of him through class notes in *Shipmate*, which was how I learned he was doing white-glove duty as assistant naval attaché in Mexico. I hadn't expected Ernie to come down, but I recognized him when he stepped out of the elevator, even though he was wearing civvies.

We exchanged an Old School embrace, and he asked me if I'd had lunch. I hadn't.

"Good. Let's buzz around the corner and reprovision. Lotta years to cover."

In a small, clean Hungarian restaurant we covered them while sharing goulash and Zinfandel. He said, "If you're having such a marvelous time in Cozumel, what brings you to this polluted city?"

"Last month I had a client who chartered for two days and skipped out without paying. Said he was an architect and gave his name as José Manuel Mendez. I'd appreciate you running him through embassy and ONI files."

"For DI?"

"For anything. It would be hopeless to sue him in Mexican courts so I'd like to learn if he has attachable possessions: plane, car, house—any property in the northern states, for instance."

"No problem," he said, and glanced at his watch. "We'll finish coffee and go back to the shop."

"Great, lunch is on me."

Ernie chuckled. "Haven't changed, Jack . . . How did things go with DEA?"

"Fine, for a while. Then I came up against a fellow who took Captain Queeg as a role model, and I turned in my suit."

"Drifting ever since," he said musingly, "in a tropical paradise. How bad can it be?"

I paid the check and walked back with him to the embassy. Ernie passed me through, and we rode up to the DOD reception room. I leafed through *El Universal*, and after a while Ernie came out with a letter-size envelope. Handing it to me he said, "What poop we have is there. Need I say, Read and Destroy?"

"My oath." We shook hands and he reiterated a promise to dive Palancar Reef with me.

As I left the embassy I paused long enough to check for surveillants, then got into my rental Ford. As I drove off I thought I glimpsed a blue *guayabera* in the sidewalk crowd, but that color was no rarity in Mexico City. Besides, why would anyone be tailing me? Hakem wouldn't want to encounter me again, and as far as I knew, Dario Casillas didn't know my face. I decided I was getting edgy, without reason.

At the old Fenix Hotel I rented a room, got comfortable with cracked ice and Añejo, and began reading the contents of Ernie's envelope. The ONI report bore José Manuel's name, DPOB—Date and Place of Birth—and the cryptic entry: NO DI.

The consular printout covered information I already

knew, plus a notation stating that when Mendez's Mexican passport was last presented for U.S. visa it bore airport entry-exit stamps showing he had spent nine days in Lebanon the previous year. That was the sole item of interest to me, and suggested that Mendez had gone there with Shari, or at her behest. Thanks, Ernie, I thought, tore up both info sheets and flushed their scraps down the toilet.

Then I turned up the air conditioner, turned off the lights and slept until well after dark.

———

Before heading up into the Lomas I drove past Mendez's office building and checked his parking slot, which was empty. Twelve minutes later I turned onto Calle Tehuantepec and drove slowly around the block, looking for the boozy *sereno* or his night replacement. Neither was in evidence, so I parked in front of a high-walled residence around the corner, and turned off the lights, and walked back to Mendez's house, hearing the sharp *whack-thock* of a jai alai game in someone's private *frontón*.

After looking left and right I climbed quickly over the entrance gate, and waited in shadows, in case a guard dog came bounding after me.

I went around the side of the house and saw that the white BMW was in the garage. So far, no attack canine. I looked in the darkened kitchen window, but couldn't see inside. Exterior stairs led up to the *azotea*, the open roof area used for washing and drying laundry. It was isolated from the house proper by an iron-faced door and a tumbler lock. I placed my ear against the door and listened. All that came through was a faint sound of music. No light showed around the door jamb, so I got out my lockpicks and set to work.

Like the house, the lock and its door were new. I opened them, my only light the quarter-moon, and stepped in. The room I entered held a cot with mattress, a washbasin, toilet and a shower stall—typical servant's quarters. The music was louder now and coming from below. The privacy door opened into a lighted upstairs hall. Through the crack I listened for a while and heard only music. I knew it was a radio program when a commercial cut in with an advertisement for disposable diapers. When the music resumed I stepped quietly into the hall and peered over the railing.

From that angle I could see part of a sitting room, unoccupied. Light fanned out from an open door where the music was coming from. I got out my Walther and went softly down the stairs. At floor level I paused, looked around and listened, but the music would have covered footsteps. I moved to the doorway and looked in.

A man in shirtsleeves was smoking a cigarette and reading a newspaper. He was relaxed in a reclining chair, one foot moving to the slow rhythm of the radio music. Covering him with my Walther I stepped in and pulled the door shut behind me.

José Manuel Mendez was half out of his chair before he saw the pistol in my hand. "Easy, Pepe," I said. "As you were." I walked around him and pulled down the window blind, his gaze following me.

I went back and sat in a rustic leather chair five feet from his right side, so he couldn't come at me without making a stop and a turn. His eyes narrowed and he said, "I don't keep money here."

"I'm not looking for money," I told him. "Where is she?"

"She? Who?"

"Shari. Your sister's friend, your friend. She's been staying here."

His eyes opened wide. "Why do you say that?"

I said, "Answer my questions and I won't harm you. No lying."

He put aside the newspaper and looked down at his hands. "You must be the man who called himself Mahan. Nina phoned Rice—they said they'd never heard of you. Your questions alarmed her. What do you want?"

Beside me on an end table stood a decorative vase. I heaved it at the radio. The vase shattered, the radio sparked, smoked and went dead. I said, "You can buy a new radio,

José Manuel. What you can't buy is new kneecaps." I sighted on the nearest one.

"Wait ... *wait*. Yes, she was here. She ... she left this morning."

"Was Hakem with her?"

"Who?"

"Abela Hakem, the arms merchant."

"I don't know him."

"But you know about him."

He hesitated.

"Maybe you met him in Lebanon last year," I suggested. "Like Shari, he moves around—Manzanillo one day, Monterrey the next. Was he here?"

He swallowed, nodded.

"All right," I said. "Now back to Shari Valour. Did she tell you she killed Ibarra? How she shot me? Emptied the safe and left town?"

"No," he said, "because she didn't. I read the story and it was as she said—a burglar shot Ibarra." He sat forward, chin up, an earnest fool. "We're going to be married."

I laughed shortly. "She told you that? She tells that to every man she manipulates. What does she want from you?"

His cheek muscles were working. I had slandered the loved one. "She's a killer," I said, "a strong-arm robber, an assassin. She'll use you, and when you're no longer useful she'll discard you, and you'll be lucky to be alive. Tell me where she is."

"So you can destroy her?" He shook his head resolutely, a man far gone in her spell.

I sighed. "I want what she took from Ibarra. Is it here?"

"She took everything with her," he said hoarsely.

"Where?"

He shook his head. He wasn't going to tell me. I leaned forward, shoved the pistol muzzle into the chair-back next to his head, and pulled the trigger. Mendez yelled and covered his ear. Even muffled the detonation was good for a thumping headache. "Where is she?" I repeated.

Behind me a voice said, "Here."

Turning, I saw her in the open doorway, and my mind flashed back to the last time her pistol had pointed at me. Now her left hand gripped a leash, checking a brown-tan Doberman. Beside it stood a man I'd never seen before. "Put down your gun," she said in a harsh voice. "If you try to use it, either I'll kill you or the dog will."

TWENTY

My pistol barrel was only an inch from Mendez's cheek. I said, "You have a way of coming up behind people, Shari." My palm was sweaty on the pistol grip.

"Put it down," she repeated. "Now!"

"Maybe I'll just blow off his head," I said. "Why not? According to you, he's been dead for years anyway."

Mendez's head didn't move but his eyes did, and he spoke to Shari. "You told him that?"

"It was a useful story, engaged his sympathy."

"Sure did," I agreed. "Want him alive, or dead?"

She shrugged. "I would prefer him alive, but I can't have José Manuel used as a hostage, Henry." A slight smile appeared on her lips. "Such a foolish name, but I will say you do know how to open a safe."

The architect blurted, "But you told me—"

"Never mind, Pepe," she said sharply, "what I told you. Now, Henry, what are you going to do?"

To José Manuel I said, "This is your lucky night, Pepe. I wasn't going to kill you, but she would make me." I lowered my arm and left the Walther in the chair beside his thigh. He stood up quickly, started toward her but she said, "Don't get in the way." More evidence of solid training. To the man beside her she said, "Tie him up, Dario, while we decide what to do."

So this was Ibarra's head honcho. A tall, burly man with curly gray hair, a sweeping mustache, and cruel eyes. He stepped around the dog and spoke to Mendez. "Rope?"

Weakly he said, "In the garage."

"Get it."

Wiping his face, Pepe Mendez left the room.

Shari came closer to me. "I was sure you'd follow me. How did you find me?"

"Long story, not important."

"It was two days before I realized I hadn't killed you, Henry. Did Nina give me away?"

"How else could I have found Pepe—and you?"

"A foolish, confused girl. Always was."

"Letting you assume her identity wasn't only foolish, it was dangerous. But then, you don't care whom you harm."

"Not when it benefits my cause," she said shortly.

"That's what Mossad told me."

"The *Mo*—I don't believe you!"

"They're concerned about you, Shari, you and Hakem and your plans for the LPA. They can chop you off faster than I ever could."

She bit her lower lip. "After I thought I'd killed you I had second thoughts. The FBI or DEA would want to know who killed you, and why, and that would inconvenience me." She turned to Dario Casillas. "We have to take him with us."

"To Atitlán?"

"I can't have him found. Not here, not now."

Mendez returned with a coil of clothesline and gave it to Casillas who tied my wrists behind my back, pushed me to the floor and ran the line from my wrists to my ankles. He trussed me so tightly my leg and arm muscles ached from the tension.

When Casillas stood up Mendez said, "What are you going to do with him?"

Shari said, "Isolate him so he can't interfere."

I grunted. "Permanent isolation—a grave."

Casillas kicked my thigh and I yelped. Mendez wasn't liking any of this. It was one thing to be an ideological partisan of the woman he loved, another to witness brutality he wasn't accustomed to. Perhaps Pepe would turn out to be an ally, passive as he was. I had no one else.

Casillas loosened my ankle ropes and jerked me to my feet. I glanced at Shari's face—immobile, indifferent. Until then I hadn't been able to think clearly about her because I'd felt a mix of admiration, lust, hatred and fear, but the illusion was over now. My thoughts were as clear and well defined as a laser ray. I had viewed her as a person, a sentient human being, whereas to her I was only a tool to be used and cast aside.

To my dying day I was going to remember the spurt of muzzle flame that seemed to issue from her mouth . . .

"Take him away," she said, "so we can talk."

Casillas didn't need a gun to steer me outside and into the garage. His thumb found the pressure point just above my right elbow and the nerve went white-hot. It was all I could do to keep from screaming.

He left me in a heap in the corner of the garage, locked the door and went away. My right arm was numb. I wondered if I could ever use it again. Gradually, feeling returned, along with a prickling echo of pain. My eyes grew accustomed to the darkness and I made out the white profile of Pepe's car. Casillas hadn't tightened the cord between wrists and ankles quite as much as before, so I rolled over the dank cement floor and came up against the rear wheel. Hunched over like Quasimodo I managed to lever myself partway up until my wrists found the curved edge of the rear bumper. I could saw the cord against the metal end for no more than two inches. It was going to take time to abrade the rope but I had nothing but time—until Casillas returned.

I hoped there'd be a long discussion in the house; Shari giving termination orders, Casillas accepting them, Mendez protesting my planned murder. I wanted Pepe to generate a courage he hadn't shown before. A slim hope, but it was all I had to go on. Meanwhile, in my cramped, pitiful position, my arms moved up and down like a ratchet, wrists scraping against the rough-sharp curving steel. Never give up, I told myself, never admit anything. They'll kill you anyway.

So I gritted my teeth and worked away, pausing now and

then to touch a fingertip to the abraded area. A few of the fibers had parted but there was much more to be done. After a while I heard a car backing toward the garage, a big vehicle, judging by the engine volume. I fell over on my side just before the door opened and Casillas strode in.

He loosened my ankle bindings and jerked me upright. Then he shoved me ahead of him and out to the moonlit drive, where a shiny Dodge utility wagon idled. Casillas opened the rear door and pushed me down into the foot well. Shari got into the front passenger seat beside Casillas. Pepe Mendez climbed into the rear, clumsily stepping on my legs. Tight-lipped, he looked down at me. Casillas hit the accelerator and the vehicle lurched forward.

The road wound downward, and in a few minutes moonlight told me we were heading westward on a fairly smooth highway. To Mendez I said, "How far to the cemetery?"

Moonlight whitened his pale face. He swallowed and looked away. I said, "You want to consider your position, Pepe. You're intelligent, think it over."

I saw Shari's head turn back so she could stare at Mendez. Neither said anything.

I estimated we'd been on the road about fifty minutes when I heard the sound of aircraft engines. The only airport I knew of west of the capital was outside Toluca, and as Casillas continued driving the aircraft noise gained volume. He slowed finally, the road became bumpy, and the big Dodge lumbered to a stop. Casillas turned off the motor and spoke to Shari. "Stay here while I warm the engines. Then bring him to the plane." He got out and slammed the heavy door. I said, "Night flight? How romantical."

Shari said, "Save your breath, Henry."

"Where are we going? One of Ibarra's plantations?"

Mendez said, "I don't think any of this is necessary."

"But I do," Shari said, an edge to her voice.

Suddenly Mendez said, "I don't want my wife to be a drug trafficker."

"Suit yourself—only remember that narcotics are the

road to the money I need. Without it my militia will fall apart, as so many factions have."

"Inspiring," I said. "Pepe, keep telling yourself the end justifies the means. If you believe that you'll feel heaps better."

"Shut up!" Shari snapped. A nearby engine popped, coughed, and revved, followed by a second. Casillas ran up the engines, and presently Shari turned to Mendez. "To the plane," she told him. She got out and opened the rear door.

Between them I hobbled toward a twin Beech whose spinning props were kicking back dust and pebbles. I recognized Toluca airport's buildings before they forced my head down, made me crawl into the plane like a caterpillar. Casillas came back and tied my wrists to a seat stanchion. At least I could stretch full length, though my ankles were still tied.

A wild thought flashed through my brain: if Casillas locked the controls on auto pilot I'd overpower him and take over. But sanity returned with the realization that while I was wrestling with Casillas, Mendez and Shari wouldn't be passive, and she was armed. Forget that one. I considered trying to saw the rest of the way through my wrist cords, but the stanchion was round and smooth, not edged and rough.

The plane began to move ahead. If we were headed for one of the border states we were in for a long flight, four to five hours, with maybe a set-down for fuel before reaching Ibarra's headquarters.

I heard the radio crackling as Casillas exchanged take-off talk with the control tower, which cleared us for Saltillo. Not our final destination, I was sure, but a cover for northward flight. During which they could shove me out at any time.

The props' sound changed as Casillas increased their pitch, then at full throttle we sped down the runway and lifted into the night.

We flew for two hours and fueled at San Luis Potosí, confirming our northern flight path. Mendez brought me a cup of water and I slobbered as much of it as I could, thanked him, and said, "Pepe, you're a decent man, but you're giving aid and comfort to murderers. Think about what's best for you."

He looked at me helplessly. "What can I do? If I try to interfere they'll kill me."

"I can't tell you what to do. But when we get to wherever we're going, look for opportunities to untie me and I'll take my chances."

He shook his head. "There are men there, laborers, *pistoleros* . . ."

"How many?"

"Twenty . . . fifty—I don't know."

"I'm not worried about the *campesinos*," I told him. "They're tillers of the soil, but the *bandoleros*—" I broke off as Casillas got into the plane, followed by Shari. As Mendez went forward, she said, "Don't feel sorry for him, Pepe. He wants to destroy everything I've worked for."

Mendez slid into a seat behind her, said, "Once I've seen the place I have to return to Mexico City. Client appointments—" He waved his hands vaguely. Shari said, "Yes, dear. As soon as it's possible." Then Casillas restarted the engines.

While I dozed and dreamed, the plane flew on through the moonlit night. Two hours and twelve minutes later I was roused by reduced engine sound, landing gear locking into place. The plane banked steeply, and through the grayness of early dawn I could see a landing strip outlined with flare pots, beyond the wide crook of a river. The land was desert-flat, uninviting. Set back from the airstrip were a series of crudely built, tin-topped aircraft shelters; farther away, what looked like barracks for laborers at the edge of tilled fields. An old, tile-roofed, two-story Mission-style house dominated the *hacienda*.

As we lost altitude, Casillas banked again, and I saw two trucks spewing dust as they moved toward the airstrip: reception committee.

After a bumpy landing, Casillas taxied back and cut the engines. He got out first, and I could hear him issuing orders to his troops. Mendez and Shari left the plane, and two ugly-looking *pistoleros* came back and untied me from the stanchion. I was almost too stiff to walk, and hobbled ankles didn't help. They prodded me into the bed of a pickup and drove off. I could see Pepe talking to Casillas and Shari, then they got into the other truck and went off toward the house. Even in early dawn the air was warmer than Mexico City, and sun would scorch the land within an hour or so.

In a few minutes the truck stopped and the men hauled me off and pointed toward an almost hemispheric mound overgrown with scrub and desert weeds. From flying over the Yucatán I recognized the mound as the bulk of an ancient pyramid. This one was about twenty feet high, forty or fifty in diameter. Taking short, shuffling steps, I managed to fall. I got up and took a few more steps, fell again. With a curse, one of the men pulled out a serrated knife and slashed through my ankle cords, then pushed me ahead. We went around the side of the pyramid to where a deep trench sliced partway under the mound. "Looking for Aztec gold?" I asked.

"Some *ladrones* were digging until Ibarra ran them off." He pushed me forward and I managed to land in the trench on my feet. The jolt was about the same as a parachute landing; I estimated the trench as eight feet deep.

Just about right for a grave.

"We'll be back, *gringo*," one of them called, and the truck drove away.

Sunlight gradually revealed my surroundings. The trench was about a yard wide, ancient pottery shards speckling the walls. On the trench floor I saw a scorpion, tail upraised, stalking a large centipede. I waited until after the scorpion struck its prey and was manipulating it with its claws; then I crushed it under my shoe, and scuffed dirt over its remains. Where there was one scorpion there had to be more, probably a large family living in the pyramid's cool crevices.

As the sun rose I heard *campesinos* chanting in the distant fields. Far above, three buzzards circled in warming updrafts from the desert floor. Waiting, perhaps, for me?

One end of the trench was an almost vertical wall, the other end extended under the pyramid and was pierced by a dark hole wide enough to admit a man. All the treasures of Cuauhtémoc couldn't have gotten me into that hole, not with bound wrists and no flashlight. Rattlers liked the warm desert surface, but other venomous *culebras* preferred slinking around where it was cool and dark; for them the pyramid's interior was ideal.

Still, the passageway deserved observation. As I knelt I glimpsed something in the sandy earth just below it. Black, thin and long, it glinted dully under its layer of dust. Stepping back I toed it partly free and saw the flaked blade of an obsidian knife. Excitedly I backed against it and tried to set my wrist cords on the edge. My fingers helped position it, but at the first sawing pressure the blade pulled out of the damp soil and dropped to the floor.

I stared at it despairingly and heard an exclamation above.

Two men were peering down into the trench. They wore rough *ponchos, sombreros,* and one held a stubby shovel. "*Qué pasa, hombre?*" he asked.

Turning, I displayed my bound wrists. "Help me," I said, "I'll pay you."

The other grave robber said, "If we help you, *Señor* Ibarra will send men to kill us."

"Ibarra is dead. The same men who would kill you are going to kill me. Help me!"

Their faces vanished. I heard muttered conversation, one face reappeared. "With great regret, *señor*, we cannot help you from your difficulty. They will come back to kill you and find us here, making three dead men in place of one." He touched his forehead respectfully. "*Buena suerte, señor.* Perhaps later we will come again . . ."

"I'll be waiting," I said, but already they had disappeared.

It was going to be ten hours until nightfall—what could be my final sunset—and even if the grave robbers returned, I had no reason to believe they would be any more cooperative after dark. Thinking objectively, their best move would be to take what money I had, continue their treasure search, and depart, leaving me alive or dead. Besides, at any moment the *pistoleros* could return, so if I was going to help myself that time was now. I decided to try something I hadn't had the opportunity to do until now.

By lying on my side I was able to work my wrists under my feet and bring up my arms in front of me. It was slow and very painful. My arms had been tied behind me so long that my shoulders felt dislocated. Finally, I could see my scraped, bloodied wrists and the abraded cord that bound them. I began chewing the cord when another idea occurred. My fingers picked up the Aztec blade and set it vertically between my heels. Thus clamped, the blade was reachable and fairly steady. Bending forward like an oarsman I began working the wrist cord up and down the blade edge, thanking the long-dead Aztec for his pains in making the stone blade sharp.

A few strands parted, the knife fell away and I had to reset it between my heels. While I was doing that a plane took off and circled above, gaining altitude. Not Casillas's twin Beech, but what looked like an old crop-dusting Stinson biplane. When it turned north I decided its spray tanks were packed with cocaine for delivery across the border. I wondered how much white gold was refined on the *hacienda*, and how much processed coke came in from Colombia and Bolivia. Ibarra had established a transshipment center, and the fact that neither the airstrip nor the marijuana fields were camouflaged meant that he'd enjoyed protection from very high up. The state governor and the regional military commander had to be involved, as well as officials in Mexico City, accustomed to taking their cut.

Shari would have to reestablish those relationships while defending her ill-got gains from takeover by someone who figured he didn't need a *muchacha* heading the system. Apparently she had already persuaded Dario Casillas to accept her as Ibarra's replacement, but a narcotics organization's continuance depended on satisfying the avarice of underlings. Shari planned on the lion's share of profits to maintain her Lebanese militia, and how well that would sit with Ibarra's lieutenants—only time would tell. Shari was a risk-taker, and so far a successful one, but it would be easy for a rival to put a bullet in her head. And she was smart enough to know it.

I sawed through the last strand and my wrists were free. After pocketing the knife blade I massaged my raw wrists and evaluated my situation. I was free of my bonds, alone and in dangerous surroundings. Other than knowing that the *hacienda* was probably more than a thousand miles to the north of Mexico City, I had no idea where I was. How far was it to the nearest outpost of civilization? Casillas had indicated we were going to Atitlán—a region, *pueblo,* or the name of the *hacienda?* How far to the border, the Rio Grande? A hundred miles? Two hundred? Five? I was hungry and thirsty and I had neither food nor water. No weapon but my obsidian blade.

If I started walking north without water across the desert, I'd be dead in a day. Even with water I'd first have to get off the *hacienda* and away from Casillas's guards and workers.

I remembered the river. If it ran northward I could follow it, perhaps to the Rio Grande. Walking in desert heat I might be able to cover twenty miles, sunrise to sunset, but fifteen or sixteen were more likely. Desert rats traveled at night, their burros warning them of sidewinders and horned vipers. I didn't have a burro; I wasn't going to walk the desert at night.

But maybe a burro could be found.

Using the stone knife, I dug toeholds in the dirt wall and stepped up until my hands reached the surface. Raising my head slowly, I looked around. As far as I could see, there was nothing but scrawny mesquite and cactus—sahuaro, maguey, and a few towering stands of organ cactus. The pyramid blocked any view of the house, the airstrip and the *campesinos* working the fields. I pulled myself out of the trench and lay at the edge, listening. My watch showed ten-fourteen; not even noon, and the sun blazed like a welding torch.

I heard a burro bray.

It brayed again, plaintively, and I fixed the source as a

thick clump of mesquite about a hundred yards away. The burro's hide blended into the desert background, but not the black-red ponchos of the two grave robbers lying in the branches' shade. Sleeping or resting? I wanted their burro and everything else they had.

On knees and elbows I began worming toward them, dust and sand covering my mouth and chin, left arm aching. After a while I paused for breath, moistened a finger and checked the slight breeze. It was coming in my direction, so the burro wouldn't scent me for a while. Dust devils spiraled up and swayed. As they vanished, others whirled and danced across the desert floor. The burro was watching them. He nickered, his ears flattened back and he lay down. So far, I hadn't seen the grave robbers move. Their heads were under their *sombreros*, protection from sun and sand. I dug in knees and elbows and kept crawling.

It was hard work and I was getting dehydrated fast; perspiration on my face and forehead evaporated as soon as it formed. My chest was damp but it was close to the ground. I needed water.

When I was about twenty yards away I rested again. The burro seemed to be asleep but you could never tell about burros. On his back was a crude wood-rawhide saddle, saddlebags on either side, a *reata* looped around the low pommel. As I studied the scene I saw something I hadn't seen before—a long gun leaning against a mesquite trunk. I licked dry lips. I wanted that, too.

Ten yards more.

The burro made a snuffling sound, yawned and went back to sleep. One of the men stirred. I lay flat, hugging the earth. When I looked again everything was motionless as before. Readying myself, I tensed in a sprinter's crouch, and began running. The burro got up, shook himself noisily, and started to bray. One of the men shoved aside his sombrero and sat up. He looked at the burro, and saw me.

Went for the gun.

TWENTY-ONE

I got to him before he was off his knees, kicked him aside and grabbed the gun. Both men were scrabbling under their *ponchos* when I covered them. "Don't move," I snapped. "Pull off your *ponchos* and lie face down."

"But *señor*," one protested, "we mean you no harm."

"*Ponchos* off," I repeated and cocked the gun. It was an old twelve-bore, battered and rusted, wooden stock chipped, split, bound with wire. I knew the piece was loaded when its owners obeyed me and began shucking their *ponchos*.

Both men wore cartridge belts and holstered revolvers. I took out the revolvers and had them toss their cartridge belts toward me. Neither one looked angry or resentful, just philosophical. They were Indians.

Their feet wore crude sandals fashioned from tire rubber and leather thongs. I told them to shed the sandals and toss them to me. While they were doing that I checked both revolvers. They were antique Colt Cavalry models, cylinders loaded with .50 caliber cartridges. I laid down the ancient shotgun, and holding a cocked revolver on them, got both weapons belts around my waist. I opened the shotgun breech and ejected the hand-loaded shell, wondering if all three weapons had come from General Scott's historic expedition.

The burro let me approach, and I took off the coiled *reata*. I made one man tie up the other, and then I bound him, loosely enough that he could free himself in a couple of hours. I leashed both men to mesquite trunks far enough apart that they couldn't reach each other, and then I lifted their canvas waterbag from the burro and drank. The water was old and hot but I swallowed as much as I could hold. I debated leaving the bag with them, but they'd know where the river was, and I had a longer distance to travel than they did. Much, much longer.

Plaintively one man said, "You leave us to die, *señor*."

"As you left me," I said. "So put your faith in the Great Spirit, Quetzalcoatl. Where is the nearest *pueblo*?"

They stared at me sullenly.

I cocked a revolver and pointed it at their legs.

One man said, "Atitlán, eight *kilómetros* west."

"And *la frontera*—the border?"

"Ah, ¿*quién sabe*? Many *kilómetros* to the north."

"Many, many," his partner agreed.

I realized they probably couldn't grasp a figure in excess of twenty, so I gave them each a drink from the waterbag, and hung it from the pommel. One saddlebag contained a paper-wrapped stack of *tortillas* not quite as hard as tin. I chewed down two of them and hunger pangs subsided. I eased both revolvers in their holsters for quick-draw, and pulled on a *poncho*. The heavy knit would ward off heat and preserve body moisture. One of the sombreros fitted me better than the other so I put it on and tied the string under my chin. I stuck their sandals in a saddlebag, and untied the burro's halter rope. "*Adiós*," I said, and led the burro away from the thin shadows of the mesquite trees.

The sun struck my hands with almost palpable force. I decided to find shelter by the river for the rest of the day, and strike north after nightfall. The burro plodded peaceably behind me, its hoofsteps a clopping rhythm from *On the Trail*.

I was about fifty yards off when I heard the engine of an oncoming vehicle. Shading my eyes I made out a distant dust plume and saw a pickup speeding toward the pyramid. Whether or not the riders were my executioners, I had to keep them from sounding the alarm. With men scouring the desert for me, planes searching overhead, I'd be found in a matter of minutes. So I turned the burro around and began walking back to the pyramid.

I was almost there when the pickup arrived in a thick swirl of dust. The driver jumped down and ran toward the trench, pulling a pistol from his pocket. When the dust settled I saw there was no one else in the pickup. I couldn't see the man's face but there was something familiar about his build. He pointed the pistol into the trench, and I saw his shoulders slump. He strode to the pyramid end and got down on hands and knees to peer at the entrance hole. The burrow whinnied, and when the man turned around he was looking at my two revolvers.

Abela Hakem.

"Put down the gun," I said. "Very slowly."

He recognized me now, and his face showed disbelief. His hand opened and the pistol dropped.

"So, you were going to do it," I said. "An eager volunteer. Take off your clothes, Abe."

He stared at me, immobile. "Now," I snapped, "or I'll drag you behind the truck."

He pulled off his dark coat, then his shirt and trousers. He stopped.

"Everything," I told him, and cocked both revolvers.

Awkwardly he got out of shoes, socks and underwear, the last reluctantly. "Into the trench," I said. "Now."

He looked down at the raw earth. The sun was high enough that the whole trench was lighted. He would have a choice of baking in the sun or crawling into the dark hole. Hakem didn't know what was in the hole, but I did. Grave robbers would toss in torches to scare off scorpions and snakes, but Hakem didn't have a torch. Let him figure it out.

Looking at me he got down and sat on the edge.

I said, "Are Ibarra's books here with Shari?"

"At the house."

While he was gazing into the trench I planted my foot on his back and shoved. He hit the far side with a scream and crumpled on the bottom. Staring up at me he began yelling.

I picked up his pistol, a nice Beretta 9 millimeter, and shoved it into a *poncho* pocket out of sight. Tipping my *sombrero* in his direction, I left the trench and went to the pickup.

The trench muffled Hakem's shouting while I tied the burro to the tailgate. I got behind the wheel and started the engine, drove slowly to the mesquite stand, and untied the burro. It ambled over to the nearest tree and began to gnaw on bark and leaves. The two grave robbers watched me sullenly. I unhitched their cartridge belts and dropped them on the sand. Now they had everything I'd taken except for one *poncho* and one *sombrero*; they could reimburse themselves from Hakem's wallet.

Atitlán was west. I'd be noticed there, and it was the first *pueblo* where Casillas's men would look for me. The gas gauge registered half. I turned the pickup and headed northeast across the desert, away from house, airstrip and *campesinos*. It was rough driving, dodging among cactus and mesquite stands, scaring roadrunners and hares, and after a few minutes I stopped to let the dust trail settle.

I got out and looked into the truck bed. Under a tarpaulin lay an assortment of field tools—bush hoes, machetes, and shovels. And a large tin cup. I took out a machete in its canvas sheath and laid it on the seat beside me.

Then I heard the sound of an airplane.

Under the sombrero brim I made out a C-47 Gooney Bird banking down toward the *hacienda*'s airstrip. I waited until it was out of sight and then I drove on, and after a while came to the river. It was low, and muddy in midstream, but the shore edge was reasonably clear, so I stooped and drank, bathed my face, and soaked the *sombrero*. Upstream the shore was eroded and overhung by a thick stand of mesquite. I drove to it, hacked off low branches, and sheltered the pickup underneath, right wheels in the shallow stream. It was the only cover offered by the barren landscape, and what mountains I could see looked about fifty miles away.

Using cut branches I walked back and dusted wheel tracks as they emerged from the cactus field. Feeling hunger again I cut into a likely looking *maguey* and collected a handful of white *maguey* worms—*gusanos de maguey*—the kind you find in *pulque* bottles along with the flies. To me they tasted a little like scallops, but it always revolted Melody to see me eat them.

Back at the truck I filled the tin cup with water, added *gusanos*, then set the cup on the hot engine block. While the cup water heated I pulled off my shoes and cooled my feet in the river. I let the worms boil for five minutes and when they were cool enough I ate them like popcorn shrimp, washing them down with warm boiled water.

After that I spread the tarpaulin under a mesquite branch, and lay back in the shade. Eventually Hakem would be missed, and someone would be sent to find him and the pickup. Then the search would be on. Either they'd find me or they wouldn't. I took Hakem's pistol and slid out the magazine. Filled to capacity. I jacked a shell into the chamber and laid the pistol on the tarpaulin under my hand.

The opposition would be much better armed: machine guns, assault rifles, grenades, even rocket launchers. They could wipe me out in seconds once the truck was spotted. And they'd spot me much faster if I were driving; dust plumes in the desert could be seen from miles away. Prudence told me that if I survived the long afternoon, I should drive toward the border in darkness, go as far as I could before the pickup ran out of gas. Somewhere out there was a road, and it would lead to a village. By telephone I could reach Sean Murphy in Monterrey, ask him to send a rescue team—non-Mexican. Then I'd be home free.

That was the prudent course of action. But back in the *hacienda* house were Ibarra's books—and Shari. If I let this opportunity slide by I'd never get so close to them again. And for all I knew she'd leave the *hacienda* with Pepe in the morning.

Light breeze from the river wafted over me. I pulled off the heavy *poncho* and made a pillow from it. Mesquite branches stirred as I slept.

An aircraft engine wakened me. Peering up through the lacework of branches I made out a high-wing, radial engine monoplane. It was circling lazily about half a mile away. From its profile, probably a Beaver. I had to hope the setting sun wouldn't glint from the pickup's metal and attract the pilot's attention. The plane was doing a search pattern of ever-expanding circles that would soon bring it overhead. I picked up the tarp and replaced it with the unfolded *poncho*, lay down and pulled the tarp over me. There was about an hour of sunlight remaining. If the pilot didn't spot the pickup on this sweep, chances were good he'd fly on and return to the *hacienda* airstrip by dark.

Meanwhile, a ground search was going on.

I was, I figured, an hour's hike from the house, and that was the one place they wouldn't expect me.

The plane was nearing. Its next turn would put it over the river—and me. Its altitude was around a thousand feet for lateral scan, and daylight was fading fast.

This time yesterday, I reflected, I'd been snoozing in an air-conditioned room at the Fenix, after which I'd done everything wrong. Now I was a hunted man, hiding on a riverbank somewhere in northern Mexico, and the Beaver was directly overhead. Automatically I held my breath. If the plane came down for a closer look I was finished. I listened for variations in engine sound, and prayed.

Blood pounded my eardrums before I exhaled. The plane was flying away. I pulled off the tarp and checked its heading. If the pickup had been seen the plane would be flying back to the airstrip; instead, it was moving beyond the river toward the purpling mountains.

At the river's edge I drank deeply, ducked my face and head, and smeared mud over my face, arms and neck. As much to keep off insects as to camouflage my skin.

The reverse side of the *poncho* was dark gray, so I put it on that way and tucked the Beretta into my trouser pocket. Before leaving the pickup I went through the glove compartment and took out a small flashlight that went into a hip pocket. Then I hitched the machete around my waist with the sheath's braided thongs, checked the Beaver's location—almost out of hearing now—and remembered the pickup's ignition key. I pulled it out and stuck it under the left front tire, where I could find it if I needed wheels again.

I took bearings from the sunset afterglow and began walking toward Ibarra's stronghold.

It's a truism that the sun sets quickly in the desert, and night drops like a purple curtain. Then nocturnal creatures begin to stir: owls and kangaroo rats, gophers, scorpions, snakes, large furry spiders that can kill and devour a sparrow. As I walked I could hear rustling in the cactus and mesquite.

The moon was rising. Off in the distance a coyote barked and bayed, others joined the plaintive chorus. I wondered if the grave robbers had freed themselves and gone off with their burro. I could use that burro now, I told myself, because with night vision better than mine it wouldn't bump into unseen cactus as I was doing. But I'd given it back to them. So much for excess generosity.

I doubted that a perimeter guard would be posted around the *hacienda*. It would be routine at the airstrip, but I was betting the house residents weren't expecting me to come back. I remembered Hakem's attack dog, Fritz, and wondered if Abe had brought him to the *hacienda*. I didn't want to tangle with him again.

Presently, the cactus stands thinned out and moonlight showed me the old pyramid off in the distance. I didn't hear Hakem shouting, so either he'd quieted down or been rescued by his partners. If he was still in the trench he'd have a cold night; I was glad of the *poncho* I wore.

As I walked, the sheathed machete slapped my thigh, the Beretta rode heavily in my pocket. Stones bruised my feet. I was tired and hungry, I could use a drink. Añejo preferably, in a glass of crushed ice. The thought of it made my mouth salivate. Because my mind was on what I'd like to have instead of on what I was doing I didn't react to the first sound of voices. But when I did, I froze.

The sounds came from two o'clock, conversational snatches between two men. One claimed Graciela was a better lay than Raquel, and Raquel's champion denied it. Stealthily I moved in a ten o'clock direction and finally saw them sitting only twenty yards away. They wore caps and baggy uniforms, and looked like young Mexican soldiers. Probably detailed to guard their general's equity in the *hacienda*'s profits. They were smoking in the moonlight, talking *macho* talk and thinking of next payday in the village whorehouse. Each had an automatic rifle across his lap, and though I wanted one badly I wasn't going to kill them to get it. So I walked quietly on and soon their voices were lost in the night.

I was now inside the plantation perimeter, I told myself, and the next few minutes would decide whether this mission was feasible or impossible. In the latter case I could make my way back to the pickup and drive toward the border. But I'd used up a lot of strength and shoe leather getting this far, and I wanted to unravel the *hacienda*'s mysteries if I could manage it without getting killed.

Ahead of me the land was cleared and I could see the ranch house lights. I sat down to rest, think and listen. Through the still air came the soft throbbing of a gas-powered electric generator. I turned my head until I could fix the directional source—beyond the dark barracks building. Field hands went to sleep early and rose before dawn.

To the left of it stood a large concrete blockhouse with lighted windows. A man came out of the door, stood to one side of the light shaft and urinated. Before he reentered and closed the door, I could see that he wore a long white chemist's coat and face mask. The blockhouse was the *hacienda*'s lab.

The old Mission-style house was lighted on the first floor where Shari and her band would gather to eat and drink and plot. A figure moved past a window, silhouetting a shouldered rifle. I checked the time.

Breeze rose, shifted, and from the airstrip came the sound of a prop plane taking off. The search Beaver? I itched to get at the controls of Casillas's Beechcraft.

The armed man passed the window again. Just under three minutes; one guard circling the house. I got up and in a crouch began approaching the house, right hand on my pistol grip. A pickup truck was parked near the back of the house, and I decided it would provide temporary cover. I angled toward it and when the guard was on the far side I went quickly to the truck. No ignition key.

A bunched tarpaulin covered whatever was on the truck bed. Weapons? I heard the crunch of the guard's boots and moved out of sight behind the cab. When he disappeared around the corner I lifted the tarp.

Moonlight showed a naked body, swollen and covered with strange purple spots. The face was hideously contorted as though the man had died in agony, teeth bared in the unmistakable rictus of death.

Abela Hakem had met kismet far from his native shores, bitten repeatedly by scorpions, vipers, or both. I wondered if he'd crawled into the trench hole or if the creatures had come out for him. While it lasted, I thought, it must have been a frantic scene.

I replaced the tarpaulin, waited until the guard came and went, and covered the distance to the nearest window. The inside room held a dining table with plates and dishes that hadn't been cleared away. Beyond, three people were in a sitting room: Casillas, Shari, and Mendez. The men had glasses in their hands. Shari stared stonily at Casillas who was gesturing with his free hand. I couldn't wait for more, and ducked back behind the pickup until the guard went past again.

Then I moved to the sitting room window and heard Casillas's loud voice. "If you hadn't let Hakem try to kill the *gringo* he wouldn't be dead now. Instead the *gringo* is out there driving to safety." He lifted his glass and drank.

Shari said, "You said your search parties will find him."

"They haven't yet, have they? Not even the plane that looked all afternoon. No, it looks like the *gringo* got away. And you know what that means, *señorita*."

She shrugged. "I don't see there is much to fear. If he goes to the police they'll arrest him as Abela's killer. Isn't that what you've arranged?"

"Yes. But if he doesn't contact the police?"

"Army, then. Isn't it the same? You pay for protection, don't you? A great deal of money. If I don't get full cooperation from the army I'll make different arrangements."

Casillas, who had been pacing, stopped abruptly. "*I'll* deal with the general. Me, not you, understand?"

I had to go back to the truck then. I waited until the guard was out of sight, and was about to leave when something hard jammed into my spine. "*Manos arriba*," came a coarse, cruel voice I recognized as one of the *pistoleros* who had dumped me in the trench. Slowly I lifted my arms. "We looked for you in all the wrong places, *señor gringo*, so I did what I thought you might do—come back here. And so we have you now."

TWENTY-TWO

They had me.

Legs tied to a heavy straight-backed chair under the living room chandelier, wrists handcuffed behind the chair back. I wasn't going anywhere until execution time.

Casillas had cuffed me around before tiring of it. My face was swollen, jaws ached. One eye half-closed. They had my stone knife and my Beretta. I wanted to kick myself for not having driven to the border.

Pepe Mendez sat at the far end of a sofa, Shari at the other; they seemed to be staying apart. Casillas ignored Mendez and addressed Shari. "This *gringo* has been only bad luck to you, bad luck to me."

"What are you afraid of, an American invasion to rescue him? Don't be foolish, Dario. Nothing will happen in consequence of his disappearance."

"Don't believe her," I said. "She doesn't know what arrangements I made from Atitlán."

Shari said, "You didn't go to Atitlán, you don't even know where it is."

"Eight kilometers west," I said, "with a telephone and telegraph office."

She looked up at Casillas. "You said the truck hadn't been seen there."

"I walked in," I said, "for that very reason. Helicopter gunships will be here after dawn."

"Not Mexican," Casillas sneered.

"American. And they expect to find me alive, not dead like Hakem."

Bitterly, Shari said, "You killed him, killed my friend."

"He was going to shoot me, wasn't he? By your leave, too. But *I* didn't kill him—nature took care of that. And as for Abe being your friend, he was everyone's friend. He used your money and bought arms for your enemies."

She shot to her feet. "You lie!"

"I tell you what Mossad told me. And they keep track of those things."

Casillas looked at her with contempt. "A traitor at your right hand, eh? And so soon—"

"Don't believe him," she snapped. "He would say anything to save his life, no lie too great."

"Perhaps, but he seems to know hidden things about you and your organization. That makes me nervous, *señorita*. It makes me unhappy."

I looked at Mendez. "Tell them what I told you—that last year you were in Lebanon for nine days."

Shari swallowed. "Did he, Pepe?"

"Yes, he knew about that," he said uncomfortably.

"What else did he tell you?"

"Abela was betraying you."

"Even if he said so I don't believe it."

Casillas grunted. "If it were not so, why would he say it at that time? I think you lack experience in rooting out traitors. In my organization that ability is very necessary."

"*Your* organization? It is my organization now."

Casillas shrugged. "I am feeling less receptive to you as a partner. I think our agreement is going to be changed."

"Oh, no, I have the books essential to distributing everything that goes out of here. Without them this place is useless except to grow sorghum."

"Not entirely," he said mildly. "It would be inconvenient and time-consuming to reestablish Pedrito's network, but I could do it. Where are those records, by the way?"

"Where you'll never find them, I assure you."

Mendez sat forward. Earnestly he said, "Shari, give them to Dario, get out of all this. We'll marry and have a wonderful life together."

She stared at her lover. "Did Dario *pay* you to say that? I can't believe you expect me to abandon the cause I fought for for so many years, risked my life for time and time again. No, Pepe, find some docile Mexican girl for yourself, but don't tell me what I must do. Frankly, being a housewife and mother of your children has no appeal for me."

Mendez paled. Casillas uttered a short laugh. "It's not my habit to intervene in lovers' quarrels, but the *arquitecto* has the correct idea. I endorse it."

She said, "Naturally you would. And since we are getting nowhere I think we should rest and talk again in the morning."

"Sleep late," I said, "and you won't hear the choppers come."

She turned to me with a thin smile. "Bluff, Henry, pure bluff and you know it."

Casillas's face had a thoughtful expression. I said nothing, wanting him to think it over. Shari got up and strode toward the doorway, stopped suddenly because it was barred by Casillas's two *pistoleros*. "Out of my way," she snapped, but one pushed her back into the room. Mendez shot to his feet and Casillas turned to him. "She's forgotten you," he said. "You're part of her past and I'm not sure she has a future." He gestured, and the two men walked her backward into a chair.

"Tie her," Casillas ordered, and one man went off for rope.

Shari said, "You'll regret this, Dario. Harm me and a hundred men will avenge me."

"From Lebanon? Lebanon is far away and news travels slowly from this *hacienda*. But who said I would harm you? I simply want your attention, Shari, until our discussion is over."

"To yield to you would be to betray my people."

He sighed. "There are worse things than betrayal, *señorita*. Consider Hakem's body . . . horrible, was it not? The creatures that killed him so painfully are still out there, lest you forget."

"*No!*" Mendez yelled in agony. "You can't do that!"

"Her choice." Casillas stepped back while his men tied her to the chair. Mendez stood with clenched fists glancing from his love to Casillas and back again. In my frankly uncomfortable position I was glad for the entertainment.

To Mendez, Casillas said, "Don't try to free her, *muchacho*, don't interfere. This is not your affair. Take a stroll in the moonlight." When Mendez didn't move, Casillas said, "*Go!*"

Slowly, the architect left the room. I heard his soles on the stone steps.

Casillas motioned the *pistoleros* to leave and drew up a chair facing Shari. "*My* men," he said, "and they obey me, not you, Shari. Pedrito was a difficult man to deal with, and his reluctance to pay good wages infused a spirit of mutiny in our organization. I am changing all that because I believe not only in loyalty but in rewarding those who take the risks necessary for success. It was impudent of you to think that you could be my *jefe*, that I would serve you as I served Ibarra. But because you disposed of him I owe you something, even though you killed him for your own needs."

I saw a shadow cross the nearest window. Mendez? A *pistolero*? The young architect was no match for even an unarmed gunman, let alone two with big revolvers. But maybe he was infatuated enough to try.

Casillas said, "Well?"

Surlily, Shari said, "Well, what?"

"Are you going to give me what you stole from Ibarra or do you prefer the rest of the night in that infested trench?"

I didn't like the thought of her beautiful naked body swollen like Hakem's, but she'd brought this on herself. She said, "If I turn everything over to you, what will I get?"

"Your life—and Pepe's."

"Why should I trust you?"

"What choice do you have?"

She moved and a cord cut into the swelling of her breasts. "I trusted you when I came here, and look at me now."

"Where are the records?"

"In a *very* safe place." She was a tough, dedicated fighter and I admired her resistance. Clearly, she was resolved to die before submitting.

Casillas leaned forward and pulled off her shoe. He flicked on a butane lighter and moved it toward the sole of her foot. I wondered if he'd bought any part of my tale about armed choppers coming for me. If he did it would only add urgency to his work. Once he extracted the records from Shari he could abandon the plantation and set up shop at another. The flame moved until it was directly under her flesh. As her face tightened, he said, "Once the tendons contract you'll never dance again—or walk without limping."

A spot turned black, began to crackle and smoke. The smell of charred flesh carried to my nostrils. I wondered how long she could hold out. My handcuffs bit into my wrists.

She turned her face to the window and screamed.

Casillas drew back the lighter. "Where, Shari?"

She shook her head violently, tears streaking her cheeks. "Very well," he said, "before you're taken to the trench my men deserve a treat. Thirty-seven *campesinos* and fourteen soldiers. None has seen a woman in a long time." He stood up. "You might die of pleasure."

Through set teeth she grated, "I was tortured by the PLO, raped."

"Then you'll do well tonight. Fortunate you're not a tender virgin."

Pepe's face appeared at the window, pale, eyes demented. Casillas followed my gaze, but Pepe's face vanished. Where was the patrol guard, the two *pistoleros*? Pepe might have taken out one, but not all three.

Something was troubling Casillas. He looked from the empty window to Shari, to me. He knelt, and I thought he was going to roast her foot some more, but he began untying the cord around her knees. I thought of Hakem's body under the tarp, of the nonexistent assault choppers, and the mass rape ahead for Shari.

192

Her knee cords dropped, and from outside came the dull sound of an explosion, like a truck backfire. But it wasn't that because house lights flickered, went pale and died out. Casillas yelled, *"Hijo de la gran puta!"* and rushed out of the room. Lights came on, but weakly, drawing on emergency batteries. I said, "Where's the handcuff key?"

"If I tell you will you help me?"

"Don't bargain with me, Shari, you're no good at it."

"Casillas—shirt pocket."

"Try to move your chair behind mine, maybe I can untie your wrists."

We began rocking and edging our chairs together until they were back to back. My fingers found her knots but I hesitated. "Go on," she said urgently, "untie me."

"I'm thinking," I said, "about how you shot me in Ixtapa, delivered me here last night, sent Hakem to kill me. Not your fault I'm alive."

"Doesn't this change everything?"

"Only slightly," I said. "Where are the records?"

"If I didn't surrender to Dario why should I surrender to you?"

"He'll rape and kill you; I can set you free."

She considered. "We'll discuss it, but not now, there isn't time."

"Then there's never time," I said, and edged my chair away.

"No, *no*. What are your terms?"

"The books, that's all I want."

"Hurry, he'll be back. What about me? I have to get away from here."

"With Pepe?" I began heeling my chair back against hers.

"Up to you. How can we get away?"

My fingers resumed working on her wrist knots. "I'll tell you a little secret—yes, I still have a few—I can fly that Beechcraft."

"Are you *sure*? It's got two engines."

Lights were dimming again. The batteries were draining fast, probably because of neglected care. After they were gone, no more light. "Do you suppose Pepe blew the generator?"

"I hope so," she said peevishly. "It's the least he could do to help me."

I laughed hollowly. "After you castrated him? For God's sake, Shari, he owes you nothing." Her knots were open but she didn't know it because I held the free ends in my hands. "Where are Ibarra's records?"

"I . . . I left them in Pepe's house"

"That's a lie. Hakem said they were here."

Outside there was a lot of shouting and running around, *campesinos* and soldiers confused by the generator destruction and darkness. She said, "If you don't untie me they'll come back and kill us both."

"You'll stay here until you tell me about the books."

"They're upstairs, hidden in my mattress."

"That's the first place Casillas will look and you know it. Where are they?"

Finally, she sighed defeatedly. "Hakem's suitcase."

The light surged blindingly, turned orange, pale yellow, gray, flickered out. "*Please,*" she begged, "finish untying me."

"And you'll untie my legs?"

"I *promise.* You know I will—I need you to get me out of here." With that I let go the cords. She made a startled exclamation and stood up, scraping the chair aside. "Untie me, Shari," I said.

"Fuck you, Henry," she hissed, and ran from the room. As expected. Well, I was no worse off than before, and now Casillas would have to hunt her down, distracting his attention from me. That extended my life expectancy an hour or so; Shari couldn't get far on one shoe and a burned foot.

Pepe was also a target of course. If Casillas had his way, we were all dead. I tensed my thigh muscles and coughed.

From beyond the doorway I heard a quick intake of breath. Shari? Pepe? A thin light beam struck the floor. A hoarse voice: "Novak? Mr. Novak?"

194

"In here, hurry." I didn't care who it was, he knew my name, the only one on the plantation who did. The light struck my feet, raised and stopped on the bindings. The light went out. I felt sawing pressure on my bonds. They parted, and he began working on the thigh cords. "Easy," I whispered, "that's awfully close to my privates."

The knife blade lifted, and my thighs were free.

"Can you walk?"

"Can you run?"

I followed him out the back of the house and saw an immense fire billowing around the generator house. My rescuer guided me to the pickup with Hakem's body. When he realized I couldn't open the door he opened it for me, boosted me in.

Firelight showed him to me for the first time: a small, wiry man wearing black trousers, heavy boots, a black *guayabera* and a black straw hat. He got behind the wheel and started the engine.

"Where'd you get the key?"

He gestured at the folded sunvisor. "Where they're always hidden." He turned to face me and I made positive ID. "Damn! You were tailing me at the airport—Mexico City—in a blue shirt."

"I was pretty sure you spotted me, so I laid back. Didn't tail you again until you left your embassy."

We were bouncing over the desert—where, I didn't care. "Who are you? Who do you work for?"

"You can call me Saul," the small man said, "and Issar Levi asked me to look out for you."

"Then you tailed me to Mendez's house . . ."

"And saw all of you leave. Followed you to the airport. I don't suppose you have a weapon?"

"They took it. And from Toluca . . . ?"

"I hired a plane to follow yours."

"But you didn't land here."

"I don't think that would have been wise." I heard a low chuckle over the bouncing springs.

"*Watch out!*" I yelled, as we hit the big sahuaro head on.

Pulp spattered the windshield, the cactus toppled, and we went on.

"No," Saul continued imperturbably, "I came overland, penetrated at dusk."

"And blew the generator."

"To attract their attention."

"You got it," I said admiringly. "And where are we headed now?"

"The file says you can fly. Can you, Mr. Novak?"

"Anything with metal wings."

"Then we'll go to the airstrip." He slowed. "I think we're far enough away now." Braking, he said, "Come to the headlights."

"Why?"

"You can't fly—even drive, with handcuffs."

So I got down and backed up to the headlights. I heard the scrape of metal, felt a handcuff spring retract, and Saul pulled them open.

I brought my arms around in front of me and rubbed my raw wrists. "That was fast work."

He held up a thin case of lockpicking implements. Among them were three small shiny keys. "There are only three basic handcuff locks," he said, "and I carry the keys to all three. Get in and we'll find a plane."

I reached inside and turned off the headlights. Just then there was a very loud explosion from the direction of the house, then another. Saul said, "Reserve petrol drums. I punctured one hoping it would blow—before now. What's with the lights?"

"You rescued me, and my thanks to Mr. Levi, but I have to go back."

"Because of the woman, Shari?" Moonlight showed his mouth twisting.

"Because of Ibarra's records, what I came for."

"They're back there? You're sure?"

"The odds say so."

"What about Mlle. Valour?"

"If I can find her I'll bring her along."

196

"She shot you and left you for dead."

"I can't leave her to Casillas and his animals." I looked around. "Where are we? How far to the border?"

"You want I should give you coordinates? A navigator I'm not." He faced north. "Forty miles to the river. Del Rio, Texas, about seventy miles east."

"Close enough. Coming, or staying?"

"My brief is limited to you, Mr. Novak. If you make it back I'll be near the airstrip." He handed me a silenced automatic pistol. "Your chances are better while they're confused and in the dark."

I looked at the pistol in my hand, weighed it. "What about you?"

One hand dropped under the *guayabera* and brought out a thin black commando knife. He must have used it to cut my ropes. "I'll be all right," he said. "At night a knife is a good companion. Did you not perhaps wonder what happened to the two *pistoleros*?"

"Ah," I said, and got behind the wheel. I turned on the dimmers and saw him standing to the left of the front fender, small and sinewy, perfectly self-contained, and old enough to be my father. He was doing his job, had *done* his job, and if I could do mine and get to the strip, he'd be there.

I backed the pickup around and drove toward the orange flames shooting skyward into the night.

TWENTY-THREE

As I drove I remembered Hakem's body bouncing around on the truck bed behind me so I steered to the pyramid. I backed the pickup close to the trench, dragged the body off and let it drop. I followed it with the tarpaulin to hide it from buzzards' sharp and ever-watchful eyes. Then I drove closer to the ranch house and left the pickup in darkness outside the lighted zone, ignition key in my pocket.

I got out the silenced pistol and jacked a ready shell into the chamber. It was a nicely made piece, Czech or East German, copied from the standard Beretta 9 millimeter. I wondered if it was Mossad issue or if Saul had picked it up in Mexico.

Nearing the flame-lit area I made out two lines of men. At first I thought it was a water chain, but then I saw they were facing each other. They formed a gauntlet, and they were kicking and pummeling a victim staggering along the line. When he'd drop they'd pick him up and keep him going, turn him around and shove him down the line again. They were going to kill the poor bastard, and they were enjoying it. Casillas was at the head of the line, egging them on, and as the half-conscious man fell against him, Casillas shoved him away—but not before I saw the tattered, dirty clothing of Pepe Mendez.

So, I thought, they blame Pepe for the sabotage. I wanted to help him, but my eight cartridges would hardly dent the crowd of tormentors. I needed more firepower. I began looking around.

Ahead, leaning against a maguey, was a soldier. The butt

198

of his automatic rifle was on the ground between his boots. He was staring fixedly at the torture scene and didn't notice me come up behind him. Gripping the silencer I slammed the pistol butt against the side of his head. His hat popped off as he fell forward, and I caught the M-16 barrel before it hit the ground. From his belt I took the spare magazine and began moving forward. My plan was to rake the gauntlet and kill them all, then I realized I could easily kill Pepe, so I stopped and scanned the buildings.

The workers' barracks was dark, probably all of them were outside taking part in Pepe's killing. I shouldered the M-16 and took a wide flanking track that brought me to the end door of the barracks. I went inside, pistol first, flattened my body against the wall and looked around. Cots, blankets, hampers . . . and a lighted kerosene lantern on a table between the two rows. I dragged cots together, piled them with work clothes and blankets and smashed the lantern on the pile. The kerosene exploded, flames soaring blindingly. I ran to the other end and stepped outside.

From the shadows I saw the men looking up at their barracks. The gauntlet dissolved as they ran toward the building that held their burning possessions.

I left the shadows in a low crouch, saw one man standing over Pepe's fallen body.

Casillas.

Behind me the barracks filled with shouting men. Casillas took out a pistol and pointed it at Pepe.

From my knees I sighted Saul's silenced pistol on Casillas and pulled the trigger. A breathy *pop*, and Casillas staggered backward, left hand clutching his gut. He went down on one knee, looking frantically around, pistol moving, but drooping toward the ground. I came up behind him and kicked the pistol away, slammed the rifle stock on his chest, dropping him backward. Flame light showed blood bubbling from his mouth, staining his chin. It spread across his shirt from under his hands. I said, "Where is she?"

His mouth opened, but no words came out, just a hoarse rattle. Paramedics might still save him but there were none around. His eyes rolled, he coughed, and blood spattered his chest.

I left him and knelt beside Pepe, "No more," he moaned. "No more. Please, God, no more . . ."

His face and arms were bruised and bloody. His hands pressed his belly, but I saw no blood. Nearby, Casillas coughed wetly and tried to get to his feet, fell back. The barracks was roaring, men running from it. I got my hands under Pepe's arms and dragged him toward the house. "Don't hurt me, Dario," he pleaded, "I can't take any more."

"You'll be all right," I told him. "Can you walk?" Stooping, I levered him to his feet, helped him stagger forward toward the flame-lit house.

The laboratory door was open, I saw, men in chemists' frocks standing away from it, watching flames consume the barracks. I got Pepe to the porch of the house, and he dropped inside the door. I dragged him into darkness and left him.

I went up the stairs.

Flames from two angles lighted the bedrooms as I began searching. No one in the first two rooms. Then the third

Shari was lying on the floor, her arms and legs bound fast. On the bed was an open suitcase. A man's clothing—Hakem's—and the three books I'd come for. I peeled off a pillowcase and dropped in the records. Bitterly, Shari said, "You've got what you wanted. Are you going to leave me here to die?"

"Like you did me? Tempting," I said, but I bent over and untied her legs so she could walk. Both shoes were missing.

She got up slowly. I steered her along the hall and down the stairs. Flames made bizarre moving shadows on the walls.

I led her to where Pepe lay, and said, "Stay with him."

She raised her bound hands. "No," I said, "I like it that way," and paid a brief return visit to Hakem's room.

Outside again, I walked toward the laboratory. As I neared it, two chemists saw me, my rifle and pistol and moved away. Men of science, they had no weapons. They made death with tubes and retorts. I stepped into the lab.

The cloying smell of cocaine struck my nostrils. There was very little light but I could see blue flames flickering from Bunsen burners. There was a big copper vat over a lighted gas ring where coke was cooking. I fired the M-16 twice and liquid spurted from bottom holes. I used the rifle stock to smash retorts and Pyrex containers. Their chemicals caught fire. I was getting giddy from coke fumes. I broke windows on both sides of the lab, letting in more air to feed the flames. No one could stop them now. Eventually the gas tank for the burners would go up and blow the place apart.

I stepped outside and filled my lungs with pure night air.

Campesinos were sitting on the ground staring at the remains of their barracks. A few saw me but no one made a move. I walked over to where Casillas lay. He was still alive, foam on his lips, blood bubbling between his fingers.

I wondered where his soldiers were.

He was trying to say something but only bloody froth came from his mouth. It would have been merciful to finish him off as *toreros* do a dying bull, but I wasn't in a merciful mood. I walked back to the house.

As I reached the porch, the lab's butane detonated, fragmenting the cinder-block walls. What was left of the roof shot skyward as though elevated on a blanket of flame.

Pepe was sitting in the doorway, Shari beside him. His eyes were closed. Shari's glinted in the billowing flames. I was glad to see that her hands were still bound; from now on Pepe wouldn't be giving her much help.

She said, "You've destroyed everything, haven't you?"

"With a little help from a friend."

"Who?"

"You'll meet him. Where are the soldiers?"

"They come from the post in Atitlán. You didn't go there, did you?"

"No. How many soldiers here now?"

"Six, I think. Two at the airstrip." I'd knocked out one so

three were still out on the *hacienda* perimeter. I knew where two of them were.

"Where is Dario?" she asked.

"What's left of him is over there." I gestured with my thumb.

"Dead?"

"Sooner or later. All right, I'm going for the pickup. When I drive up, get in fast." I looked at Pepe. "How bad is he?"

"Broken ribs, I think, and his stomach hurts."

"He can thank you for everything," I said, and went back to where I'd left the pickup.

When I drove back to the house, clusters of *campesinos* were moving around, staring disconsolately at barracks embers. Part of the lab walls still stood, but there was nothing left inside. Everything combustible had burned.

There was nothing I could do about the fields of poppy and ganja, nothing except hope DEA could get the Mexicans to spray the plantation with defoliants. The general wouldn't like that but perhaps he'd have to agree.

Bent over, Pepe limped slowly to the pickup. I got down and helped him into the front seat. Shari stood in the moonlight as though waiting for me to make room. I lowered the tailgate and boosted her into the flatbed. She looked around and I knew she was thinking of Hakem's body. I said nothing, and closed the tailgate. Then I went to where I'd dropped the pillowcase beside the house, and placed it on the front seat beside Pepe.

I steered mainly with my left hand because Saul's pistol was in my right. Pepe's eyes opened and his swollen mouth moved, but I couldn't hear any words. I wondered if he'd have anything to say to Shari.

The airstrip was unlighted, but I could make out aircraft shelters and what passed for a control tower. Between the hangars and the runway were the high-wing Beaver and Casillas's twin Beech. As I steered toward it I saw a soldier get up from under its wing and point his rifle at my lights. I stopped ten feet in front of him and got down. He expected Casillas and I was a stranger. It troubled him. I wondered where Saul was. Ignoring the soldier I helped Pepe down and began walking him toward the plane. The soldier backed away and ordered me to stop. I opened the cabin door and heard the metallic *snick* as the rifle cocked. Supporting Pepe, I turned to talk peaceably with the soldier but from under the fuselage crept a dark ninjalike figure. Noiselessly he got behind the soldier and kicked his spine. The rifle discharged skyward, and as the soldier fell my rescuer hand-chopped the back of his neck.

Good ol' Saul. He came toward me and I said, "There's another guard somewhere."

His head turned toward the crude hangars. "In there. Now, what can I do?"

"Pepe is in a lot of pain, let's get him into a seat and strap him in."

"And Shari?"

"We'll tie her for our own safety."

Together we accomplished both maneuvers. I closed the cabin door and got into the pilot's seat. Saul thought it would be interesting to ride beside me, but I told him I'd rather he stayed close to Shari until we landed. He agreed it was a good idea and buckled up beside her.

Using Saul's penlight I studied the checkoff list and began working toggle switches in order. The port engine fired first, and while it was revving I started its twin. Even without the reserve tank there was plenty in the main to get us where we were going.

Wing lights on, I taxied to the end of the runway and turned around. The striped windsock hung lifelessly from its pole atop the low tower; one takeoff direction was as good as the other. I let the engines rev and took an air navigation chart of northern Mexico from the copilot's seat. It showed flight lanes and tower radio frequencies. I turned the transponder to Del Rio's megs and fitted on the headset, expecting to pick up controller chatter in the next few minutes. Unless the Texas airport was closed until dawn.

Before takeoff I looked back and saw Pepe Mendez in his seat, gazing at me through swollen eyes. Saul looked alert and attentive, and Shari stared back at me without expression.

I set flaps, waggled ailerons and rudder and released the brakes. The plane accelerated, gathered lift speed, and presently I could feel the wings taking our weight.

I went up to five hundred feet before circling back over the glow of smoldering buildings, and then I drew back the control column and turned east.

Assuming 200 mph airspeed I expected to reach the Texas border in around twenty minutes, and I felt plenty glad I hadn't had to walk. I climbed to four thousand feet to make sure I was on border radar because I didn't want a pair of F-14s forcing me to land where I didn't want to go. Radar controllers would realize that if I was carrying contraband I'd come in low and try to sneak under their beams, as happened all the time.

There had to be a DEA office at Del Rio; I didn't know who was in charge but I wanted to keep arrival low key, and landing at San Antone would create much more of a stir than I wanted. I had three illegal aliens on board and I didn't want to try explaining them to inquiring reporters at a major airport.

So far nothing from the Del Rio tower. I called in, but there was no response. A few minutes later I heard a controller asking me to repeat my message, and when I asked for landing clearance he said he'd hand me over to San Antone. I told him I lacked fuel to divert and had an injured passenger on board.

Because it was an "emergency" he agreed, located me on his radar, gave me a new heading, wind direction and landing instructions.

On my final approach I asked him to have an ambulance pick up a trauma patient, and requested that a DEA agent meet the plane.

I touched down on the east-west runway, braked and taxied off to the General Aviation building. After I cut the engines Saul came forward and said, "I have to get to a phone, Mr. Novak."

"Issar Levi?"

"If I can reach him at this hour." He opened the cabin door and jumped down. I saw ambulance lights flashing, the siren growled and whinnied as it sped toward me.

While we were getting Pepe into a Stokes stretcher I saw a black sedan draw up beside the ambulance. A man in shirtsleeves got out and came up to me. "Fogarty, DEA," he said. "You want me?"

I nodded. "This is Manny Montijo's operation, and I'm Jack Novak. I have a prisoner in custody."

"Yeah?" Sleepy eyes opened wide. "From where?"

"Ask me no questions," I said, "until Manny verifies. Got a holding area?"

"Sure, main building. Marshal's office."

After we got Shari into his car, I went back for the bulging pillowcase. I held it on my lap, thinking how far the books had traveled since that night in Ixtapa when Shari had taken them from Ibarra's bedroom safe, over my almost-dead body.

The U.S. Marshal's airport office was like every marshal's den I'd ever seen: old desks, banged-up chairs, a Telex and telecopier, WANTED flyers on the wall, overloaded ashtrays, trash baskets that needed emptying a week ago, cigarette stubs on the floor, tangled phone wires between punch phones and conference speakers, crushed coffee containers, crumpled McDonald's bags, and a glass-front weapons cabinet against a marred and pitted wall. The air smelled of old cigars, sweat and acid stomachs.

Three deputies were finishing night shift, a black, and two redneck whites. They wore reg shirts, and parts of their Monkey-Ward jackets were shiny where .45 revolvers, and handcuff sheaths had relentlessly rubbed the polyester. None of the deputies liked putting Shari in a holding cell. The shift supervisor said, "What's the charge, pardner?"

"I'll think of something, cousin—how about obstruction of justice?"

He grinned. "Sounds good."

"And resisting arrest."

205

"Read her her rights?"

"She hasn't any."

Fogarty came over, handed me coffee in a plastic cup—last week's coffee, still warm. He said, "It'll be a while before Mr. Montijo gets on the horn. Why don't you flake out, you look all done in."

He was right, and I felt worse than I looked. They gave me a cell near Shari's, a pillow and a mattress sheet. The cell smelled rankly of ammonia, or maybe it was Lysol. I pulled off my shoes and stretched out. Eyes closed, I said, "If a small man in black comes looking for me, let him in."

"Little man in black, eh? Who would that be? Death?"

"How right you are."

———

Someone shook me. Daylight whitened the cell's thick frosted window. I sat up, felt pain in stiff muscles, and blinked at Fogarty. "Conference call," he said. "Mr. Montijo in Washington, and Mr. Hagopian from Miami."

I moistened dry lips, tried to swallow. "The Hag? Whose idea was that?"

"Mr. Montijo said you wouldn't like it but that's the drill." He handed me a plastic cup. It was steaming hot and the black liquid tasted very old, but it helped me focus. I got off the bunk and trudged to the telephone desk. Fogarty punched two buttons and said, "Here he is, sir—Mr. Novak."

I sat in front of the speakerphone and glanced around. Saul was sitting next to the wall, arms folded. He looked at me but his face told me nothing. The inscrutable Mid-East, I thought, and said, "Novak here."

Hagopian spoke first. "What's this about a prisoner, Jack? What are you holding her for?"

"General principles," I said. "Manny, I've got Ibarra's books."

"And a stolen plane," Hagopian cut in. "Plus three illegals, right?"

"One's a compassionate case, check the INS rulebook.

Casillas beat him up pretty bad." I looked at Fogarty. "He's in surgery now." Fogarty nodded agreement. "José Manuel Mendez," I said, for Manny's benefit.

"That makes two," Hagopian said sternly. "What about the other guy?"

"Ask Issar Levi."

Saul left the cane chair and strolled over. He shot a bird at the speakerphone. Fogarty smiled.

Manny said, "We'll get it straightened out, Jack. I got a call from Issar. He was worried about you. I confirmed you were home safe."

Saul went back to his chair, folded his arms and closed his eyes. Under the fluorescent lights I saw something on one forearm I'd never noticed before—a tattooed number. That explained a lot.

Hagopian said, "People aren't going to like this unholy muddle, Jack; you were under strict orders to . . ."

He broke off as Manny asserted himself. "Merle, why don't you let me handle things? Jack's a private citizen, and I don't recall any 'orders' given to him."

"Well, there was certainly a consensus, but if you want to unsnarl things, be my guest." His line clicked off and Fogarty punched the kill button. After a moment, Manny said, "As I understand it, Jack, the only apparent problem is the young woman."

"So it seems."

"Saul there?"

"Yes."

"Good. He'll tell you what's been arranged." He paused. "What are your plans?"

"A soft bed, a bottle of Añejo, and back to Cozumel."

"Sounds right. Shall I tell Melody?"

"Please do."

"*Hasta.*" He hung up and Fogarty killed the line.

I was still drunk with fatigue. I stared dully at Saul, who came over and motioned me into an empty office. After closing the door, he said, "Turns out to be a good thing you brought Shari along."

"Why?"

"Issar wants her, Mr. Novak, and it goes like this. First, she won't be prosecuted, because she's committed no crime in the U.S."

I thought it over. "Maybe not."

"But it's leverage over her. Good female agents are hard to find, and you will admit that Shari Valour is a trained and competent agent. Her dream of drug profits is over. Between us, we ended it."

I remembered the burning buildings, Casillas dying on the ground, dull eyes reflecting the flames. "Go on."

"I'm going to talk to her now. Tell her she can work for me or go to prison."

"What kind of work?"

"Mainly among Arabs. She has Arab blood, speaks Arabic. Properly inserted and controlled she can be worth half a dozen men. As a bonus I'm going to offer limited support for her LPA."

I ran a hand over my dirty beard. "If she's smart," I said, "she'll go for it."

"She's not Israeli so she is . . . expendable. But she should be able to accomplish a number of worthwhile tasks."

"Killing?"

"She is certainly no stranger to it, Mr. Novak, but we also require information."

"Well," I said, "as long as I don't have to handle her."

"No, I have been assigned that role." He looked at his wristwatch and I glimpsed his extermination camp tattoo. By daylight his all-black costume was jarringly out of place. "If Shari agrees, I'm taking her back to Mexico. From there . . ."

I sighed. "I've known her a while, my friend, and she's a lass of endless artifice. Heed the voice of experience: when you're around Shari, watch your ass."

"I intend to," he said. "And I'm glad to have been of service."

"Much obliged," I said. "Regards to Issar Levi."

Saul went out of the office and I heard him walking off to

her holding cell. I drank from the water cooler and when I turned around Fogarty said, "I booked a room for you. Ready to go?"

"Presently." I went slowly back to the holding cells.

Saul was sitting beside her on the bunk. The door was open, her hands were untied, and she was listening to every word he said. At first she didn't see me, but when she did she looked up at me with blank eyes that told me I didn't exist. I walked back to Fogarty and we got in his car. By the time he drove up to the Holiday Inn I was nearly asleep.

Añejo helped ease bodily pain, but it did nothing to blot Shari from my mind. I remembered how we'd gone into the surf together and surfaced, bodies touching, welded together by desire . . . her face across the candlelit table . . . the smooth perfection of her caramel skin . . . and after a while I was swimming near Palancar Reef, breasting strong current as I struggled to get back to shore. But my muscles tired, arms and legs grew heavy, useless. Undertow swept me down . . . down . . . until I lay among curious fish and coral fans . . .

That evening I went to Pepe's hospital room. There were wires in his lower jaw and his chest was tightly taped. An IV bottle fed into his left arm, and drains extended from his abdomen. They'd had to take out his ruptured spleen.

He was coming out of sedation, the nurse whispered, but when I looked at his pallid face I couldn't tell. After a while his eyes opened and fixed on me. His lips moved but I heard nothing. Moments later I heard him whisper, "Shari . . . ?"

"She's gone," I told him. "You'll never see her again. Count yourself lucky."

"I love her," he said in a distant voice, and I saw tears welling in his eyes.

"She has that talent," I said, "but she feels nothing for anyone. She's a robot, a mechanical creature without human feelings."

I heard him sigh. Then, "She suffered so much."

209

"Did she? Who can tell? If the truth was inconvenient she banished it, created a useful legend. Try not to think of her, Pepe."

His head turned on the pillow, away from me. I said, "Has anyone told your sister—Nina?"

"No."

"Tell her the truth, Pepe, about Shari."

"Nina . . . won't believe . . ." His voice died away.

That was true, also. No one wanted to believe what Shari was. She was so bright, so beautiful, so alluring, yet for her everything was a weapon to use against friends as well as enemies. She was magnetic, hypnotic, and she got her way. She survived.

"Pepe," I said, but his eyes were closed. The nurse came in and told me I had to let him rest.

As I left the hospital I wondered why I'd come. I hadn't convinced Pepe, no one could. A waste of his time and mine.

———

Fogarty had the office pilot fly me to Dallas airport in a souped-up Cessna that had belonged to a drug ring operating out of Galveston. I sat beside him in the copilot's seat but didn't touch the controls; last night's flight was still too much on my mind . . . and all that had brought it about.

At the duty-free shop I bought a jug of bourbon and one of scotch to replenish hospitality supplies, and then I boarded a Mexicana 727 for the night flight to Cozumel.

There was no one at the airport to greet me. The *aduana* waved me through. I took a taxi along the shore road to my house.

Behind the chain-link fence my dogs set up a joyful clamor. Lacking a gate key I was wondering how to get in, when floodlights went on and Melody burst out of the front door, running toward me, key in hand.

She was wearing a short lacy nightie, and when I picked her up I was afraid it was going to tear. But she hugged me and covered my face with kisses. Her cheeks were wet with tears.

"I missed you, you wonderful bastard," she blurted, "don't ever go off again."

━━━━━━━━━━

Under cool sheets our shower-damp bodies met and joined. We made love, and afterward as I lay beside her I thought that it was the kind of homecoming I needed—and deserved.

TWENTY-FOUR

A week later Manny Montijo joined us. We took deck chairs out on the pier because workmen were excavating the lawn for an enclosed pool, designed by Melody. The backhoe rumbled down the packed incline, scooped, and chugged up, giving off loud chuffs of blue-black smoke. Manny sipped from his glass and said, "Anywhere in the States all this would cost a lot more than forty thousand, Jack."

"I know," I said, "but it's only money."

"And he earned it," Melody remarked, got up and went off to refill our drinks. When she was out of hearing range Manny said, "Ray Maguire asked me to put a question to you . . . what ever happened to that authentic million?"

"Tell him I've thought about that myself. Maybe the question should be put to Shari, via Issar Levi and Saul. She was the last holder of record."

"That's it? No further comment?"

"Well, maybe *El Ratón Perez* took it." That was what Mexicans called the tooth fairy. Manny grimaced and I looked away. "Things were happening fast that night," I told him. "Buildings burning, men running around . . . I had to get out of there with three people. Much confusion."

"I'm sure." He gazed thoughtfully at my Seabee, snubbed and bobbing gently in the water a few yards away.

I said, "Now I've got a question for *you*. What about all that shit growing on the plantation—ganja and opium poppies. Is it going to be left there to thrive on the sun-drenched plain?"

"I don't know," he said after a while. "My impression is the Mexican authorities are going to kick around our request and do nothing. As for sending in our own choppers to spray the crops . . . well, you know how Mexicans react to anything they can misconstrue as a Yanqui invasion."

"I know," I said, "and it's all so hopeless."

"Also," Manny said, "there's a complicated question of *hacienda* ownership. Ibarra's widow claims inheritance, and has gotten a federal court to issue an *amparo* against another claimant, one of Ibarra's shell corporations in Panama. Meanwhile, no one is allowed to live on the property or work the plantation."

"And litigation will drag on for years," I remarked. "At least Shari won't get the *hacienda*, even though she murdered Ibarra for it. That pleases me."

Manny got out a cigarette, looked at it longingly and threw it away. "You wanted her jailed."

"Damn right I did."

"But maybe it's worked out for the best. Mossad will run her hard as long as she lives. Surely that's more useful than having her stitch pillowcases at Alderson?" That was the federal women's prison.

"I guess," I said. "Anyway, I wasn't consulted. And it's over with."

Melody heard me, and when she was handing us our drinks she said, "Darn right it's over, Manny. And if any more choice missions turn up, please leave Jack out. I've retired him. Permanently." She sucked noisily on her piña colada straw."

"That right, Jack?"

"What can I say? I wouldn't displease my fiancée for the world."

She smiled, leaned over and planted a frothy kiss on my chin. "Every now and then, dear, you say exactly the right thing."

I relaxed in my chair and closed my eyes. They thought I was sunning but I was thinking back to that wild night when I'd found Shari in Hakem's room and recovered the record books. I'd left her below with Pepe and gone upstairs again. Under Hakem's folded suit, bundles of currency were packed in the dead man's valise. It was the money Shari had taken from Ibarra's safe. Chato's money by way of Eddie Wax.

I remembered shoving it into another pillowcase and finding a hiding place that would be secure until I decided to come back.

The money was uncounted and unaccountable. And in the entire world, I was the only one who knew where it was hidden.

Ice tinkled in my glass. Melody hummed snatches of *"Solamente Tú."* The backhoe chugged and snarled. Trucks arrived empty and drove off filled. Melody was going to have her enclosed pool.

I opened my eyes and saw a chevron of pelicans skimming the offshore water. Life at that moment was very good.

And it was going to get even better.